LETHBRIDGE-STEWART

THE LAUGHING GNOME
RISE OF THE DOMINATOR

ROBERT MAMMONE

CANDY JAR BOOKS · CARDIFF

The right of Robert Mammone to be identified as the
Author of the Work has been asserted by him in accordance
with the Copyright, Designs and Patents Act 1988.

Rise of the Dominator © Robert Mammone 2019

Characters from 'The Web of Fear' and 'The Dominators'
© *Mervyn Haisman & Henry Lincoln*
Lethbridge-Stewart: The Series
© *Andy Frankham-Allen & Shaun Russell 2014, 2019*

Fiona Campbell created by Gary Russell
Doris Lethbridge-Stewart created by Ben Aaronovitch
Dominic Vaar created by Nick Walters

Doctor Who is © British Broadcasting Corporation, 1963, 2019

Range Editor: Andy Frankham-Allen
Editor: Shaun Russell
Editorial: Keren Williams
Licensed by The Haisman Estate
Cover Art by Adrian Salmon

Printed and bound in the UK by
CPI Anthony Rowe, Chippenham, Wiltshire

ISBN: 978-1-912535-41-5

Published by
Candy Jar Books
Mackintosh House
136 Newport Road, Cardiff, CF24 1DJ
www.candyjarbooks.co.uk

All rights reserved.
No part of this publication may be reproduced, stored in a
retrieval system, or transmitted at any time or by any means, electronic,
mechanical, photocopying, recording or otherwise without the prior
permission of the copyright holder. This book is sold subject to
the condition that it shall not by way of trade or otherwise be circulated
without the publisher's prior consent in any form of binding
or cover other than that in which it is published.

PREVIOUSLY...

AFTER FINDING A MYSTERIOUS GARDEN GNOME IN A *churchyard, Sir Alistair Lethbridge-Stewart's mind is catapulted back in time. Trapped in the body of his younger self from 1981, Alistair is unsure what has happened. But he is soon embroiled in an adventure he barely remembers; it becomes apparent he's back in time to clear this foggy memory, sent back by the gnome! He eventually comes-to again in 2011 and attempts to explain things to his visitors, Dame Anne Bishop and her husband, Brigadier William Bishop. But the explanations do not get far before he is once again pulled out of his body by the laughter of the gnome, only this time he is not alone. Anne and Bill are pulled with him!*

They all come-to in 1969, where they are forced to relive the London Event, the trap set for the Doctor by the Great Intelligence. Once again, Alistair finds himself in his younger body, and learns why it had to be him who met the Doctor. Meanwhile Bill finds himself in the body of a boy, unable to do anything useful. Anne is in the body of a woman fated to die. She attempts to save her father's life, but along the way discovers that no matter what she does, she can't change the past. She, and no doubt Bill, are simply caught in Alistair's temporal wake. Whatever is going on, it's all about him!

They continue to travel, astral projected throughout Alistair's timeline. Trapped in other peoples' bodies, their paths never seeming to cross, they know, they hope, that they will eventually return to 2011. Meanwhile Alistair starts to uncover the purpose of his journey: his past is filled with mistakes, regrets, things he wishes he could have done differently. Unanswered questions. Now, guided by the gnome, he has a chance to get his house in order...

Casting her gaze around the room, Fiona Campbell noted that there was no sign of a struggle or forced entry; no indication of immediate danger, no foreign item in evidence, save that ghastly gnome Alistair had picked up earlier in the churchyard. It was now on the floor by Brigadier Bishop's feet. He must have dropped it.

Such practicalities established, there was little else Fiona could do, save make her charges as comfortable as possible. Falling back on her Girl Guide training, she set about putting the Bishops into the recovery position, taking care to support their heads correctly as she did so. Next, she took the blankets from Alistair's bed, tucking one securely around his waist and legs, and used the others to cover Brigadier Bishop and his wife.

Smoothing the blanket over Dame Anne's shoulders, Fiona studied her sleeping face. A few strands of grey hair had been dislodged from her usually neat bob, and Fiona gently tucked them back in place behind her ear.

Pushing herself up from the floor, her knees clicking with arthritis, Fiona crossed back to Alistair's bedside and pressed the emergency call button. With the sound of hurried footsteps approaching down the corridor, Fiona sat down to worry, and to wait.

She remained there, as nurses and staff busied themselves around Alistair and his friends. The conclusion was that they were all simply sleeping. But the why was beyond the nursing home staff. Fiona told them she had an idea who could help, all she had to do was make a phone call.

The administrator of the nursing home agreed; he did not know everything, but he was aware about enough of Sir Alistair's past to allow his ex-wife this courtesy.

Unfortunately, it turned out Kate was out of the country, busy with work. So, Fiona had no choice but to turn to the only other woman who might be able to wake Alistair up...

An hour later, Fiona stood by the window of Alistair's room, looking down at the courtyard. And she smiled. A taxi pulled up, and out of it climbed a petite woman in her early seventies, wrapped up against the cold winter air. She looked up, caught Fiona's eye, and waved. Fiona returned the wave, and felt old resentments bubbling up inside. She forced herself to put them aside for now; Alistair was more important.

Fiona turned to her ex-husband's sleeping form.

'No need to worry now,' she told him. 'Doris is here. Hopefully she'll know what to do.'

CHAPTER ONE
Hang on to Yourself

LONDON, APRIL 30, 1945.

Arthur Seaton tasted the ashes of defeat in his mouth and found them to be bitter indeed. At his feet lay a discarded uniform, purloined from a nearby barracks the previous night. He crushed his cigarette out in a square of foil and sat, elbows on knees, contemplating the view through the sole window of bombed out buildings stretching towards the Thames, their roofs blown in and walls collapsed into the streets.

A Mosleyite for the last decade, Seaton had allowed his sympathies to take him further and further into plans and conspiracies that, had he been caught, would've seen him hanged as a traitor. He never considered himself a traitor, of course. Instead, he regarded himself as a patriot, intent on doing his best to ensure Britain hewed closely its natural ally, Germany, and not the mongrel nation that America had become.

And it had all come to naught. The papers were full of the imminent fall of Berlin, and with it, Hitler and his Thousand Year Reich. He shivered for a moment, and wondered bleakly about the future.

Seaton had been intimately involved in this last, most desperate gambit. He had greeted the men a week before on the beach in the dead of night. There, he handed over the sword. None of the men asked him how he had taken it from where it had been stored, forgotten. But he had followed orders from the crumbling Reich and found the weapon, hidden in a chest in a forgotten corner of a storage room in a London warehouse. The weapon nestled under books of astrology and homeopathy, which puzzled him. As instructed, he had not touched the weapon, merely walked out of the facility with it tucked under his long coat. With the war nearing its end, security had become lax.

Seaton had driven the men in a blacked-out van along dangerous roads, avoiding roadblocks and bringing them at last into London. On the journey, they ignored him, conversing in low tones as they brought out the sword and unwrapped it. He found himself growing sick looking at it, but the grins on the faces of the men carrying it reassured him, a little.

Behind him, on the bed, the weapon lay swaddled in canvas. Seaton's heart beat faster at the memory of the tumult in the Cabinet Bunker. The German agent holding the weapon to Churchill's throat. The Prime Minister's implacability in the face of his own death. And the English soldier, bleeding from a wound, yet whose aim had been true. So close, he seethed. So close…

Yet he'd had a victory, of sorts. In the confusion, he had scooped up the sword and escaped with it via the winding stairs into the afternoon light. Seaton shivered at the memory of the weapon in his hands, the voices and the visions that almost overwhelmed him until he had removed his jacket and wrapped the sword in it.

But that was the past. A new life beckoned. But not before he performed one final act of betrayal. He turned to the small radio set. It had warmed up sufficiently. Leaning over the keys, he sent a simple message; two words that would be the final hammer blow to a thousand-year dream.

WOTAN LIVES flashed across the Channel and into

France, where a lone receiver waited patiently in Colmar, aware of the noose tightening around his neck. Before abandoning his post, the collaborator passed on the message. It flashed into ruined Germany along the last thread of copper wire connecting the dissolving Reich to the Bunker beneath the Reichstag itself.

Finished, Arthur Seaton sat back and contemplated the last ten years of his life. Then he picked up a hammer and smashed the radio set to flinders. Casting the tool aside, he stood, adjusted his tie, shrugged on his jacket and picked up the canvas-wrapped sword and left the building, turning into an empty street that led to more streets that eventually took Seaton to the financial heart of London.

WOTAN LIVES. The private stared at the message on the scrap of paper at his tiny desk. The heavy radio in front of him hummed and hissed; the green-lit dials like heavy lidded eyes. Tremors shook the Bunker and dust sifted down from the ceiling, adding to the funk of the thumping diesel generators, the rank sweat and fear of dozens of people crammed within the tight confines of what the private had come to regard as a concrete tomb, populated by lunatics.

Still, he wouldn't abandon his post, even as the dying heartbeats of the Reich convulsed, here, beneath the Reichstag. He looked again at the message he had pencilled on a scrap of paper, puzzled by the words; as puzzling as anything he had witnessed down there. More tremors shook the room, this time accompanied by a long, protesting groan. He looked up, fearfully, then the tremors subsided, and the bombardment stilled.

Rising from his stool, the private left the radio room and stepped into a corridor. Officers slumped on the ground along its length, jackets undone, empty bottles of schnapps lying around them. On his left, he heard crying and laughter, and something that might have been a muffled scream. With the slip of paper grasped tight in his right hand, he crossed the corridor and stopped in front of a door.

He raised his free hand to knock, then paused, suddenly terrified of who resided on the other side. Sweat ran down his neck, and he tugged nervously at his collar. A pair of guards stalked by, their heads together, speaking in low, urgent whispers. The private stared at their backs as they disappeared into the gloom, then gathered his courage and knocked.

The door immediately swung open. A heavyset man with hard eyes glared at him. A tic pulled at his mouth, making him appear to sneer. Knowing his reputation, the private could well imagine that sneering was the man's usual pose.

'A message, sir,' the private said, standing to attention.

Boorman had no military rank, but the private had enough good sense not to provoke the Führer's private secretary.

'Hand it over then,' Boorman said gruffly. The private shot out his hand, passing over the folded paper. He saw movement beyond Boorman, a shuffling figure with his head down. The private felt a tingle down his spine as his Führer shambled into view.

One hand clutched the other, only barely stilling the trembling that afflicted the limb. The face was sallow, gone white in the long weeks spent in the Bunker, and his dark hair shot through with grey, was greasy and lank. When the eyes flicked up, eyes that had once glowed with an unholy light and commanded a nation to rise up and declare war on the world, the private only saw a blank, empty gaze.

Boorman examined the piece of paper for a moment.

The private saw his face shift, the mouth turn down. Without another word, Boorman shoved the door shut.

The private contemplated the door and the message. He turned and walked slowly back to his station.

After a while, as he monitored the hissing emptiness of the radio frequency, he heard a commotion in the corridor. People lined the corridor. He saw the Führer emerge, wearing a greatcoat, and shuffle slowly up and down the line, shaking hands, offering a consoling word to a weeping woman, before returning to his rooms.

An hour later, as the private transcribed a shouted message from a desperate commander under fire somewhere in the rubble-strewn capital, a single shot rang out. He paused, closed his eyes briefly and wondered what would happen next.

A long, silent scream as his consciousness falls from the limitless darkness of infinity, back into the mundane reality of the universe. Within the fathomless cold, colours flare and dissolve, ribbons of light twist and curl as he plunges through stars, riding the black event horizons of vast galaxy devouring black holes. He feels invisible lines of gravity wrap themselves around him like the arms of a lover and then...

Sir Alistair opened his eyes with a start and found himself staring at a low ceiling. He felt the room rock gently from side to side. Something angular jammed hard against his ribs. He smelled salt in the air. Then he heard the thump of the engines and realised he had arrived on a boat.

'How many more times?' he muttered, and swung himself into a sitting position.

The pain in his side vanished and he looked down at the holstered revolver on his left hip. His stomach turned over and over and he almost vomited. Bracing himself against a wall with one hand, he closed his eyes and swallowed.

Glass clinked at his feet. Opening his eyes, he saw empty bottles of whisky rolling along the floor. His nose wrinkled at the smell of alcohol. His throat felt coated with a thick substance, and a dull headache throbbed at his temples.

'Damn strange place to go on a bender,' he said. He shook his head, immediately regretted it, and closed his eyes again.

Despite the hangover, Alistair still found it a marvel to be able to get up and move around. Memories of sitting in that damned wheelchair, so long ago now, while others pushed him around, filled him with a dull anger.

'Not something I want to get used to again in a hurry,' he said to himself. It was a habit he'd fallen into since the first time he'd found himself in the body of another; thirteen-year old George Vine in 1929. How many jumps ago was that now? Over ten, he felt sure. But each time, although his accent remained his, the voice changed. The cadence different.

The unfamiliar face in the mirror opposite smiled briefly then stared. A swarthy, handsome face looked back at him. A clipped moustache, in a fashion Alistair dimly knew to be wildly out of fashion, was at least familiar to him. Slicked black hair. A scar through his left eyebrow that added, rather than detracted, from his looks. And roguishly charming, albeit badly bloodshot, eyes that had a definitely unfamiliar twinkle to them. All in all, a face that made him instantly suspicious.

'I dare say you've been on the wrong end of the law more than once, old chap,' he murmured.

He flexed his hands and revelled again in a body that time had not yet broken. Looking around, Alistair saw a long, rectangular case sitting on the opposite bunk. Running a hand over the lid, he unlatched it and flipped it open.

An unfamiliar metal apparatus sat nestled within

moulded foam. A long barrel connected to a mechanism housed within a metal box. Leaning closer, Alistair saw a diamond embedded into the tip of the barrel.

'Drill bit,' he said, rubbing his jaw.

Several sunken sockets were visible on the back of the metal box. A bulky cube sat in another foam pocket. A pair of short leads trailed from the cube and looked like they plugged into the box.

'This is... unusual.' Alistair shut the case, absently locking it while he rummaged through the memories of this new body; a trick he had happened upon accidentally a good five jumps ago. He found two things; one he was now Spanish (he would have to work on an accent soon!), and... His frown deepened when the second memory came to him.

Putting the disturbing thoughts to one side, he looked around the cabin. On a table beside his bunk, he saw his wallet. He flipped it open.

An eyebrow quirked at the sight of the money stuffed inside. He ran a thumb over it, and found a photo. Pulling it out, Alistair found himself staring at the image of a young girl, perhaps seven or eight. Memories and a distant anger and purpose flooded through him. The child's violet coloured eyes stared at him.

'I'm a man on a mission, it seems.' He traced the edges of the photo with a finger, then tucked it away.

The door to the cabin rattled briefly then swung open. Alistair's hand dropped to the revolver. Lifting it free in one smooth movement, he took aim at the man standing in the open doorway.

'Easy,' the sailor said, in a thick Polish accent. He jerked a shaking thumb upwards. 'The captain says we are close to land.'

Alistair lowered the revolver. He didn't like the look of fear in the sailor's eyes. 'Good,' he said, having little choice but to start working on his Spanish accent now, and slid the weapon back into the holster. 'Tell him I'll be up in a moment.'

Nodding, the sailor hurriedly closed the door. Alistair sat down on the bed and realised his hands were shaking. He clasped them together until the tremors faded. The empty bottles clinked and rolled across the floor.

'No more of that,' he said. He looked through the porthole.

The view offered a glimpse of white topped waves and a distant smudge of land. A bell rang, and he heard chains rattling.

Pulling on a leather jacket, Alistair left the cabin with the case and made his way up the steep stairs.

Several sailors hurried past him. Bracing himself against the swell, Alistair walked across the deck. He watched a pair of sailors lowering a boat. He sat the case down and waited.

Dark clouds scudded across the sky as a freshening breeze swept towards the coast. Sailors moved around him. All refused to meet his gaze. Alistair wondered at the reputation of the man he had become. A name swam up from the depths of his memory. *Matador*. The name provoked a cascade of images; of vaults and safes, gunfire and roaring cars, cities and shadows and adrenaline, swiftly interrupted by the sound of approaching footsteps.

Turning, Alistair saw a heavyset fellow with a dark face and squinting eyes. A pipe jutted defiantly from his mouth, and a thin curl of smoke trailed from it.

'You're lucky the weather is this good.'

'Lucky?' Alistair said. The accent took some getting used to. 'There is no such thing as luck. Only skill and bravery.' He smiled and raised his hands, balling them into fists. 'Usually with these.'

The Matador, it seems, thought Alistair, *enjoys playing*

the role of a hard man.

The captain nodded. 'Perhaps. I've sailed far and wide and luck sails with us.' He cocked his head and his eyes bore into Alistair. 'I wonder about you, though.'

'Why?'

'You've spent the last three days indoors. Barely eaten. Drank too much. I sent some of the crew to remove your supply of whisky, but you broke the jaw of the first man through the door. Since then, they've refused to have anything to do with you.' He stopped, and considered the horizon. 'Someone might believe a man acting this way realises his luck has run out. That he doesn't anticipate returning home.'

A chill ran up Alistair's spine. *Apt phrase.*

'Perhaps a man makes his own luck,' he said, acknowledging the concession with a shrug of his shoulders. Taking out his wallet, Alistair removed several notes, which he offered to the captain. 'Give my apologies to the fellow whose jaw I broke.'

Surprised, the captain nodded and took the money, folding it into a pocket.

By the rail, the windlass halted with a rusty shriek. The boat swayed and bumped against the side. A pair of men climbed in and waited expectantly.

'This is it?' Alistair said.

The captain nodded. 'They will take you to a cove where someone will meet you. That's all I know.'

Alistair nodded. He was already looking forward to the next stage of his strange journey, discovering why he was... well, wherever he was this time. Without farewell, he walked over to the edge of the deck and handed over the case.

'Be careful with it,' he said.

Climbing over the rail, he swung himself into the boat and found a seat. A pair of seagulls wheeled overhead, one of them screaming as they dove into the wind.

'One more thing,' Alistair called out as they began to lower the boat.

The captain looked over the rail. 'What?' He had to shout above the squeal of the windlass.

'What date is it?'

The look on the captain's face almost made Alistair laugh.

'What?'

'The date. What's the date?'

The captain opened his mouth to say something, closed it and shook his head. 'Twenty-third.'

That didn't really help. 'And the month, the year?'

Now the captain really did look at him as if he were mad. 'November, nineteen seventy-bloody-three!'

Alistair felt a shock drive up his spine. He was so close to home last time, but now he was back another thirty years... He turned his gaze to the coast, as the boat splashed into the water.

1973. The year that UNIT saw its baptism of fire!

A very busy one for me, the first time around, he thought.

Images of two Doctors, silver giants outside St Paul's, plastic dummies, cave monsters, and Doomsday clocks came to him in a rush.

Lord alone knows what it'll bring this time!

CHAPTER TWO
Boys Keeps Swinging

'SOMEONE'S FOLLOWING US, BOSS.'

Sammy Wilberforce, long known by London's Underworld as the Hammer ever since he rearranged Stan Cooper's face in the infamous Five Bell's Hotel Massacre in 1962 with said instrument, turned in his seat in the rear of the car and peered through the window. Acid filled his mouth, erasing the pleasant memory of his mum's rice pudding. Another vehicle, its lights dimmed, raced behind them. He could see several shapes crammed into the vehicle's darkened interior.

'How long?'

'Reckon since we left,' the driver said.

'Where are the boys tonight?'

'Celebrating Frank's birthday at *The Cock and Bull*.'

'Get us there. Fast.'

The driver turned his attention to the road ahead. The Jaguar's engine built up from a low mutter to a throbbing growl as they raced down Liverpool Road. Evening had come on quickly, and streetlights flickered into life as the car sped by.

Wilberforce sat back in his seat and felt his heart surge in his chest. His throat constricted, and pain developed in his left shoulder. With a shaking hand, he pulled a bottle of nitro-glycerine pills from his inner jacket pocket and shook out several small tablets into the palm of his hand. He tipped them into his mouth and held them in place behind his front teeth with his tongue. A metallic taste wormed its way down his throat.

Screwing the cap tight, Wilberforce tossed the bottle into the seat beside him. From its holster sitting under his left armpit, he pulled out a snub-nosed Smith & Wesson .357 Magnum. The silver revolver sat comfortably in his hand. Resting the weapon on his thigh, he felt his heart begin to steady and the pain in his shoulder fade. His throat loosened.

'Who do you think it is, Henry?' he called to the driver up front.

Henry remained silent for a moment as he gunned the car through an intersection as the light turned red. The other car blew through the red light.

'That's torn it,' Wilberforce heard Henry mutter to himself. 'The Big Man,' he added, answering the original question. 'No doubt. Ever since Fabulous Phil disappeared, he's been nosing around our turf.'

'We should've dealt with that upstart months ago,' Wilberforce said. He glanced at his reflection in the window and looked quickly away. The sallow face with holes for eyes looked like a premonition.

Henry wisely stayed silent as he turned the wheel sharply to the right, leaving a long rubber track in their wake and a screech like a violated woman in the descending dark. The car following them did the same, a cloud of smoke marking its path around the corner. Cars braked around them, barely avoiding a collision.

It took Wilberforce a moment for his disbelieving ears to realise they were being fired on. He saw the driver's side mirror explode. Henry flinched, and the car veered to the left before he regained control. The back window blew in with a rain of glass, the bullet travelling on and shattering the rear-view mirror. Casting a wide-eyed look over his shoulder, Wilberforce swore as he saw the trailing car close behind them.

A clash of grinding metal filled the cabin. The Jaguar swerved from side to side while Henry frantically struggled to regain control. Flung forward, Wilberforce lost his grip on his revolver, which fell into the foot well. Swearing, he groped blindly for it as the chasing car smashed again into the rear bumper bar.

Time slowed as Henry lost control. The Jaguar described a long slewing arc across the road before it slammed into a parked car, scraping the paintwork down to the metal from headlight to brake light. Stunned, Wilberforce, through blind chance, grabbed the revolver.

The car's forward momentum kept them moving. Henry, swiftly regaining his composure, ripped through the gears and slammed the accelerator to the floor. With glass trailing them in a shimmering wake, the Jaguar lurched forward, quickly gathering speed.

Cold air rushed through the cabin. Shaking his head, Wilberforce felt the familiar tightening in his chest. He looked frantically for the pill bottle, but couldn't find it amid the broken glass. He turned around, resting on his knees as he glared in rage through the gap where the rear window used to be.

The chasing car surged forward again, and he saw an arm reach out of the front passenger window. Wilberforce fired twice. Acrid gun smoke billowed into the night. Deafened by the concussive blasts, he watched, almost as in a dream, as the chasing car jerked to one side. A hole opened in the front window, and Wilberforce saw a head snap back. The pistol tumbled from the senseless grip of the dead gunman, bouncing along the road before it vanished from sight.

Wilberforce's surge of triumph vanished when he caught a glimpse of fiery eyes glaring at him from the rear of the chasing car. For a moment, he felt his heart stop as overwhelming fear gripped him. Molten eyes smouldered and bore deep into him. The day Wilberforce killed someone for the first time he had abandoned religion. However, for a moment, he thought that Lucifer snapped at his heels. Gasping, Wilberforce fell back.

'You all right back there, boss?' Henry called.

'Do your damned job and I'll do mine!' Wilberforce's chest felt ready to explode.

'We're almost there. I'll get as close to the front door as I can!'

They shot through another intersection. People on the street gawped as the car slalomed between vehicles that had braked to avoid a collision. Henry gripped the steering wheel and careened down the street. Up ahead, Wilberforce saw the unmistakeable sign of *The Cock and Bull* hanging over the door.

'Here we go!' Henry shouted. In a screaming turn, he spun the wheel to the right. A tyre burst, and he lost control of the car. It slewed around in a wide arc and came to a stop opposite the pub's front door, no more than twenty feet away.

Wilberforce threw open the door and staggered outside. Casting a desperate glance over his shoulder, he saw the chasing car lunge forward. The tendons in his neck stood out like cables as the pain in his chest grew worse. He broke into a shambling run.

Eighteen steps. Like a childhood nightmare, the front door appeared to recede from Wilberforce, no matter how much he tried to reach it.

Fourteen steps. He heard a piano playing loudly inside, and the drunken laughter of friends celebrating together.

Ten steps. He heard the whine of the Jaguar's engine as Henry reversed to intercept the pursuing car. An enormous crashing sound, of rending metal and shattered glass, filled the universe.

Seven steps. Something large and heavy flew by Wilberforce, and his dumbfounded mind only managed to work out it was a vehicle, driver's side crunched in as if from a giant's fist, tumbling through the air.

Six steps. The right side of the pub collapsed in a flurry of bricks and shattered timber.

Three steps. Screams filled the night as the front door fell into the street.

One step. Falling through the doorway, Wilberforce saw several figures approaching him from the street, eyes smouldering, promising an end to all his suffering.

And then time snapped back into place. Wilberforce rose unsteadily to his feet, the revolver somehow still clutched in one trembling hand.

'They've killed Henry,' he croaked from a throat suddenly reed thin.

Half a dozen black suited men, who had until a few moments ago been celebrating in the otherwise empty front bar, sprang into action. Two swooped on Wilberforce, and frogmarched him towards the stairs. One of the other men pulled out a sawn-off shotgun from behind the bar, while the remainder took out long barrelled pistols.

'Hang on, boss,' one of the men helping Wilberforce up the stairs yelled.

Wilberforce opened his mouth to ask him what the hell else did he think he was doing, when someone screamed. A body flew over the bar, crashing into the heavy mirror hanging behind it. Glass exploded, cutting off the screaming with an awful finality.

Up the stairs they went. The shotgun barked, twice. Another scream rose up, then another and suddenly the front bar was filled with the ear-splitting whine of ricocheting bullets.

'This isn't happening,' Wilberforce muttered as his men bundled him into a room. One jammed him into a corner and stood in front of him, pistol raised. The other waited beside the closed door. Orange streetlight filtered through the window, washing the room with a haze that reminded Wilberforce of blood.

The screaming and gunfire downstairs stopped. An awful silence gripped the building. Wilberforce realised the whistling noise in his ears was his own faltering breath. The pain in his chest and shoulder had transformed into a frightening numbness. He tightened his grip on the revolver.

'What the hell's going on?' the man at the door said, looking anxiously at Wilberforce.

Before Wilberforce could reply, the wall beside the man exploded in a flurry of plaster and shattered lathe. A massive black fist appeared, grabbed the guard by the throat, and pulled him through the wall.

The man guarding Wilberforce immediately opened fire. Flashes of light exploded in the dim room as bullets punched through the door. Something like metal cracking on stone could be dimly heard above the cacophony, then Wilberforce heard the click, click, click of the hammer striking an empty chamber.

Before Wilberforce could bring his own revolver to bear, the door smashed in. A truly massive shape filled the space, its coarse features lit by hellish eyes gleaming in hungry anticipation. The man guarding Wilberforce charged the figure. With a club-like arm, it swatted him aside like a kitten. He cannoned into a wall and the awful sound of his neck snapping filled the room.

Numb, Wilberforce raised his revolver and fired until he ran out of bullets. Sparks burst off the figure looming in front of him. He had an impression that some sort of scar sat in the centre of its forehead.

Wilberforce watched it step aside, allowing a companion to loom at its shoulder. It too had the strange scar on its forehead. Beneath them, he could hear the floor straining to support their weight.

The tension in the room grew worse. The numbness

had spread all the way down Wilberforce's left arm. Footsteps walked slowly down the corridor towards the room.

Another figure appeared, lissom where its companions were squat grotesques. Wilberforce saw a familiar face, etched with exhaustion, split into an imperious smile.

'Hello, Sammy,' the Big Man said, his voice tinged with an accent that Wilberforce had always supposed was Scandinavian.

'Y-Y-You,' Wilberforce stuttered. An unfamiliar sensation filled him. *Fear. I'm afraid* he thought. His faltering heart began to race.

'Very definitely.' The smile became predatory. 'You should have come to terms, Sammy. An empire needs good hands at the wheel.' The smile widened as the figure took out a pistol and thumbed back the hammer.

Time slowed to a trickle. In that moment, before the hammer crashed down and sent a bullet into his brain, Wilberforce fell to his knees, reaching out impotently.

'Like you,' the Big Man said, training the revolver on Wilberforce. 'Like you, they will all kneel before me.'

The barrel's cyclopean eye fell on Wilberforce. His head dropped, and then he heard a bang that swept him into darkness.

'Another down.' The Big Man, Dominic Vaar, coughed. It was a long hacking sound, and he sagged against one of the figures. He looked wearily at the creature holding him up.

'Come,' he said, signalling with a wavering hand. 'Return me to the vehicle.' With the creature's aid, he made his way from the room, its companion lumbering after them.

Outside, a little of his old strength returned. Vaar walked around his car, examining the damage. The front had caved in, but the engine miraculously ran. His driver slumped over the steering wheel. Human physiognomy wasn't his strong suit, but he thought the man, face splashed with blood, looked dead. He shrugged and signalled to one of the creatures. It pulled the body from the car, and dumped it into the street.

Slipping into the driver's seat, Vaar waited for the creatures. He watched them lumber to the rear of the vehicle. Despite his exhaustion, he felt a sense of triumph at how these creatures had performed. His ally had proven useful after all.

They lurched to the rear of the vehicle and got in. The primitive suspension sagged as they settled into place. With all the doors shut, Vaar turned the car around and drove away, as police sirens filled the night.

CHAPTER THREE
Ashes to Ashes

'RUTH? RUTH! CAN YOU SEE IF THERE'S ANY COFFEE LEFT?' bellowed a detective from across the room. The men around him laughed.

Ruth Winters looked up from reading a report; her lips pressed tightly together, her eyes narrowed.

'That's Detective Winters, you pig,' she whispered under her breath. Then her eyes widened and her back arched, as if fighting against a sudden weight across her shoulders.

Panic gripped her, sending her heart slamming against her ribs. The world wavered, and she thought for a moment that she might be dying. Then, as quickly as the sensation had arrived, it vanished.

Ruth closed her eyes and felt her heart slow…

…and when she opened them again, Dame Anne Bishop looked out over a room full of desks and men, the air thick with cigarette smoke.

The walls were stained nicotine yellow, the paint peeling in places. Several girlie calendars, opened to November, were pinned up. Ashtrays sat on every desk and most were full. A refrigerator rattled quietly to itself in a corner. Anne was willing to bet good money that it was filled with cans of lager.

'Ruth? You okay? You've gone pale.'

Looking across the desk Anne saw a black man with

tightly cropped hair, sprinkled with grey, sitting opposite her. Concern wrinkled his forehead. Smoke curled from a cigarette sitting in an ashtray beside his typewriter. The name on the desk read: Harry Champion.

'I'm fine,' Anne said, and looked at the wedge on her side of the desk. Ruth Winters. She felt a hand rest on her shoulder.

'You're all tense, Detective Winters. Fancy a back rub?'

The sour smell of whisky filled her nose and her eyes watered.

'No more than I fancy dating Reggie Kray,' she said loudly. She wondered at the reference, and felt an odd memory drift away. The clatter of typewriters fell silent.

'Don't get your knickers in a twist.'

Anne looked up at a hulking figure in a cheap suit, his face adopting a look of wounded pride, which soon dissolved into an embarrassed grin. One of the detectives sniggered and Anne felt her face turn hot. She lowered her head, trying to calm herself.

Her eyes alighted on a small desk calendar. November 23rd, 1973. Well, at least she knew the date. She was, apparently, a police detective.

She looked at Harry Champion, presumably Ruth's partner. He stared at her, looking like he was about to choke. His hand convulsed, snapping the pen in two. For a moment he looked like he didn't know where he was, as if someone had just put on his skin...

Could it be? Anne didn't want to attract attention, but she'd been astral projected into too many bodies now to not see the signs. Could it really be that, finally, either Alistair or Bill had arrived in proximity to her?

'Leave off, Tom,' the man said, and stopped, a look of unfamiliarity crossing his face. As if he didn't know where the name had come from.

'Well. What do you know?' Tom said. 'Old Man

Champion. Who'd imagine you'd be a white knight, eh?' Laughter spread across the room.

'I'm just saying,' Champion said, unsteady and unsure of himself. 'We're all a team here–'

'Team? The Crouch End Team, that's what we are?' Tom shook his head. Sweat stood out in fat beads on his forehead. 'Can you imagine Ruth pulling on the boots for a kick on the pitch this Saturday? Spare me.'

Laughter now, but less of it, as interest in the confrontation waned. Quickly, conversation and the clatter of typewriters filled the air once again. Tom lumbered back to his corner of the room.

Anne watched Champion lean over his typewriter. She saw his nose wrinkle at the cigarette smoke curling from the ashtray.

It had to be him, nobody else's nose wrinkled like that.

'Harry?' No response, so she said, quieter, 'Bill, is it you?'

'What?' He looked at her, really studied her, eyes disbelieving. 'Anne? After all this time…'

She nodded, shaking with relief. 'It's been so long since we've… Thank God you're here.'

He smiled, and despite the stranger's face, it was a smile she'd recognise anywhere. That of her husband, Brigadier William Bishop.

'Where are we?' he whispered. He looked around the room, trying to take it all in.

Quickly gathering her thoughts, Anne turned the desk calendar towards him. 'Back where we first met,' she said, then smiled wryly. 'Give or take a few years.' There was more laughter from the other side of the room. Anne felt her cheeks flame again. She stood. 'Come on,' she said. 'Let's get out of here. We need to talk.'

They exited into a corridor. A sign pointed to the front desk. There, they found an old officer haranguing a greasy looking teenager with lank hair and a cigarette hanging from the corner of his mouth.

'It's Sergeant Clifford, you little blighter,' the officer said loudly. The teenager smirked and shoved his hands deeper into the pockets of his ragged flared jeans.

Anne felt a pang of sympathy for Clifford. She too had experienced the indifference of colleagues much younger than her. She also knew that in 1973 teenagers like this one would have little care for what she said. Which was why she turned to Bill.

'Give him both barrels, why don't you?' she said with a smile.

'Been a while since I've needed to strip new recruits, but I think I remember how.' He winked at her, and stepped towards the teenager. 'What's all this?' he barked into the teenager's face. The boy flinched at Bill's sudden outburst.

'Nothin',' he said, uncertainly.

Bill flicked a glance at Clifford, who looked at him with relief. Bill nodded at him, and smiled. 'If it's 'nothin, then why the bleedin' heck are you givin' the sergeant a hard time? Or do you fancy a spell in the cells downstairs? The rats won't mind who they nibble on, even someone as useless as you.'

Spots of colour rode on the teenager's cheekbones. He ducked his head and mumbled something.

'I can't hear you,' Bill almost shouted.

The teenager looked ready to cry. 'Sorry,' he managed.

'Right then.' Bill winked at Clifford. 'He's all yours, Sarge.'

'Good job,' Anne said, as they stepped outside.

'Feels like old times.'

A chill wind blew down the street. The hum of traffic filled the air. Bare trees reached for the sky, and fallen leaves clattered along the footpath, gathering in drifts in the gutters.

'Crouch End. 1973,' Anne said.

'Or 1979, depending on the dating protocols.'

'Oh yes, them.' She looked back at the station. 'Well, that calendar said '73, so let's just go with that. The enfolded decades are confusing enough to be in as it is.'

'Agreed.' Bill smiled at her.

Anne shook her head. 'It's been so long,' she said, almost choking on the words.

Bill nodded. Impulsively, he grabbed her hand, holding on for dear life. 'Too long,' he said, his voice thick. He looked aside, blinking furiously. When he turned back, he smiled at her. '1973? I was last in 2003, if you can believe it,' he said.

'I can, I was there, too. In London.' Anne said. 'Where were you?'

'Malebolgia.'

'The American State? What were you doing there?'

'Do you remember that Gideon Crane fella the Brig told us about?'

Anne nodded.

'That was me.'

'Didn't he lose his marbles back then?'

'Yes, but it must have happened just after I left. Or because I left.' Bill shrugged. 'I dread to think. What about you? What do you remember?'

'I was in the body of a nurse called Claire Thompson. I think we're being dragged along in the—'

'Detectives?'

Anne and Bill looked to the station entrance. Clifford stood in the entrance, watching the teenager stalk away.

'What's up, Sarge?' Anne asked.

'That meeting with Inspector Pearson. It's about to start. He's been asking for Detective Champion's presentation.'

A quick search of their desks elicited two pieces of useful

information. Champion's presentation, and a thick file Anne pulled from a drawer in Ruth's desk.

'What do you think?' Bill asked, as they headed for the conference room.

'Right now, not much.' Anne frantically paged through the file. 'Though whatever this investigation is into, it's big. Very, very big.' She smiled at him as they entered the room. 'You present, and I'll read. Good luck.'

The narrow conference room looked out onto an empty, weed-choked yard. A uniformed officer with the rank of inspector stood at the front of the room. Beside him stood a table with a slide carousel. Someone had set up a projector screen.

'At a guess, I'd say that's Inspector Pearson,' Anne said to Bill, leaning closer to him so they wouldn't be overheard. Bill watched her brow wrinkle. 'Alfred, I think his first name is,' she said. Her forehead smoothed. 'It is. Trace memory.' She tapped her temple then bent her head to examine the file.

Bill nodded. After all this time apart, he was glad to be standing with Anne. He had discovered a lot about what was happening to them, and their link to the Brig, but having Anne with him made the ordeal tolerable.

As he walked to join the inspector, Bill's eyes flicked around the room, taking in the strangely familiar faces.

'As you know,' Pearson began, his nasally voice eerily like Kenneth Williams, 'our cousins in Central London are overwhelmed with investigating a number of recent incidents. I don't need to tell you all if the MOD wasn't so obstructive, those cases would have been cleared up well before now.'

There was a rumble of agreement. Bill and Anne shared a glance over the heads of the audience, but kept their own counsel.

'As a result, we have been tasked with investigating a new gang that has sprung up in Soho. Since we have been unable to confirm the boss's actual name, we will use the honorific his colleagues in the underworld use – the Big Man.' A deep chuckle rose in the room. It came from Tom. 'If you could keep your schoolyard comments you yourself, Detective Hartigan, it would be most appreciated.' The inspector waited. Tom Hartigan's chuckle died away. 'Very good. Detective Champion, if you could do the honours?'

Gripping his notes tightly in one hand, Bill made his way to the front of the room. A sea of faces stared expectantly at him. Anne nodded encouragement. He smiled, briefly.

'Thanks, Inspector,' Bill began, the deeper timbre of his voice startling him again. He rubbed his suddenly sweaty hands on his jacket. 'All right then.' He felt Pearson's presence looming beside him, and thought for a moment about what would happen to Champion's career if he mucked the presentation up completely.

For God's sake, he thought. *You're a damned brigadier. You've handled your fair share of briefings. So, you're in a different body, you don't know the case... How many jumps now? You're an old hand at this. Come on, Billy, pull yourself together.*

'Lights, please?'

One of the detectives lowered the lights. Bill picked up the selector and pushed a button. A grainy image of a hulking figure in a pin-striped suit, its face turned away from the camera, leaped onto the screen. The figure wore a black hat jammed low. Bill glanced at it, found he didn't recognise the image, and felt his stomach tighten. *Think,* he said to himself. He glanced down at his notes, ignoring the rustling in the room. Pearson cleared his throat. Frantically scanning the front page, Bill managed to pull several thoughts together.

'We have no idea what his real name is. As the inspector said, in the underworld they refer to him as the

Big Man. His gang, for whatever reason, styles itself the Black Sons.' Bill frowned. There was something very familiar about this. A distant memory... Maybe he'd read about it back in '73?

'He appeared literally from nowhere six months ago,' Bill continued. 'There's no record of a passport, or birth certificate or driver's license. Not even a damned library card, which I suppose shouldn't surprise us.' Soft laugher filled the room, and he grew in confidence. 'Safe to say, his origins are a complete mystery. That said, what's most important is stopping him. His gang deals mainly in financial crimes. He has steered away from the customary vice activities his type usually engages in.'

Bill clicked the button. The carousel rattled around and another image, this time of a ruined entrance to a high street betting shop, appeared. There were blown out windows, with obvious smoke damage. Pausing for a moment to let the image speak for itself, he turned the page on his notes and scanned them.

'When I say financial, I don't mean he's fiddling the stock market, as you can see. He started with armed robbery. Used the proceeds to build an organisation from scratch, then diversified into other areas. He's even invested in a trucking company. Landry's, I think it's called. He may be angling for contracts in the armoured lorry cash delivery field.'

'Talk about a fox in the henhouse,' Hartigan said loudly.

'He's spent the money wisely, Tom. Unlike some I could name,' Bill said, looking Tom in the face. Knowing chuckles filled the room. Crossing his arms over his chest, Tom glanced around and grumbled to himself. 'We know he used it to pay off some of the gangs that came sniffing around in the early days. Those he couldn't buy off, he intimidated, or killed. We believe, without any actual proof, that his organisation is responsible for the deaths of the Merton brothers and the disappearance of Philip Fitzsimons.'

In succession, separate images of the two dead men appeared. They stared blindly, their bodies crumpled, found in the street, and on a roof, the London skyline apparent in the background. The third image showed a mug shot of a severe looking fellow with swept back black hair and piercing eyes.

'Fitzsimons has been missing for the last two months. None of his associates will tell us where he is, assuming he's still alive. It's no surprise the Big Man has moved in on his territory.' Bill looked up and surveyed the room. 'Any questions?'

Heads shook.

'Good. As these photos attest, the Big Man is utterly ruthless. And deeply secretive. We believe, based on tips we've received, that he's headquartered somewhere in the Chinese quarter of Soho. We have a surveillance team stationed in the area, working to gather evidence to get a warrant for a raid, but that day is still some time away. We haven't been able to pin any of his men to any of the crimes linked to the Black Sons. They've intimidated or bought off all the witnesses we could use.'

Bill clicked the button again and the grainy image of a figure in the back of a car appeared on the screen. The same black hat was visible.

'As you can see, we have some photographic evidence of the person we believe is the Big Man, but nothing conclusive. Similarly, we lack any insight into the organisation itself. The lads in Financial Crimes have been useful, but the Big Man is very careful with what he does with his criminal proceeds. The funds for the Landry business, for instance, were laundered with great skill. For all intents and purposes, his organisation is a black box.'

'How about we just go in guns blazing and see what

shakes loose?' Hartigan called out.

'Assuming we even knew where he is, going in all guns blazing like the Wild West would taint the evidence we would need to convict him. No matter how much I might agree with you, Tom.' Bill didn't want to alienate the man, who seemed to have sway over the other detectives. 'No. We do this the right way, no matter how long it takes. We follow up on leads and keep our ears to the ground. Winters and I will continue pressing our contacts.' He turned to the inspector, who nodded.

'Thank you, Detective Champion. Like you, I appreciate the difficulty of this investigation. I'm sure I can bore you all with my war stories of smashing some of the underworld gangs back in the '50s, but we don't have enough time or alcohol. Back to work then.'

The lights went up and as the rest of the detectives left the room, and Inspector Pearson beckoned to Anne, who joined him and Bill at the front of the room.

'Good work, both of you. You'll appreciate I've got pressure coming down on me to get results. Is there anything else, anything you can tell me that will ease that pressure?'

Anne shook her head. 'I'm afraid not, sir. The Big Man operates under a reign of terror and he remunerates his men very, very well.'

Bill was impressed at Anne's quick response. She had always been a quick reader. He wondered just what she'd been up to since the first jump to 1969, all those… what, months ago?

'He doesn't even have a girlfriend or wife we could try to dislodge from his grasp. As Harry said, we'll continue the surveillance. That's the key. No one in the Big Man's game can carry on much longer without making a mistake. When he does, we'll be there.'

Pearson pursed his lips. 'Very well. But I need something. If you don't have a breakthrough soon, the operation may be taken from you.' With that, he nodded to them both and left the room.

Bill looked around the empty conference room and frowned. 'Talk about riding the whirlwind.'

'You did very well, dear,' Anne said, smiling and patting his arm.

Bill chuckled. 'Blimey.'

'That's one word,' Anne said. She placed the file down on an empty chair. 'I've got the barebones of the case, from your presentation and the file.'

Bill nodded. 'Investigation into the criminal underworld. Be like *Special Branch*, won't it?'

'Hopefully not. Loved the theme tune. Now about this case—'

Distant shouting caught their attention.

'Sounds like another happy customer,' Bill said.

'Get me to a hospital!' a male voice shouted.

'Let's go have a look,' Anne said.

Several of the detectives stood in the corridor leading to the public area. Anne pushed her way through, with Bill behind her.

A pair of uniformed officers dragged a struggling man, yelling at the top of his voice, towards them. Blood covered his face and an ugly bump stood out on his forehead.

'Get me to a hospital, for pity's sake.' The sparse remnants of his hair stuck up at odd angles. 'I've cracked my skull open. Let me go, you—'

One of the officers slammed the man into the wall and his face knotted in pain.

'Listen here, Carnarvon,' the officer said, his face creased into a scowl. 'Shut yer trap or I'll shut it for you.'

'What's going on?' Anne asked.

The officer glanced dismissively at her. 'Nothin' that need concern you!' he snapped, returning his attention to Carnarvon.

'You watch how you speak to a superior,' Bill said, scowling.

'Superior?' the officer said, laughing. 'Leave off, will ya?'

Bill stepped forward, so that his chest touched the officer's shoulder. Anne stood back, watching the scene with a growing smile on her face. Bill so loved being a brigadier.

'Leave off? I'll bleedin' well give you leave off, son,' Bill said, almost shouting. 'You will give Detective Winters the respect her position deserves, or I'll make sure you're down at Crouch End Canal pulling dog carcasses from the water.'

The officer's eyes went wide. Carnarvon, despite his position, smirked.

'Right,' the officer managed to choke out. His face had gone beet-red. 'Sorry, guv. I mean, ma'am.'

'Very good,' Anne said smoothly. She nodded to Bill, who winked at her and stepped back. 'What's this man charged with?'

'We reckon he's one of the Big Man's foot soldiers.'

'Get me to a hospital!' Carnarvon shouted.

'Shut it.'

'What's the charge?' Anne repeated.

The officer rolled his eyes. 'Murder, ma'am.'

Oh, good, Bill thought. *And here was me thinking things would calm down around here for a bit.*

CHAPTER FOUR
This is Not America

ALISTAIR PAUSED AT THE TOP OF THE BLUFF OVERLOOKING the beach, and looked down. White capped waves crashed onto the shore in a distant, hissing rush. He saw the boat heading for the trawler, the little craft rising and falling in the swell. Without its running lights, it was little more than a black speck against a star-spangled sky.

Turning up his collar against the freshening breeze, Alistair looked inland. A black ribbon of road followed the coastline. Shadowy copses of trees dotted the landscape, and tendrils of thin mist rose from the ground. He picked up his case and walked towards the road.

The sound of waves crashing on the stony shore faded, replaced by a brooding silence pockmarked by the crunch of his boots. A bird cried distantly, a long, mournful sound that wound down into silence. The darkness fell swiftly upon him and it was more by luck than design that Alistair found the macadam.

He stopped beneath a wooden sign and placed the case by his feet. Checking his watch, Alistair was surprised it had been only thirty minutes since his departure from the trawler. He half turned to look back towards the beach when he heard the low rumble of an approaching motor car. Twin powerful beams from the vehicle's headlights washed over him. Raising an arm to shield his eyes, Alistair was acutely aware of how exposed he was out in the open.

'Probably half the point,' he said to himself.

The car came to a stop beside him. Its engine throbbed with a soothing rumble. It was a Rolls-Royce. Someone was on a good wicket, Alistair reflected. The windows were black, and only a hint of movement in the driver's seat indicated the car hadn't driven itself out to collect him.

'Though I've seen *that* before,' he said to himself, with no little humour.

A door opened, and light from the interior dome slanted out into the night. A figure unfolded from the driver's seat and walked around the front of the car towards Alistair.

The driver, charitably, looked like a shaven gorilla dressed in a Saville Row suit. Arms as thick as thighs swung from shoulders broad enough to carry an ox. A business shirt barely constrained a barrel chest. Deep-set eyes buried under a thick, bony forehead swept over Alistair.

'You're the Matador,' the driver said, the rumble of his voice eerily like that of the car engine.

'I suppose I am,' Alistair said, managing a weak smile. 'And you are…?'

'Max.' The driver was truly huge. His feet had half sunk into the mud beside the crumbling macadam. Alistair wondered idly if a bazooka could stop the man if his temper turned foul, and then decided it would be a dicey proposition at best. Max peered at the case by Alistair's feet. 'Travelling light?'

Alistair nodded. A little of the Matador's anger trickled into his voice. 'I am here only because your boss has kidnapped my niece. If there's any honour among thieves, he has none.'

Max stared indifferently down at Alistair. 'I do what I'm told, and get paid well for it. Do the same, and the boss will give your niece back to you.'

'Where is he?'

A broad, frightening grin swept across Max's face. 'He's in a... How did he describe it? A business meeting. That's right. Let's go.'

Max turned on his heel, gouging out a chunk of mud, and stalked around to the driver's door. Alistair opened the passenger door and lifted the case into the back of the car. He had just enough time to slide into the seat and shut the door before the car began to move. The driver turned the Rolls-Royce in a wide arc. Gears shifted smoothly as the car picked up speed.

Alistair settled back into the plush leather seats. He closed his eyes for a moment, then they snapped open. He leaned forward and spoke through the open glass partition dividing the Rolls-Royce's interior in two.

'You don't happen to have the paper, by any chance?'

Max's eyes filled the rear-view mirror. He shifted slightly and raised a folded newspaper to the gap.

Alistair took it and sat back. In what remained of the light, he shook the paper open and found he held a copy of *The Times*. He flicked a glance to the front, and decided that he truly shouldn't judge a book by its cover.

The headline on the front page reported impending oil shortages due to machinations in the Middle East. A sidebar examined an experimental drilling project in Eastchester seeking alternative energy, and a familiar name appeared. Professor Eric Stahlman. Shaking his head, thinking of the disaster awaiting England next summer, Alistair continued through the newspaper.

And then he found it. Buried on page twenty-four, tucked awkwardly beneath an advertisement extolling the virtues of Beluga Caviar, Alistair found the article.

Headlined *Tremors Detected on Wenley Moor*, Alistair read the article with a sense of mounting shame. The article was uncredited, a tell-tale sign it had been handed to a copy boy on the up, and briefly interviewed a visiting

American seismologist, who pronounced the activity nothing unusual for the British Isles.

'We paid him enough to keep the public calm,' Alistair muttered. He looked out the window, the Matador's ghostly reflection staring back at him. The article sparked a profound sense of age and disappointment.

Entombing the colony of Earth Reptiles had been a mistake he long regretted. He'd tried to atone for it in the dying days of 2004, but thanks to Captain Andrea Winnington and the Internal Counter-Intelligence Service, the results had been mixed at best. The shame and bitterness lingered. He crumpled the newspaper and tossed it aside.

'How long before we reach London?' he called out.

Eyes flicked up in the rear-view mirror. 'A couple more hours,' the gruff voice replied.

A wave of tiredness swept over Alistair. Temporal fatigue, an all too familiar side effect of his astral journey through time. He tilted his head back, closed his eyes, and fell asleep, while the Rolls-Royce passed through the countryside with all the smooth menace of a hunting shark.

Anne and Bill watched a whirlwind descend upon the squad room.

Hartigan, beaming, stood in the centre of the room, ordering men around with the aplomb of a field marshal.

'We need four cars down at *The Cock and Bull*. Make sure uniform has both ends of the street blocked off. And someone ring bloody Teddy at *The Sun* and Hampson at the *Mirror*. I want pictures in both papers first thing tomorrow!' He rubbed his hands and his face lit with delight. 'Bloody Sammy Wilberforce, dead.' He looked at Anne. 'Don't look so upset, luv. Wilberforce had it coming. He's lucky it wasn't us!'

Guffaws greeted Hartigan's joke and he joined in. Quickly, the detectives formed up and marched through the squad room.

'Hang on,' Bill said, stepping in front of Hartigan. 'You're not going off and leaving me and Ruth holding the baby.'

'That's exactly what we're doing, Harry, me lad,' Hartigan said. He positively radiated glee.

'Missed the jungle drums, our Harry has,' another detective said, laughing as he lit a cigarette. Bill's eyes narrowed, and the detective took half a step back.

'Easy, Harry. Just a joke, okay?' Hartigan said.

'Tommy Cooper's funny, you're not!' Anne snapped. 'And we're still waiting for an answer.'

'All right, luv, keep your knickers on. It's not every day someone like Sammy Wilberforce and his gang get wiped out. We've been asked to help with the clean-up.'

'We're coming,' Bill said.

'I'm afraid not, Detectives.'

Bill and Anne turned to Inspector Pearson, who had remained behind when the news came of Wilberforce's death. He had stood back, watching preparations like a hawk.

'Why's that, Inspector?' Anne asked.

'You saw Carnarvon. He's the only survivor of the attack - left for dead by the Big Man. Since he's important to the gangland investigation, someone will have to babysit him.'

'Surely there are men we can spare?' Bill asked.

'It's all hands on deck, Detective Champion,' Pearson said. 'The Big Man has stumbled here. We'll have eyewitnesses, evidence we can gather and use. Plus, we have Carnarvon.' He turned to Anne. 'Keep an eye on him. Mother him a little, if you want. Once we have Wilberforce squared away, we can start asking Carnarvon some questions.' Pearson's sallow features lit up with a predatory glow.

Bill frowned. He looked at Anne and reluctantly nodded.

'Tom, where did you put Carnarvon?'

'Interview room three,' Hartigan called over his shoulder as he exited the room.

Pearson followed the detectives out, their departure marked by receding echoes.

'1973.' Anne shook her head. 'Bad enough the first time around.'

'It wasn't all bad, as I remember. Our first anniversary trip to Niagara Falls, for example.'

Anne smiled. It was strange; it was her smile, and yet it wasn't. 'Just think, we're there now.'

Bill sighed. 'So,' he said, changing the subject. 'What do we do? Warehouse ourselves until we move on again?'

'I did think that the first time, but I've learned that's not how it works. We can't put the lives of our hosts on hold. We can't sit around and wait until Alistair solves whatever it is he's been pulled here for.'

'Agreed. I... *learned* that in 1999. Well, when I say learned, I really mean I was told in no uncertain terms. How we were always a part of events.'

'1999...? But that was four jumps in.'

Bill smiled softly. 'I did have some suspicions before, but...'

Anne nodded grimly. 'I learned it in 1969, the hard way.'

'You'll have to tell me all about it. When we get home.' Bill laughed. 'You wouldn't believe what happened the first time. I ended up in the body of a boy, caught up in London when the Yeti invaded; I was even rescued by the Brig!'

For a few minutes they exchanged stories, comparing experiences. Between them they were able to pin down all previous thirteen temporal locations, all of them within the Brig's timeline.

'The Gnome has sent him here for a reason,' Bill said. 'And here we are…'

'…Caught in his wake. Yes, I worked that out too.'

Bill wasn't surprised. Anne had always been sharp, and she was no stranger to time travel. 'Have you discovered who's behind the Gnome, though?' Anne shook her head, and Bill said, 'I have. Only one person it could be, really.'

'You don't mean…?' Anne smiled. 'Of course, that explains the engravings on the base of the Gnome. It's his handwriting. What do you think, a parting gift for an old friend?'

'Seems likely. The Brig doesn't have much longer left, everybody knows that.'

'Well, whatever he's doing out there,' Anne said, 'helping out at UNIT, reliving one of his greatest hits, I'm just glad you're here with me. Again.' She reached out to hold Bill's hand, and for a moment he let her. Then he pulled his hand away. She briefly looked stung, then she nodded her understanding. 'No, you're right. These aren't our bodies. Ruth and Harry are in the midst of a big investigation into gangland crime. Seems too important to just hide away, or indulge in our proximity.' She smiled, and Bill recognised the twinkle in the stranger's eyes. 'What do you think about playing police officers for a while?'

'You're right. These two have struggled hard enough as it is to get to where they are. We'd kill their careers if we played a dead bat.'

'Good then,' Anne said. 'So, what do you recommend?'

'We're flying blind at the moment. We need to look over the case files. Research our hosts while we're at it. There should be personnel files in the station. Need to play these roles as best as possible. And, on top of all that and helping with the gangland investigation, we're looking into a murder.'

'A murder?' Anne's forehead crinkled.

'Yeah, took a quick look at the files on Harry's desk. Richard Perkins. An ugly death.'

'Richard Perkins? Do I know that name? It sounds familiar...' Anne shrugged. 'It'll come back to me. But, what does "ugly" mean in the context of murder?'

'He was tortured and then drowned in the Crouch End Canal.'

'Delightful,' Anne said, with as much distaste as she could muster. 'Come on then. Let's get to it.'

Two tall stacks of files sat on Harry's desk. He flipped to the end of an open file then closed it and added it to the nearest pile. 'They're hip deep into this investigation,' Bill said.

Anne looked up from poring over the newspaper. The office was empty. A telephone had rung half an hour before, but since then, nothing.

'What have you found?'

'The Big Man plays for keeps. This morning's hit isn't the first one, but it is the most brazen.'

Anne looked around. 'The other detectives aren't coming back, are they?'

'I wouldn't think so. Chances are they're down the pub by now. Beer was a great form of therapy for coppers back in the '70s. Other ranks too, come to think on it.'

'I remember. The trouble some of your men caused.' Anne shook her head. Something in the newspaper caught her attention. 'There's a mention of Wenley Moor. Something about the damage caused by an earthquake a few weeks ago. Wenley Moor...?'

'Earth Reptiles,' Bill supplied.

'Of course. Speaking of Alistair's greatest hits, and not-so-great moments. For such a beige year, 1973 was a busy time for Alistair.'

Bill pulled a folder from a different pile and opened it. 'This Perkins fella. The murder victim. There's something very strange about it.'

'The torture isn't strange enough?'

'Surprisingly not. The mortuary report indicates he was tortured in a different location to where they found his body. The symbol carved into his chest suggests either a grudge, or a message. Or both.' Bill held up a black and white photo. 'Do you want to look?'

Anne nodded.

'It's not pretty,' Bill said.

'I may look different, but I'm still me. I'm sure I've seen worse.'

'True.' Bill handed over the photo.

In the photo, a dead man sprawled on the ground. In a corner, Anne could see water lapping at his feet. His face was turned away, but there was enough detail in the picture to show the heavy bruising.

'Seems like they worked him over for a while,' Anne said, grimacing. She peered at the grainy image, and frowned. She tapped the desk with a fingernail.

'Anything you recognise?' Bill asked, after a minute.

'It could be a religious symbol,' she said. 'I'm missing the internet more than I thought possible. Even some books would be helpful. I think the symbol looks Sumerian.'

'Sumerian? Doesn't that have something to do with the Middle East?'

Anne nodded. 'One of the earliest civilisations. Certainly one of the most mysterious. Gods and magic. The first Flood myth, actually. Some mystics claim the Sumerians spoke directly with the gods, and their writings, in part, relate to the magic they used...' She stopped. 'What? Why are you looking at me like that?'

'I've missed you.' After a moment, Bill cleared his

throat. 'Will we ever return to our bodies, do you think?'

'Alistair did, the first time, so I can't see why we won't. Eventually.'

They let the silence sit between them.

'Tell me about Ruth,' Bill said.

A thin file stamped PERSONNEL sat at her elbow. Anne flipped the folder open.

'Detective Ruth Winters. Second woman in the MET to make detective. You can only imagine what it's like for her since she made the grade. I mean, I had to put up with some stupid stuff back in the '60s, but at least it was within academia. More than any other institution at the time, the police force was *the* personification of a boy's club. With the manners to match.' She shuddered. After a moment, she nodded to a similarly marked folder on Bill's side of the desk. 'What about Detective Champion?'

'Detective Harry Champion. Age... fifty-five.' Bill looked down at his hands and turned them over. 'A middle-aged man of African descent with the rank of Detective in the MET. God help me... Us. Is Ruth married?'

Anne shook her head. 'Harry?'

'Yes,' he said. 'Though his wife is visiting an ill aunt in Jamaica. She won't be back for another week or two.'

'Good,' Anne said, a half smile quirking her lips. 'Otherwise it would be a little... awkward.'

'Awkward doesn't begin to describe what we're going through.' Bill paused, and they stared at each other for a long moment. 'So, that's us. What about this murdered man? The photo seems to indicate possible links to... what, a magical ritual? In 1973?'

'Quite a year, 1973,' Anne said, her eyes distant. 'Satanists in Highgate Cemetery and the Sunday tabloids. Mysticism gone awry, especially after the Age of Aquarius turned sour. Even the sciences were looking into fringe stuff. Even as we speak that damned fool Eric

Stahlman is preparing to pierce the Earth's crust.'

Bill swallowed and looked down. 'I'm starving,' he said suddenly. 'I haven't eaten since 2003.' He patted his pockets. Unrewarded, he pulled open desk drawers until he found a wallet. 'We can come back to Perkins later. I fancy a curry. I discovered a taste for it again on my travels; younger metabolism and all. What about you?'

'Food safety standards aren't what you've come to expect.'

'It didn't kill me then... or now, actually.'

'No, I suppose it didn't.' Anne put the paper down. 'I'd murder a Rogan Josh, actually.'

'Good. I'll explore the High Street, see what I can find. I should be back in... half an hour?'

'I'll hold the fort.'

Snapping a salute, Bill pulled on his jacket and left. His footsteps echoed in the chill corridor and a light fitting fizzed overhead. The night seemed to press on the building, and Bill was glad when he reached the front desk.

'See you soon, Sarge,' Bill said, lowering the countertop. 'I'm getting a curry; do you want anything?'

Sergeant Clifford blinked his eyes into focus. 'Can't stomach any of that muck,' he grumbled. Unconsciously, he ran a hand through his thinning hair. 'Give me a ham sarnie any day.'

'Indian is the future of cuisine,' Bill said breezily as he walked to the door. 'You'll see.'

He smiled at the memory of the old London fogs, then trotted off into the night.

CHAPTER FIVE
Lazarus

MID-EVENING, AND THE ROLLS-ROYCE CROSSED Westminster Bridge. Refreshed after his nap, Alistair stared raptly out the window at the City, memories washing over him as they drove past familiar buildings. Westminster loomed out of the darkness, the old palace slumbering by the Thames.

Max turned a corner and drove north. The Rolls slid past a pair of armed police officers standing at the familiar entrance to Downing Street, before racing to the roundabout in front of Nelson's Column. So strange to see Trafalgar Square open to traffic; it had been pedestrianised for so long in his time, no cars up by the National History Museum, that Alistair had almost forgotten what it was like to drive all the way around Nelson's Column. Max waited for a break in the traffic, tapped the steering wheel impatiently, then darted into a gap and swung the car around to the right, passing St Martin in the Fields.

The streets were largely empty, the gathering fog lit at intervals by the sodium glare of street lamps. Gradually, however, ghostly colours began to light the sky.

Soho. Neon signs covered every inch of the looming buildings and the footpaths became crowded with people. Restaurants, cafes, nightclubs and theatres all declared their names in lurid light. Heads turned to stare at the Rolls-Royce as it rumbled by, then returned to their shouted conversations over the din of other shouted conversations as London's youth partied late into the night.

For a moment, Alistair had an image of a silent London, corpses carpeting the streets as the virus, unchecked in his nightmares from so long ago, swept the capital. In those black dreams, Britain's new masters lurked in their bunker, waiting for the virus to burn itself, and humanity, out.

'Perhaps sealing them away was right, after all,' he murmured, ignoring Max's quirked eyebrow. He glanced at the crumpled copy of *The Times*, and shook his head.

The neon signs changed, their characters growing more Eastern as the driver took them deep into Chinatown. Banners covered in Chinese script hung from buildings and flapped in the breeze.

They paused at an intersection, and Alistair stared at a window filled with plucked ducks. His mouth filled with saliva.

'I trust your boss has laid out some food?' Alistair asked.

'Maybe,' Max said, turning the wheel. 'Never seen him eat, to be honest. If he did, it wouldn't be any of that Spanish muck. How you wogs can stomach it I'll never understand.'

Alistair ignored the racial slur, and returned his gaze to the street.

Western faces had become the minority, replaced by the denizens of Chinatown. Even late at night, the restaurants were open, packed with friends and family dining out. He caught glimpses of old men playing mah-jong at tables on the footpath, unperturbed by the cold or the crowds milling around them. A smile flickered across his face as he remembered a rare night out in the not-so-distant past relative to his current temporal location, dining with Sally as she laughed at his clumsy attempts with chopsticks.

Then he thought about what had happened after. The smile died on his lips, and he sat back. He didn't look out of the window again until the car turned into an alley and came to a stop.

'Out we get,' Max said, opening his door and disappearing into the night. Alistair stepped outside. 'Follow me.'

Nodding, Alistair trailed behind the driver as he led him around the front of the Rolls-Royce. Orange haze lit the rectangular view of the sky overhead. Stepping around bins overflowing with rubbish, Alistair watched Max bang on a blank metal door half way along the alley.

A metal slot slid open and suspicious eyes squinted at them. The slot slammed shut and the door creaked open on rusted hinges. A dark figure filled the doorway, and a shaved, bullet-shaped head swivelled to look at them like a tank's gun turret.

'Got the Big Man's guest,' Max said. 'Are they back?'

The man on the door rumbled an answer too low and deep for Alistair to understand. Max chuckled. He turned his head.

'Sounds like the Big Man is back from his... meeting. He should be in a good mood. Come on.'

Ignoring the guard's hostile glare, Alistair followed Max down a tiled corridor. The temperature and humidity began to rise, until Alistair felt sweat trickling down his collar. Machinery clanked as light spilled into the corridor. They emerged into an industrial laundry. The sharp smell of chemicals filled his nostrils as Alistair dodged around a crowd of men and women hard at work, filling machines and emptying dryers. Large wheeled wicker baskets lined one wall, packed with linen, awaiting delivery across the city. Blank faces carefully avoided catching his gaze and, soon enough, they had crossed the damp concrete floor and plunged down a precipitous set of stairs.

Pipes burbled overhead. Condensation ran down the walls, and Alistair heard the faint squeals of rats. They entered another corridor, narrower than the last. It led to yet another metal door, this time braced with rivets and metal bands.

'Your boss is concerned for his security,' Alistair said.

Head brushing the ceiling, Max smiled humourlessly. 'He's got a target on his back, that's for sure. Bigger after today's... ahh, meeting.' He raised his fist to bang on the door then paused, looking over his shoulder. 'You carrying?'

Alistair nodded.

Max held out a hand. 'Give it to me. Don't look like that; I'll give it back to you after you meet the boss.'

Reluctantly, Alistair pulled his revolver out and handed it over. Max hefted the weapon in his hand, nodding appreciatively. He slipped it into his jacket then banged on the door and looked up at a bulky security camera staring at them. Alistair saw the lens adjust slightly, and the camera moved on whining servos until it centred on him. After a long minute, bolts were thrown, then the heavy door silently opened.

Immediately, a man in a tight suit and wielding a pistol confronted them. Behind him stood another armed man. Max raised his arms. He looked over his shoulder and nodded to Alistair.

'You'd best do the same.'

Alistair raised his arms and watched impassively as the guard checked Max.

'As you can see,' he said wryly, as the guard roughly patted him down, 'I'm not armed with anything other than—'

'Shut it,' the guard said, his mouth turned down in a scowl. He shoved the door and it closed with a hollow boom. He jabbed a thumb over his shoulder. 'He's waiting for you.' He slid his pistol into a holster under his jacket.

The corridor opened into a dark room, lit by a single lamp sitting on a table. The only other exit was another door on the far side of the room. Large paintings, of men at war, hung on the walls around the room. Otherwise, the room was as Spartan as it was material.

As his eyes grew used to the dim light, Alistair's became aware of a large figure seated at the only table. Only one hand was visible. Thick blunt fingers tapped restlessly on the green felt. Alistair became uncomfortably aware of how isolated he was down there. *If they wanted,* he thought, *they could make me disappear from the face of the Earth.*

The armed guards and Max silently exited through the far door. Time stretched around Alistair. The figure shifted in his chair. The fingers ceased their tapping. Alistair waited, then the man stood and moved into the light.

And Alistair found himself face to face with a nightmare from his past.

Tall, taller than Max, and taller than Alistair by a full head and shoulders. A chest that spread wide, pulling at the seams of a pinstriped jacket. A cruel face, with the full, sensuous lips of the most degenerate of Roman emperors. Brooding brow, a squared off nose, and eyes that had seen the light of alien suns.

'Vaar!' Alistair breathed, and watched as the Dominator reached for him with a hand that had crushed skulls.

'So, you are the Matador,' Vaar said, holding out his hand.

Dumbfounded, Alistair looked at the hand as if he had never seen one before. Hurriedly, he shook it. Thick, powerful fingers grabbed his hand, and Alistair felt his bones grind under the powerful grip. Images of September 1970 rushed through his mind; images indelibly burned into the hippocampus. Sally, Bill, Chorley, Sebastian Collins... Vaar! It was all Alistair could do not to strike the blasted Dominator there and then.

Vaar released his hold, a ghost of a smile on his face. He returned to his seat with a long, winded sigh. Beckoning, he indicated that Alistair should bring up a chair himself. Fighting every instinct, reminding himself he was back in 1973 for a reason, Alistair obligingly sat at the table, waiting with unaccustomed nervousness for Vaar to speak.

'You come highly recommended.'

'You gave me little choice,' Alistair said. He could sense the Matador's outrage.

'I made you a fair offer. You chose to make it personal.'

Alistair leaned forward, jabbing the table with a finger. 'I chose? You kidnapped my niece!' The anger was real, and it didn't all come from the Matador. 'You sent men to my sister's home and took her. If not for the gun they held to Lucia's head, her father would've killed all of them.'

Vaar looked impassively at him. 'Have you finished?' he said at last.

Alistair nodded.

'Good. We are men of destiny, are we not? Men of destiny keep their agreements. Once you have accomplished your task, then she will be returned to you.'

Alistair sat back. He found himself breathing heavily. He ran a hand down his jacket, smoothing it as he fought to control his temper. Finally, he nodded. 'I want to see her. I want to see Lucia now.'

Vaar's eyes narrowed slightly. After a moment, he nodded. Reaching for a tiny silver bell sitting beside the lamp, he rang it, the tinny noise at odds with the room's heavy atmosphere. After a moment, the rear door opened and Max entered.

'Bring the girl. And hurry. My guest and I have business to discuss.'

Max glanced at Alistair. He nodded and left the room.

'You will see we have taken good care of her. I'm a business man. She is... an asset.' Vaar smirked, then he coughed. He ignored Alistair's look. 'Do you drink?'

Startled, Alistair nodded.

'Good. What will you have? I myself do not drink, but I understand that many men do.'

'Scotch,' Alistair said immediately. 'Neat.'

Vaar rose slowly to his feet. He tottered for a moment, then gained his balance. Alistair watched him cross the room to a heavy sideboard, where several bottles of alcohol and empty glasses sat. He noted with some amusement that Vaar dressed in the garb of 1930s America mobster; black shoes, dark, three-piece pin stripe suit. On the table, a black fedora with a red headband rested by the lamp.

Looking more closely, he noted Vaar had little of the raw vitality he'd exhibited when they had last met. The Dominator seemed to be ill, in a way Alistair didn't understand. Perhaps he could learn why; he never did find out what had happened to Dominic Vaar after... after Sally.

He swallowed down the anger and asked, as politely as possible, 'Are you unwell?'

Vaar poured two fingers of scotch into a tumbler then sat the bottle down heavily.

'I am... fatigued,' Vaar said, returning with the tumbler. 'The last four years have not been kind to me, and I have a number of interests that are reaching fruition.' He placed it before Alistair and sat down with a grunt. 'It is of no matter,' he said, waving his hand irritably.

'I want to make sure my employer doesn't drop dead before the job is done. It will do my niece no good if your organisation collapses without you, and I can't get her back.'

'Do your job and you will have no fear of that,' Vaar said.

'You can rely on that,' Alistair said, almost spitting the words.

'Professional pride? That I can appreciate. You have prepared well, then?'

'This is not the first time I have broken into a vault.' The question nettled him. 'I have the equipment and skills, and you have given me the motive.' Alistair leaned forward. 'When do you want it done?'

'Over the weekend. Business will be shuttered. A perfect time to take what is rightfully mine.'

'And that is...?'

'An artefact,' Vaar said. His eyes were dark hollows, the spark Alistair had become familiar with gone. After a moment's hesitation, Vaar went on. 'I am a... collector, shall we say?'

'Why not do it yourself? You have the men.'

'My attention is taken up with other matters,' Vaar said. 'You are not aware of it, but you sit at the centre of a vast machine whose parts are beginning to align.'

Alistair sipped more scotch. His mind raced. He sensed this was the reason he had come to 1973. To foil Vaar's plans, whatever they might be. No matter the cost.

The rear door opened. Alistair felt unfamiliar emotions well up when he recognised the girl framed in the doorway. Her eyes widened in recognition. She broke free of Max's grip on her shoulder and ran towards Alistair, launching herself into his arms.

Weeping, she buried her head into his shoulder. Hitching sobs wracked her thin body.

'*Tio*,' she cried. 'Oh, *Tio*.'

Awkwardly, Alistair patted her on the back. Vaar watched him impassively.

'Here, little one,' Alistair said. He pulled a handkerchief from a pocket and dabbed at the tears streaking her face. For a brief second he saw Kate as a child, and with a sting he realised that his daughter was indeed out there in England. A child, unaware that soon, oh too soon, she would be taken away from her father. '*Tio* is here, all right?'

'Mama? Papa? Are they here too?' Lucia looked avidly around the room, shrinking back into Alistair's arms when she saw Vaar. Fresh tears welled in her eyes.

'They are at home, *sobrina*,' Alistair said.

'Are we going home?' Lucia asked, her bottom lip quivering.

Alistair frowned. 'Not today. *Tio* has something to do first, then we will go home. Together.'

Lucia nodded, but Alistair sensed how deeply traumatised she was. He glared at Vaar. 'I will do this thing for you, and nothing more. As soon as it is done, my niece will be returned to me. Unharmed. You may be a man of business, but I am a man of honour. Yes?'

Inclining his head, Vaar motioned impatiently to Max, who came forward. This prompted a fresh bout of tears from Lucia. Alistair wiped them away, then hugged her close.

'Remember your brother? He would laugh to see you cry like this. Be strong, and you will have a great adventure to tell him all about, yes?'

She sucked in a shuddering breath and nodded. Max took Lucia by the hand and led her away. The door closed behind them with a soft thud.

An uncomfortable silence descended over the two men. Alistair finished his scotch and set the tumbler down. Vaar seemed to sink into himself, disengaging from his surroundings. In the silence, his ragged breathing was noticeable. Alistair noted the chalkiness of his skin. The very air of vitality the Dominator had exuded on their previous encounters was absent.

Time stretched. Alistair waited to be dismissed, but Vaar did nothing. The gloom was suddenly lit by a crimson light bursting into life above the entrance. Vaar stirred from his stupor. The door creaked open and a man in a business suit entered.

'Mr Holcombe,' Vaar greeted the man. 'A solicitor,' he said to Alistair. 'I am not sure what a solicitor does, other than take money to send messages on my behalf.'

Alistair wasn't entirely sure, but he suspected Vaar had made a joke.

Holcombe came forward. Alistair sensed the man was incredibly nervous. Vaar, it seemed, evoked extreme emotions.

'It seems my driver, Carnarvon, is not dead,' Vaar began, without preamble. 'A pity, but we work with the hand we are dealt. He is in custody at the Crouch End Police Station. I have a message for him I want you to pass on.'

Holcombe nodded. 'We should keep as much distance between Carnarvon and yourself, Mr Vaar. He is–'

Vaar raised a hand and Holcombe immediately subsided. Alistair felt a little sorry for the solicitor, who had the look of a man trapped in a burning house.

Vaar pulled an envelope from his jacket and slid it across the table towards Holcombe, who nervously snatched it up.

'See what Carnarvon says,' Vaar said. 'If he is amenable, tell him he will be taken care of in the morning.' He paused, and the silence grew ominous. 'If he has formed a different view of how he should proceed, pass him the letter. Tell him it is… severance pay, yes?' Vaar watched Holcombe slip the letter into his jacket pocket. 'If it is required, make sure only Mr Carnarvon receives the letter.' He smiled. Alistair saw Holcombe shudder. 'Do not be too curious about its contents, Mr Holcombe.'

Holcombe went a little pale. He nodded jerkily, then turned and scuttled towards the rear door.

'It should be an interesting experiment,' Vaar remarked. If he wanted a reply from Alistair, he didn't wait for it. 'One of my plans...' His voice trailed off, and the ghost of a smile played on his full lips.

'So then,' Vaar said after a moment. 'You are ready to fulfil the task I have set?'

Alistair nodded. He twisted the tumbler around on the table. 'What about the police?'

Vaar shook his head. 'What about them? I have built my operation from nothing, and they have not had the intellect to stop me. Only a fool would allow himself to be caught. I am many things, and certainly not a fool. There are police on my trail, detectives at the Crouch End Police Station who have been investigating me and my organisation for some time.' Vaar sneered. 'Most of the detectives in the unit are lazy. All they think about is drink and women. Some are more perceptive, tenacious even. A part of me admires those few dedicated to their cause. However, their efforts will come to naught. They, like all who stand in my way, will be crushed.'

It took a moment for Alistair to realise the grimace that crawled across Vaar's face was in fact a smile.

'And these other detectives? The perceptive ones?'

'Outsiders from their own kind. They hold no sway, have no influence. They cause me no concern.'

'I'm sure,' Alistair murmured, then paused. He glanced at Vaar, who stared back at him. And thought of Bill who was out there somewhere in 1973, in some poor innocent's body. He was glad Bill was not here; he'd have a harder time containing his anger than Alistair did.

Just then, the light above the door lit up once again. The red glow washed crimson across the room. Alistair twisted in his chair.

'We have another visitor?'

'*I* have other visitors,' Vaar said. 'My plans begin to bear fruit.' His eyes grew distant, distracted. He rang the bell. 'Max will see you to your accommodation. Rest, and prepare yourself. I expect full success, do you understand?'

Alistair nodded. He was intensely keen to see who the visitor was. He drained his glass, then slowly rose to his feet. Max entered the room.

'Take our friend to his lodgings,' Vaar told Max. 'Afterwards, I am afraid our association with Mr Holcombe has come to the end of its usefulness. See that he is dealt with, in the usual way.' Vaar pressed a button sitting beside a lamp, and a buzzer sounded.

Alistair didn't miss the undertone. Max nodded. He beckoned to Alistair, who rose and followed him to the rear door.

Alistair paused on the threshold when he heard the door at the other end of the room open with a clank. Two men, one tall, the other short, stood framed in the doorway. He couldn't see the latter, but when a spill of light fell across the former's austere, ravaged face, his breath caught in his throat and he froze. The two men entered and Vaar stood to greet them.

A hand clapped on Alistair's shoulder and turned him around.

'No hanging around, mate. Not when the Big Man is seeing those two. Come on; let's get you to your lodgings. Tonight will be the last good sleep you'll have for a few days.'

Alistair nodded absently.

The scarred face, a memento of the Eastern Front. The aristocratic mien, product of generations of Prussian rule, was all too familiar. Memories of his encounter with Schädengeist, so long ago now, rose to the surface. In the aftermath, he had made sure to familiarise himself with all the other potential Nazis in hiding. He had sworn to never be caught off guard again. He had seen the photos, had studied them with grim fury.

That face, and the shocking crimes attached to it, had remained with him for many years.

Von Werner.

Alistair felt a shiver, a mingling of unease and excitement, worm its way up his spine.

CHAPTER SIX
One Shot

THE VILLAGE BURNED. IN THE TWISTING DARKNESS, WHERE shadows jumped as flames leaped, men and women and children ran, screaming. Men clad in black stalked them, machine guns barking ferociously. A building collapsed in a great belching of flame and cinders, sending a cloud of choking smoke into the street. A tall officer, face striped red and black by flames and shadow, limped back and forth across the entrance to the main square. The cane he used had a silver wolf's head, which winked in the flickering light.

'Where are they?' he screamed at a group huddled in front of him. A number of his men stood menacingly behind him. The officer waved a pistol about, and the villagers cringed.

One of the cowering men looked up, his face a mask of terror. 'We don't know. How can we know, when—'

The man's broken German descended into panicked Polish and a moan came from the crowd.

'Stop speaking that pig language!' the officer roared, spittle flying from his mouth.

Bloody light sparked from the lightning bolt runes on his collars and the skull badge in his black cap. When the villager continued his panicked pleading, the officer raised his pistol and shot the man through the head. The body toppled into the arms of a sobbing woman.

'German!' the officer yelled. 'Speak German or you all die!'

'They have gone,' a young man said, stepping forward. The light rendered his head into a skull, drained of life but not defiance.

'They were here? The man, his wife and the child?' asked

the officer eagerly. He holstered his pistol and stepped close. Shadows crawled over his face. Only his eyes shone, a silver quickening in the ruddy light.

The young man nodded. Gunfire roared, more screams filled the night, and another building collapsed.

'Where are they? Tell me, and you live.'

Amid the carnage, the young man smiled. A strange calm settled over him. 'You have missed your chance, Nazi pig!' he sneered. 'Whatever knowledge you sought, it has vanished with him. There is nothing for you here. Nothing!' He spat at the feet of the officer, whose face contorted with rage.

They stared at one another for a moment, then the officer stepped close, so that their chests almost touched.

'I will build an empire on your corpses!' he snarled, and then his arm jerked forward.

The man's mouth contorted into an 'O' of agony. Blood gushed from the wound in his belly, and the officer kicked him backwards.

Banshee keening filled the air. Ignoring it, the officer turned to his men.

'Full auto!' he screamed, waving his dagger and spraying blood through the air. 'Kill them all!'

Machine guns roared, the endless chatter only stilled when the final screams drifted away into the darkness and the hungry crackle of flames filled the night.

Von Werner shook his head, dissolving the memories that he found increasingly claimed his distracted moments. He sat uncomfortably close to his companion, who whistled tunelessly to himself as they waited. He felt breathless in the waiting room's humid grip. Tightening his hold on his cane, he felt the wolf's head bite into his flesh and was glad of the distraction. He shifted in the chair, aware of the dull, grinding pain in his hip.

'Daydreaming of the good old days?'

'What?' Von Werner looked at his companion, smoothing the sneer curling his lip.

'You went away for a little while there. You looked... happy.' The other man, with a face many in the press described as cherubic, smiled a secret smile that made von Werner wince inwardly.

'Mr Arbuthnot. I think... I think the sooner our plans come to fruition, the sooner we will all be happy.'

Arbuthnot nodded, his floppy brown hair rising and falling over a pink scalp. Von Werner couldn't stand the man. However, he did recognise his almost demonic political skills. Von Werner didn't mistake the man's glad-handing as anything other than what it was. The almost pathological need for power shone just beneath the surface.

He straightened when the door opened, and a guard lumbered into the room, reducing the space with his bulk.

'He will see you both now.'

Von Werner looked at the guard, his lip curling slightly. *Gangster scum,* he thought. With some difficulty, he levered himself to his feet. Arbuthnot joined him and they both followed the guard down the corridor. They waited a moment while the door was unbarred, then entered.

The room was familiar. The figure exiting at the rear of the room was not. For a moment, their eyes locked, and von Werner felt a sensation he hadn't felt in many years.

Recognition.

Then the man disappeared through the door, which closed, leaving them with Dominic Vaar, who stood to greet them both.

'And my old friend Mr Arbuthnot,' he said, smiling tightly. 'Colonel,' he said, turning and taking von Werner's hand. He beckoned them to sit at the table.

Only Vaar dared openly address him by his old military title. Von Werner had come to marginally tolerate it.

'Vaar,' von Werner said, sliding gratefully into the chair. He set his cane across his knees.

'A drink?' Vaar asked both men.

Arbuthnot nodded eagerly. Von Werner had smelled gin on him earlier. He had remarked, early on in his relationship with Vaar, that Arbuthnot's excessive drinking made him a problematic vessel for their plans.

Vaar had simply shaken his head. 'You are incorrect, Colonel,' he had said. 'A man with that sort of weakness is more easily led. You will see.'

'Gin, is that right?' Pouring for him, Vaar handed Arbuthnot a glass.

He swallowed a mouthful and sat back, sighing contentedly.

Without asking, Vaar poured out a glass of schnapps for von Werner. It had unnerved him, the first time they had met, that Vaar knew his drink of choice. Capping the bottle, Vaar settled back in his chair, which creaked under his weight. Von Werner looked at him carefully. Vaar had grown worse since they had last met.

Toasting him, von Werner took a careful sip of the schnapps. The grinding pain in his hip lessened somewhat as the warmth spread through his chest.

'Only the best, eh?' he said, nodding his thanks to Vaar.

'What is power without its small luxuries?'

Arbuthnot giggled.

'Power is the privilege of the strong,' von Werner said, ignoring Arbuthnot.

Vaar nodded in acknowledgement. Von Werner could tell Vaar was in some discomfort. Vaar turned to Arbuthnot.

'You will declare your hand against the Prime Minister early in the week?'

'Tuesday,' Arbuthnot said. He looked into his empty glass and then stared hopefully at Vaar, who ignored him. Arbuthnot's smile slipped a little. 'The numbers are coming in for me now.'

'They will come faster when my... demonstration has the intended effect.'

'I am not keen that my ascension to the prime ministership will be sanctified in blood,' Arbuthnot said.

'Why, it will be perfect,' von Werner said. '*Blut* and *stehlen*, as we used to say in the old days.'

Arbuthnot subsided, turning the glass in his hands.

'Who was the man leaving as we arrived?' von Werner said to Vaar, abruptly changing topic.

'The solution to our problem,' Vaar said. A satisfied smile spread across the harsh planes of his face.

'When will he begin?'

'This weekend. By Monday, our man will have broken into the vault and liberated the item. We are very close, Colonel. Very close.'

'And then we can perform the ritual,' von Werner said, his eyes shining behind his glasses.

'Oh yes.' Vaar's face slipped into shadow as he sat back. 'Yes, indeed.'

Inspired by the song blasting from a passing car, Bill returned to the station whistling *The Laughing Gnome*, not at all ironically, a plastic carrier bag in each hand. From inside each bag wafted the most mouth-watering aromas he had smelled in decades. The sergeant dozed at the front desk, his snores filling the reception area like a gasping, wheezing chainsaw. Above him, the clock ticked closer to 10pm.

Bill looked on the old man with some sympathy. As quietly as he could, he crossed the floor and eased up the counter flap. Lowering it, he entered the corridor, making his way to the squad room. He looked around, nonplussed at the quiet. Anne had vanished.

Dumping the food onto their shared desk, Bill

scratched his scalp. The short, tight curls felt strange under his fingers.

'Anne!' he called. Then hissed at his lapse. 'Erm, Ruth!'

Outside, a car's horn blared for a long moment before it faded away. He heard a distant, attenuated conversation, as if a radio had been half-tuned to a frequency. A light came from beneath a door at the far end of the room. Bill moved down the aisle between desks and pushed open the door.

Anne sat watching a number of small black and white monitors stacked on a desk. Empty rooms showed on all but one, which revealed two men sitting at a desk, deep in conversation.

'What's going on?' Bill asked, closing the door.

'A pretty big civil rights violation, I should say.' Anne's eyes were locked on the screen showing the men.

'They've got the interview room wired for sound?' Bill asked, pulling up a chair and sitting down.

'Audio and visual. The Law Society would have a field day if they knew this sort of carry-on was happening.'

'Who's that with Carnarvon?' Bill leaned in closer.

'His solicitor. Someone named Holcombe. Arrived a few minutes after you left and demanded to see his client. Clifford signed him in.'

'How's Carnarvon?'

'Angry. He's not putting up with what the solicitor's saying. Listen.'

Anne twisted a knob and the low mutter of voices resolved into a heated disagreement. Carnarvon stabbed his finger at the solicitor.

'Tell the Big Man to get me outta here, do you understand? Bleeding coppers won't even take me to the hospital.' He touched the bump on his head. 'Bloody head's killing me.' He jabbed the table with his index finger. 'The Big Man left me for dead and took off.'

The reference to the Big Man jolted Anne and Bill.

'Holcombe isn't representing Carnarvon at all,' Anne said, as the two men on the screen pointed at each other.

'You need to calm down,' Holcombe said. He looked nervously around the room. 'Come the morning, this will all be sorted.'

'Don't tell me to calm down!' Carnarvon stormed. He bared his teeth. 'I'm already out on parole. If the Big Man won't get me outta here, I'll cut a deal with the filth.'

A hush descended over the interview room.

'Parole?' Holcombe said, breaking the silence. 'You didn't tell anyone that when you were recruited.'

Carnarvon must have seen something in the Holcombe's face. He raised his hands. 'I didn't mean to say what I said, Mr Holcombe,' he stammered. 'You know I didn't mean it. Of course, I wouldn't say nothin' against the Big Man. Tell him... Tell him I'll sit tight as long as he wants, until he sorts out that other thing.'

'And what other thing would that be?'

Carnarvon could only stare mutely at the solicitor. Holcombe looked down at a buff manila folder sitting on the desk in front of him. He reached for it, then hesitated a moment. He glanced at Carnarvon, and his eyes narrowed slightly. He flipped open the folder, revealing an envelope.

Bill shared a glance with Anne. 'When Holcombe goes, I want to find out what that other thing is.'

Anne nodded, but didn't speak.

'Our mutual employer values your efforts,' Holcombe said, pushing the envelope towards Carnarvon. 'He regrets the haste of his departure. He has instructed me that your association with him regrettably must come to an end. This is your... severance pay. As a gesture of goodwill, he will post bail for you tomorrow morning. Until then, sit tight, Mr Carnarvon. All will be well.'

Holcombe stood while Carnarvon stared first at him,

then at the envelope. Holcombe was almost at the door when Carnarvon yelled out.

'You make sure he understands that I'll do whatever is needed! I'm a good soldier, tell him.'

Holcombe nodded. 'I'll be sure to do just that.' The door closed with a snick.

'Should we speak with the solicitor?' Bill wondered.

Shaking her head, Anne pointed at the screen. 'I want to take a look at that letter.'

'Why? It's probably just a note to stay quiet.'

'Then Holcombe should've told him that. Let's go see Carnarvon.'

'Wait.' Bill's skin prickled. The air felt cold.

On the screen, he watched Carnarvon reach for the envelope. He tore it open, the sound mixing with the static so harsh it hurt Bill's borrowed ears. Gingerly, Carnarvon removed a piece of paper and unfolded it.

More static filled the speakers, the sound of nails on a blackboard. Anne winced and then the image on the screen warped. Carnarvon's body slid back and forth and his mouth opened wide in a silent scream. White light enveloped the screen, so bright Anne's and Bill's shadows were pinned to the wall behind them. The static rose to a shriek and the image resolved itself. Carnarvon had disappeared, leaving behind a room roaring with flames. Distant screams filled the speakers as Anne and Bill ran from the room.

Smoke seeped from beneath the door leading into the interview room. Bill grabbed a bulky fire extinguisher off the wall. Inverting it, he tore out the pin as Anne reached the door.

'It's too dangerous to go in!' she called. She snatched her hand away from the door handle, wincing. She could hear fire crackling on the other side the door, which had begun to char.

'We'll lose the building if we don't contain it. Are you ready?'

The two exchanged a look for a precious moment, then Anne nodded. Stripping off her jacket, she wrapped it around her hand then groped for the door handle, turning it with a fumbling effort. The heat from the other side was enormous. Anne kicked the door open, and dived aside as flames roared out.

Bill triggered the extinguisher and fire retardant billowed out. Flames leaped back, and a choking ball of smoke filled the corridor. Bill advanced, spraying retardant into every corner of the room. Anne followed, her jacket held to her mouth, eyes stinging and running.

The interview room lay in ruins. In the inferno's brief life, its heat had buckled chairs and left the table slumped over like a dying animal. Chunks of melted glass from the shattered two-way mirror lay in shimmering pools on the blackened floor. Part of the ceiling had collapsed, exposing charred joists and the chalky underside of the roof tiles.

'Where is he?' Bill called, looking frantically around.

Smoke and retardant rolled across the floor in a slow-moving fog. An alarm rang hollowly. Anne had the terrifying image of a charred body emerging from the miasma, a blackened arm pointing accusingly at her.

'I don't know,' she said, coughing. She shoved the remains of the table aside with her hip, and the melted slag that had once been an ashtray fell to the floor with a soft thud. She stepped back and almost tripped over. She looked down at her feet.

'Bill.' Her eyes grew wide as she waved away the smoke with her jacket. It eddied around the twisted object lying on the ground.

'Ah, there he is,' Bill said, standing beside her. A streak of ash-mingled sweat marked his brow. He dropped to one knee, ignoring the heat rolling around them. 'It's a trick, surely?' he said, looking up at Anne. 'The Master wasn't operating on Earth at this time, was he?'

Anne shook her head, staring at the thing on the floor. 'As I recall he'd been on Earth at least a year before making himself known, setting up his Emil Keller identity. But it can't have been him. Carnarvon was the only person in the room. You saw the monitor.'

'Then what happened to him?'

A voice disturbed them from the doorway. 'What the bloody hell's that?'

It was the old desk sergeant. His face was white, and he clung like a drowning sailor to the charred doorframe.

'It's a body,' Bill said, his voice rasping from smoke inhalation.

He looked first at Anne, then down at the twisted doll on the floor, its face twisted in agony.

CHAPTER SEVEN
China Girl

'It's not much,' Max said, opening the door and flicking on a light switch. He stepped aside to allow Alistair to enter.

'That's an understatement,' Alistair said, surveying the tiny room. 'But it will do.'

He placed his case on the narrow, sagging bed. A cracked basin stood beside it, and beside that was a small, round table with two mismatched chairs. A blackened window looked onto a brick wall. The ceiling sagged in places and the paint colour could only charitably be described as mustard.

'Mr Vaar wants to keep you at a distance. He doesn't want any links between him and your job.'

'The feeling's mutual,' Alistair said.

'Right. Toilet and bathroom are down the hallway.' Max indicated the corridor with a nod of his head. 'Mrs Chin serves breakfast at eight sharpish, and if you miss dinner, well, there's a grand place that sells dumplings down the road if you're peckish.'

From the floor above, they heard muffled shouting, and then the sharper sound of something shattering against a wall.

'I see the evening's entertainment has started,' Alistair said.

Max looked at him incomprehensibly for a moment, before his face lit with a delighted grin. 'I've known a few

Spaniards in my time. None had a sense of humour,' Max said. 'Must be living under that arse Franco.' He looked around. 'I know it's late, but I'm starving. What about you?'

'The Big Man doesn't mind me moving around?'

'As far as I understand it, no one knows who you are. Tell you what, if anyone asks, you're my long-lost cousin from Majorca. Happy with that?'

Alistair nodded. He was beginning to warm to the knockabout fellow. And truth be told, he was absolutely famished.

'Good then. So, what do you want to eat?'

'How about Chinese?' Alistair suggested. 'I haven't had one in… Well, it feels like decades.'

'Not paella? Come on, surely you want something homegrown? No?' When Alistair mutely shook his head, Max grinned. 'Well, we're in the right part of London for Chinese. A bit partial to it myself. Not much choice since Mr Vaar set up shop here.'

'Will my case be all right?'

'Mrs Chin runs a tight ship. You're right as rain here, even if it is on the cheap side.'

'And my revolver?'

'Almost forgot.' Smiling, Max took the pistol from his jacket. 'Handsome piece.' He handed the weapon back to Alistair, who slipped it into its holster. 'Come on,' Max said. 'Let's get some nosh.'

It was late. The two men walked through a thin drizzle that had driven the earlier crowds away. Neon signs cast distorted images across the slick roads. Banners snapped in the fitful gusts of wind. A haunting, reed thin sound, as of a flute, floated somewhere overhead. In the distance, the sodium haze of Central London lit the sky, lending the night an otherworldly aspect.

After a few minutes, Max stopped in front of a narrow

shopfront. 'This is it,' he said.

Peering inside, Alistair saw several people dining, while shapes moved behind a long counter. Entering, they were seated at a table at the rear of the restaurant by an unsmiling waitress. She handed them both a menu, then disappeared behind a black lacquered screen.

After a few minutes spent perusing the menu, a young woman, her black hair pinned high, emerged from behind the screen and approached them. The men gave their orders. After she left, Alistair settled back in his chair and closed his eyes for a moment.

'Long day?' Max asked.

When he opened his eyes again, Alistair saw Max staring at him. He shrugged. 'In my line of work there are many long days. It would be the same for you, yes?'

'Yeah,' Max said. The waitress reappeared and poured each a cup of green tea, and left the pot behind. Max took a sip of his and sighed. 'Wouldn't have thought I'd take to this sort of grub,' he said, turning the cup around in his hands and staring into the depths. He looked up. 'Why do you call yourself the Matador?'

'Because I lead my enemies a merry dance and then I kill them,' Alistair said. The words sounded rehearsed, as if the Matador had been asked the questions dozens of times before.

Max chuckled, and thumped the table with the knuckles of one fist. 'Good. Very good. I like that.'

'Are you a local?' Alistair was keen to change the subject.

Max shook his head. 'Mr Vaar only set up shop in the last six months. Before that, I drifted from place to place. Had some steady work up north a few years back, until there wasn't. When they let everyone back in after what the tabloids called *the London Event*, I followed. Thought there might be work down here.'

'How did you meet him?' Alistair was desperately

aware he knew very little of Vaar's plans and operation.

'He needed men to build out his operations. Heard he needed some muscle. Best job I've had in a while.' Max paused, and leaned forward. 'Turns out Mr Vaar's got a few fingers in a few pies.'

'Has he?'

'Oh yeah,' Max said. 'He's built some sort of factory on the outskirts of London. None of us know why, but we think it has to do with expansion plans he has.'

'Drugs?'

'None of that. Mr Vaar broke the legs of one of the new men who tried to peddle it. Didn't he scream.' Max laughed, a little unpleasantly. 'No, I'm sure Mr Vaar will tell us in his own time what the factory is all about.'

The food came out in a cloud of steam and multiple plates heaving with food. The two men toasted one another with their small white cups of green tea. A memory of a dinner date with Fiona came to Alistair's mind, the beginning of the end of their marriage. It wasn't that far away, in relative terms. Perhaps it was a result of the time jumps, but he found himself naturally pondering contemporary things wherever he ended up, remembering events he hadn't thought about in, in some cases, decades. With a slight grimace, he forced the memory away and concentrated instead on his meal.

'What did you do before?' he asked.

'Army,' Max said, dextrously wielding a pair of chopsticks to pluck a dumpling from a plate.

'Really?' Alistair frowned slightly.

'Did my bit when I came out of school. A pity it coincided with Suez...' Max's voice trailed away, and he shook his head.

'Bad business?'

'Bad enough.' Max's eyes were distant for a moment. 'I didn't hang around after, that's for sure. What about you? Why are you in the business?'

'Money,' Alistair said. The Matador's memories spoke of an early life of war and deprivation, and a deep-seated desire to never be hungry again.

'Only money? There are easier ways to earn a crust.'

'Maybe... Risk, I think you would say. The quiet life is not for me.' Alistair stabbed a dumpling with a chopstick. 'I have no choice, though. Your boss, Mr Vaar, is holding my niece captive. I refused his first offer and now I must accept his second.'

An uncomfortable silence descended over the table. Max wiped his mouth with the back of his hand, and contemplated his cup of tea.

'You know,' he said, eager suddenly to change the subject. 'The Limehouse Ripper operated in this area? Sometime in the late 1800s.'

'It's no surprise, I suppose, that a criminal is interested in true crime,' Alistair said, managing a smile. The brief tension dissipated.

He didn't want to alienate the man. It would be hard enough to rescue Lucia and thwart Vaar's plans without having to look over his shoulder. Von Werner's meeting with Vaar also troubled him, but he put that aside for now.

'What I'm saying is, we could take a walk,' Max said, his face transformed with boyish enthusiasm. 'I've often thought that when I get out of the game, I might start up a tour. Here's where the Ripper's last victim was found, or, what sort of creature could tear someone apart like that?'

'Perhaps it was simply a ridiculously large rat,' Alistair said, genuinely amused, remembering a story Leela had once told him long ago in 1981.

'Nah, you're having a lend of me.'

'Believe me,' Alistair said. 'I'm deadly serious.' He smiled disarmingly, and for a moment Max looked unsure.

'You are,' Max said finally, breaking into a chuckle. He shook his head and contemplated the empty plates scattered across the table. 'Let's walk this lot off. Once around the block and then I'll take you back to Mrs Chin's finest establishment.'

'Her finest? I'd hate to see what her worst looked like,' Alistair said, feigning astonishment.

Max laughed. He pulled a couple of notes from his wallet and tossed them onto the table, waving away Alistair's offer to pay.

Outside, Max led Alistair down the street. A thin fog had replaced the drizzle. A distant horn sounded, drifting eerily from the Thames. A cat screamed in the distance.

'You get a sense of the place now, don't you?' Max said.

A tall building loomed over them, the nearest wall thickly clustered with pasted bills. The weather had ruined most of them, the cheap ink running, faces and names distorted as the elements did their work. One of the stencilled figures resembled a melted waxwork, and the image of shop window dummies running amok suddenly came to Alistair. Almost two months ago now, of course. He shivered, hunching his shoulders against the chill.

They ventured into the fog. Buildings smeared and windows turned hollow. Max turned his head at the sound of scuffed boots. Alistair glanced over his shoulder and saw several indistinct shapes moving in the mist. His skin prickled.

'Someone's tailing us,' Max murmured.

'Who do you think it is?' Alistair asked.

In unconscious agreement, both men began walking quickly.

'Might be Wilberforce's men looking for some payback.'

Alistair peered into the fog. 'Is there an alley up here?'

'Yeah. About thirty yards. What are you thinking?'

'We can lose them, if we hurry. I'm not interested in a fight, unless we have to.'

They walked on, Alistair feeling like a target had been pinned to his back. His senses screamed that their pursuers were closing in rapidly. The revolver riding at his hip gave him some comfort, even if the idea of a gun battle in the streets of London filled him with horror.

'There it is,' Max said from the side of his mouth. Tension showed in his face.

Quickly, Alistair chanced a look over his shoulder as they darted into the alley. The figures had receded a little into the fog.

'Back,' Alistair said, withdrawing from the mouth of the alley.

Max joined him. They retreated until the entrance vanished in swirling fog. Alistair began to breathe a little easier, just as Max bumped into a bin, the metallic rattle like machine gunfire in the alley's tight confines.

'Damnation,' Alistair breathed. He closed his eyes for a moment to compose himself.

He opened them in time to see the first of three men emerge from the fog. Alistair swept up a rubbish bin lid. Holding it like a shield, he charged the lead figure. Startled, the man had just enough time to raise his weapon before Alistair sent him flying, the metal clang sounding like the pealing of a hammer on an anvil. The man knocked one of his companions aside before disappearing with a meaty thud into the fog.

'No guns!' Alistair said harshly, as Max came up to him, his weapon drawn.

Max, sensing the note of command in Alistair's voice, reversed the weapon and smashed it into the head of the second assailant who had stumbled to his feet. His eyes glazed over, and he fell bonelessly to the ground, groaning incoherently while the remaining assailant watched stunned as his support vanished.

He pulled a revolver from beneath his jacket and aimed it uncertainly at the two men. Alistair saw a familiar look on the young man's face – uncertainty and bravado warring for control.

'Easy there,' Alistair said, trying to calm the situation. 'We can resolve this—'

A loud report filled the narrow confines of the alley. Alistair flinched, waiting for the pain to erupt. But it didn't. The younger man's face transformed into a rictus of agony. His gun fell to the ground as he clutched at the wound in his chest. Blood spilled over his fingers. Alistair knelt quickly by his side, feeling for a pulse. He felt a flicker. A groan escaped the injured man's lips.

'You bloody fool,' Alistair said, looking up at Max. Lights along the street bloomed, and he saw shadows moving behind a curtain. 'Why'd you have to do that?'

Max's earlier affability had vanished, replaced by stony-faced indifference. 'The Big Man warned us there would be retribution for what happened at *The Cock and Bull*,' he said. He took a step towards the groaning man, whose eyes fluttered. Max stood over him, his weapon trained on his head.

'No,' Alistair said, standing to confront Max. For a moment, he grappled with him, the two men chest to chest. 'You've woken up half a dozen witnesses!' Alistair hissed. 'No more shooting.'

Max's eyes bulged for a moment, surprised as Alistair's strength matched his. He shrugged himself free of Alistair's grip.

'You Continentals are a soft touch,' he said, holstering his weapon. 'No bottle about you at all.'

'Shut up and let's go.'

In the distance, a siren wailed. Together, the two men ran the length of the alley before emerging onto a silent street.

By stages, they ghosted their way across Soho, until they returned to the boarding house.

'I'll be here at eight,' Max said curtly, going to his car and opening the driver's door. He didn't act like a man who had shot another barely fifteen minutes ago.

Alistair, who had earlier thought Max was someone within Vaar's organisation he could deal with, rapidly re-evaluated the man and his situation.

'You risked everything because of your temper. Do it again and the job is off.'

Max stared at him over the roof of the car for a moment, before he broke into an unfriendly grin. 'You're forgetting we have your pretty little niece. It would be a pity if she was found shot dead in the street like a dog.'

Without waiting for Alistair to reply, Max slammed the door shut, started the engine and drove away, his brake lights flaring for a moment before he turned the corner and vanished.

Seething, Alistair contemplated the night and the distant sounds of converging sirens several streets away. The horn on the Thames sounded again, its mournful drone doing nothing to lift his spirits. He abruptly turned on his heel and entered the boarding house, stumping up several flights of stairs to his room.

He shucked off the holster. He considered replacing the revolver in the case, then remembered the look in Max's eyes in the alley when he had shot the man. Alistair shoved the revolver under his pillow, took off his shoes, jammed the back of the chair under the doorknob and then settled himself onto the bed.

In a few minutes, he was fast asleep.

CHAPTER EIGHT
Let's Spend the Night Together

IT WAS WELL AFTER MIDNIGHT. THE LAST OF THE FIRE engines had trundled away into the fog, red lights a fading smear in the air. A number of detectives, called out of whatever pub or bed they had found themselves in, milled in front of the entrance. Occasionally, one would shoot a venomous look at Anne and Bill, as if they had lit the fire themselves.

'What in God's name were you two up to?' Hartigan asked. A cigarette dangled from his mouth. The sour smell of whisky hung over him, and his clothes were more rumpled than usual.

'Trying to stop the station from burning down,' Anne said hotly. 'Whereas it smells like you were looking for your keys in a vat of whisky,' she added, playing the part of Ruth. 'Drink it, Tom, don't bathe in it.'

There were a few chortles at that, until Hartigan's glower silenced them. 'You do know what you've done, don't you?'

'Why don't you tell us,' Bill said, softly and with an edge of menace.

Hartigan paused then. Anne watched him carefully; it was clear that he was unsure at the new tone Harry Champion had adopted. 'Well. You've lost our prime witness.'

'We've not lost anyone,' Anne said. 'He's dead. Inside.'

'That shrivelled thing? That's someone's idea of a sick

joke. It's a doll. No, you let him escape. That's what happened.'

'We did, did we?' Bill held up his hands, displaying several blisters. 'And I suppose I did this deliberately to myself, right?'

'Our best chance at nailing the Big Man is gone. Without Carnarvon, we're back to square one.'

'You can barely see the nose in front of your face, Tom,' Anne said. 'The solicitor. Are you blind? He's our lead.'

'How?' Hartigan sneered. 'Did Holcombe pour petrol on Carnarvon and flick lit matches at him? Whatever the hell happened here, you can't pin it on anyone.' He leaned in so close, Anne flinched at the alcohol on his breath. 'And you know it, luv.'

A chorus of laughter rose up.

Bill took Anne by the arm to stop her taking a swing at Hartigan.

'Let it go,' he hissed, as the other detectives returned to their conversations. Someone mentioned the name of a pub, and there was a rumble of agreement.

'I could so easily slap him in the face,' Anne said, watching the other men begin to disperse.

'You could. But you won't. It would cost Ruth her job. We're here to achieve something, not to compromise the people temporarily hosting us.'

Anne nodded, tightly. 'I know.' She chewed on a thumbnail, her forehead creased in thought.

'Something's up,' Bill said, a half smile on his face.

'How can you tell?'

'Different face, same frown. Tell me.'

'I want to look at the body again. Carnarvon's.'

'Why?'

Anne's frown deepened. 'The fire didn't kill him.'

'Really? You could've fooled me.' He glanced at the other detectives talking among themselves. 'There's nothing useful happening out here. Let's go have a look.'

The front desk stood unattended, the counter flap standing up. Sergeant Clifford rattled around like a marble in a bottle, unable to fathom what had happened. A uniformed officer stood beside the desk, instructed to keep members of the public, indigents and the press away from the building until the coroner arrived.

Bill nodded to him.

In the corridor, the smell of smoke grew stronger as they approached the interview room. Soot and ash marked the ceiling and walls, and cinders crunched underfoot. Scorch marks like black fingers marked the doorframe.

Swept clean of the remains of the furniture and the shattered glass, the empty interview room echoed hollowly. The harsh smell of smoke hung in the air. Bill and Anne lingered for a moment in the doorway, eyes drawn to the huddled, twisted figure lying on the floor.

'Tell me your theory,' Bill said, as he walked over to Carnarvon's corpse.

'I think we can discount the Master,' Anne began. 'None of the descriptions of his weapon mentioned an inferno as a by-product. The flames didn't kill Carnarvon. You can see the body is unmarked. No, heat was a by-product, released as his cells collapsed in on themselves. Energy is never lost, only converted. The fire was the result of cellular collapse.'

'If not a weapon, then what caused it?'

Anne shrugged. 'The room was empty. Just Carnarvon and...' Her eyes narrowed, and she leaned closer. 'Is there something caught in his right hand?'

Bill leaned in. He pulled a pen from his shirt pocket and gently prodded the tiny fist. 'Whatever it is, it's charred.' He looked at Anne. 'The letter?'

They heard a noise at the far end of the corridor.

'Sounds like the coroner's here,' Bill said.

'Quick, give me the pen.'

Bill handed it over to Anne, who used the tip to pry open the fist, finger by finger. A wadded piece of paper dropped to the floor. As footsteps approached, Anne hurriedly picked up the paper and rose to her feet. Bill joined her as a short, rumpled man with a terrible comb-over walked into the room. He held a battered Gladstone bag in one hand, and wore a scowl that he shared with everyone in the room.

'Where's the body?' he barked. To Bill, he looked like he'd been rousted out of bed after a hard night at the pub.

'Here,' Anne said, pointing at the figure on the floor.

'That's not a body.' The coroner turned to the police officer who had accompanied him. 'If this is some sort of joke?'

The officer shrugged his shoulders.

'It'd be a poor show if it was,' Bill said.

The coroner glared at him, then sighed gustily. 'Very well. Clear the area. I need some space to work.'

Anne and Bill watched the coroner kneel beside Carnarvon's remains. Bill shivered when the coroner moved the body from side to side, the stiff limbs sticking out at odd angles, its clothes rustling like dry leaves.

The coroner pulled a magnifying glass from inside his bag and held it over the body. He looked closely at the twisted features. Bill caught a glimpse of bulging eyes under the lens and looked away, swallowing the bile in his throat. Putting the magnifying glass away, the coroner took out a tape measure and pulled on the metal tongue. The rasp of it sounded loudly in the room.

'Six inches,' the coroner said, retracting the tongue with a rattle and snap. He looked up at Anne and Bill with a mixture of annoyance and confusion. 'Tom Thumb was taller than this,' he said, shaking his head. 'And you're saying this was a man being held in custody?'

Bill nodded. 'Suspicion of murder.'

'Well, there's something a damn sight stranger here than murder,' the coroner said. 'Bernard bloody Quatermass would have a fine time working this out.'

'I bet,' Bill agreed. 'But I'm sure the British Rocket Group has its own problems right now.'

'Yes, I read about that. Losing a Mars Probe. Careless of them.' The coroner shook his head, then looked up at Anne and Bill. 'Anyway, never mind the small-talk. Were either of you on duty tonight?'

Anne nodded.

'Did you see anything?'

Anne opened her mouth to speak, but Bill cut her off. 'Nothing,' he lied. 'We were having a meal when we heard screaming. Barely stopped the fire from spreading.'

'Good work, good work.' The coroner flipped open a notebook. He stood over the corpse and began taking notes. He looked up. 'Make sure your statement is in my office by lunchtime tomorrow... Um, today,' he corrected himself, looking at his watch.

'Will do.' Bill threw Anne a glance which, even with their different faces, she understood.

'We'll leave you to it,' she said.

Stooped over the twisted remains, the coroner mumbled a response and absently waved his hand.

Back at their desks, Anne gently smoothed the scrap of paper across her blotter.

'I'm surprised it survived,' she said, looking at it closely.

'Any idea why it wasn't affected by whatever happened to Carnarvon?'

Anne shrugged. 'Perhaps the process that killed him only affects flesh and blood. The important thing is that it survived.'

'What are those markings?' Bill leaned in for a closer

look.

'I'm… not sure,' Anne said. She pushed the scrap of paper across to him.

'Looks like a job lot of geometric shapes.' Bill turned the piece of paper around. 'That could be an L, but as for the rest of it…'

'The Warehouse held a library of books.' Anne hadn't been to the Warehouse for a few years, and she now realised how much she missed it. She missed a lot about her old life. A consequence of being abruptly ripped from it, no doubt. She considered the man before her; so very different from her husband, yet his mannerisms, his body language… She was so grateful to have him back. It seemed like such a long time since she'd really been touched by her old life.

'Old tomes, really,' she continued. 'A real mixture of sources. Treatises, mainly. Mathematics, very early biology, obscure religious writings. Some even about magic.'

'Magic?' Bill laughed, and Anne smiled in response.

'I know, no such thing as magic, just old sciences. There was a ton of material collected after Operation: Maypole. That said; much of it was fit only for the silverfish, to be honest. A large portion of the collection was liberated after the fall of the Reich. High Command had teams in Berlin before the Soviets arrived. The Annenerbe had some very queer ideas, and were prepared to go to the ends of the Earth in search of artefacts to prove them.'

Bill held up a hand. 'Hang on, the Annenerbe?'

'Himmler's supernatural shock troops. Dedicated to all things mystical and the occult. Father met some in Tibet. Up to all sorts of strange things.' Anne looked at the paper again. 'We both saw Holcombe hand Carnarvon the envelope. Carnarvon opens it and takes out this piece of paper. The room explodes in flame leaving behind Carnarvon's shrunken corpse.'

'There are no burn marks on Carnarvon's body. Could it be something as simple as the heat of the fire?'

Anne shook her head. 'That sort of desiccation requires a far higher temperature, which would damage the body. Or, a longer baking time at a lower temperature. Neither fits the evidence.'

Bill tapped a pen on the desk. 'Magic is simply mathematics, right? A distortion of the physical world through the manipulation of the underlying fabric of reality.'

Anne smiled. 'Yes; if you can't understand a natural phenomenon, you ascribe a magical reason to it. Thunder is created by molecules of air collapsing together, not Thor riding his goat drawn chariot across the sky.'

'Clarke's Law. The reverse is also true, of course.'

'Yes, advanced magic is indistinguishable from science.' Anne nodded. 'But that doesn't get us any closer to how Carnarvon died.'

'How he died isn't really the issue here.'

'Really? The possible use of magic isn't something to give you pause?'

'It is. The easier question to answer, though, is who wanted him dead. He was abandoned after the attack on Wilberforce. They say the Big Man is ruthless. We've seen the reports into the other murders he's alleged to have ordered. Perhaps he thought Carnarvon died at the scene and didn't care to take the corpse with him? Imagine his surprise when he discovers Carnarvon is alive and probably furious at being left for dead.'

Anne could well imagine. 'But why kill him in such an exotic way?'

Bill shrugged. 'Sends a message? An experiment? Testing the process, maybe?'

Anne chewed on a thumbnail. She stopped, and looked at Ruth's hand. She'd seen this happen before, the host body's habits asserting themselves, even since Rachel Ashcroft. She shook her head, wondering if she'd ever get used to astral projection through time.

'In the wrong hands…' she began. 'Well, we've seen the evidence. If they have found other applications for this knowledge…' She paused, thinking hard. 'Most of these writings are scattered. Some are in the Warehouse, and you may recall it's around this time that UNIT started using the Warehouse, too.'

'We could speak to Liz. She's still there at this time, right?'

Anne shook her head. 'Let's not overcomplicate things, even if I could convince her I'm me. No. I believe there are some held in museums. I know for a fact the Vault made a point of tracking these tomes, using the records found in Berlin as a baseline.'

'So, you have a good idea of what was under lock and key?' An idea was forming in Bill's head; Anne knew that look anywhere.

She nodded and tapped the scrap of paper. 'All of that isn't to say that other texts aren't in private hands. If texts were sent out of Germany before the final collapse of the Reich…?'

'Taken by fleeing Nazis?'

'It's believed the Annenerbe had the largest collection of magical texts in the world. Other nations were playing catch-up in the ruins of Europe. If you work the numbers, chances are any texts that aren't documented are likely held by fugitive Nazis or their supporters.'

Bill nodded slowly, clearly slotting this into his idea. 'It's a bit of a leap to think they've stayed solely within those circles.'

'True, but look at it from their perspective. We've seen enough over the decades to know that some of this stuff actually works. If you had a taste of absolute power over people, you'd want to hang onto a possible means of gaining it back.'

Bill narrowed his eyes in thought. It was... odd, seeing his tics on the face of a stranger. Anne knew she'd never get used to it. How long before they returned to their own bodies?

'So,' Bill said, 'someone who studied it for long enough has decided after all these years to start using the knowledge contained in the books.'

'And leagued themselves with a criminal gang led by a ruthless killer keen to use that knowledge.' Anne ran a hand through Ruth's short hair. 'What a mess.'

'How do we find out who holds these books? The number of Nazi war criminals in public view is somewhere between none and none...' Bill trailed off. 'Hand me the Perkins file,' he said.

Anne handed it over, and Bill frantically paged through it. He removed a photograph and compared the image to the scrap of charred paper.

'Tell me I'm not crazy,' he said, handing Anne the photo of Richard Perkins' corpse and the scrap of paper.

For a minute, Anne considered both. Her frown deepened. When she looked up, her eyes shone with excitement.

'They're the same, aren't they?' Bill said. 'Sumerian?'

'They're definitely in the same style. Remarkable.'

'That links the Big Man to Perkins' death, surely?' Bill rubbed his jaw. 'Why would the Big Man expose himself so blatantly by sending Holcombe? He must know it would lead back to him?'

'It would. But perhaps he doesn't care?' Anne shook her head.

'If he's making some sort of move, what is it?'

'I don't know,' Anne said. 'What I do know is we should interview the Perkins' family. It's clear to me he was killed on the Big Man's orders, same as Carnarvon. Perkins left a wife and son. They may know something about his connection to the Big Man.'

'What about the person using this knowledge? Our theoretical Nazi?'

'We'll need help if we're to track down our fugitive magic wielding Nazi.' Anne smiled. 'It sounds ridiculous when you say it out loud.'

'Very,' Bill said. 'But what's new there?' He sat in silence a moment, rapping his fingers on the desk. 'The Brig had a contact in the Imperial War Museum. He mentioned him a few times. Fowler? Foley, I think. He was involved in a war crimes committee that met regularly in Geneva in the early '70s. Said he was a bit of a prig, but knew his stuff.'

'Are there any decent men in this benighted decade?'

'Benighted?'

Anne shrugged. 'I'm tired.'

'Fair enough,' Bill said. 'We speak with Perkins' family first and then we contact Foley.'

Decided on a course of action, they both stood. Bill shrugged on his jacket, and his eyes fell on a tray sitting on his desk.

'Who put that there?' he asked, picking up the envelope and showing it to Anne. It was stamped SURVEILLANCE.

'Someone must've dropped it on your desk this morning.'

Bill opened the envelope and pulled out a sheaf of grainy black and white photographs. A note had been pinned to one.

'What are they?' Anne asked.

'Surveillance photos. The team thinks they may have located the Big Man's lair.'

'Where?' Anne walked around the desk for a look.

'A Chinese laundry. Hang on. *Under* a Chinese laundry.'

'When were they taken?'

'According to the note, tonight.' He checked his watch and he whistled. 'About three hours ago. They don't muck about.' Curious, Bill fanned through the photographs, pausing at one and showing it to Anne.

'That's Holcombe,' she said. 'Arriving for his riding instructions for dealing with Carnarvon?'

'Likely,' Bill said. He looked at Anne. 'Do you think he knew what was going to happen to Carnarvon?'

Anne shrugged. 'Probably not. The Big Man would want to keep knowledge of this sort of stuff close to his chest.' She nodded to the photographs. 'What about the rest?'

'Let's see. Most are laundry workers. There is this old fellow, though.' Bill held up the photograph with a flourish.

'Looks like he'd murder you in your sleep,' Anne said, leaning in for a closer look.

'None of these people are Sunday school teachers,' Bill said. 'Hang on...' He held up a photograph of a stocky figure with thinning hair to show to Anne. 'Isn't this... Oh, what was his name? That politician? Used to be a right pain when I had to front up to parliamentary committees. Arbuthnot?'

'Could be,' Anne said. Such things had never been her problem. After ostensibly leaving the Fifth in late 1970 she was lucky enough not to have to deal with politicians. But the higher Bill climbed, the more he did. Especially after Alistair help set up UNIT, when Dougie took over the Fifth and promoted Bill.

'What the hell is he doing anywhere near the Big Man's HQ?' Bill wondered.

Anne shrugged. 'It wouldn't be unusual for a crime boss to have powerful friends.'

'Powerful friends? He has oversight at the Ministry of Defence!'

'One thing at a time, Billy. What about the other

photos?'

Bill shook his head. 'Just this swarthy gent.' He held a photograph of a moustachioed man with a carefully combed coif.

'Quite the Casanova,' Anne said, her lips quirking. 'Without names though, they get us no closer to working out what's going on. Can't we raid the place?'

'Even for the '70s, the evidence here is flimsy. We *suspect* the Big Man has criminal connections. We *suspect* he has been involved in murder. We suspect a lot of things, but where's the proof?' Bill shook his head. 'There were a lot of scandals in the '60s about police undermining civil liberties. The tide turned, and a decade later judges were demanding concrete evidence before they'd agree to issue a warrant.'

Anne looked around at the empty room. A horn sounded outside the station, before a car roared off.

'Then we're stuck doing the legwork,' she said.

'Tomorrow.' Bill rubbed his eyes. 'Today, dammit. Temporal lag.'

A common problem Anne had noticed too. 'We both need some rest. We've barely stopped since we arrived here. And I didn't get much rest in 2003, either.'

'Same. Okay, we'll start at sunrise. Harry will be grateful for the rest, too. He's got a bad back and a dodgy knee, both of which are screaming for a lie down.'

'Ruth's flat is nearby,' Anne said. 'Her car's in the garage downstairs. A few hours' sleep would do us both good.'

'I'd kill for a bed.'

'Bed? No chance, I'm afraid. Ruth's landlady would throw a fit if she brought a man home. I'm afraid it's going to have to be the car for you.'

Bill's look of astonishment soon gave way to understanding. 'At least give me a blanket,' he said. 'It's getting on to winter.'

'I'll see what I can manage,' Anne said sweetly. 'Now, come on.'

They descended the stairs into the bowels of the station, and exited into a small garage. The fluorescent lighting flickered and fizzed. Their footsteps echoed sharply on the concrete floor as they crossed the largely empty space. Reaching into her purse, Anne produced a bundle of keys as they approached a small yellow car.

Bill whistled. 'Look at that little beauty,' he said.

'It's a car, Bill,' Anne pointed out.

'It's not just a car. It's a two door Ford Capri,' he said, circling the vehicle and trailing his hand over the smart paint finish. 'Ruth certainly travels in style.'

Anne shook her head as she unlocked the car. Bill and his cars. He had quite a model collection of vintage cars at home. Or will have one day, she supposed. The Ford Capri wasn't vintage yet. She climbed inside.

It wasn't until after she'd put the key in the ignition that she realised Bill was still standing outside. She frowned at him, and he pointed at the small button beside the passenger door window. Anne laughed. Of course, central locking…

She reached over and released the button on the passenger door. 'Sorry,' she said. 'It's like living in *The Flintstones*.'

Bill patted the dashboard. 'Don't listen to her. You're wonderful.' He winked at Anne. 'Fire her up.'

'I'm trying to remember how to drive a manual,' Anne said, staring with deep suspicion at the gear stick beside her left knee.

'If you can't remember, I'm happy to get behind the steering wheel.'

'I get the sense Ruth doesn't like anyone driving her around, especially in her own car. As a member of the Sisterhood, I agree. Buckle up.'

'Yes, ma'am,' Bill said, smiling as he drew the belt across his chest.

Anne twisted the key and the car roared into life. Hesitantly, she put the car into reverse. It jerked backwards, throwing Bill forward, before coming to a stop. The sound of screeching tyres echoed around them.

'Like I said,' Bill said drily. 'I'm very happy to drive.'

Anne held up a warning finger and Bill subsided.

The second time around, Anne was able to get the car up the ramp and into the street. The engine rumbled softly, and Anne smiled broadly.

'Any chance I can turn on the radio, Captain?' Bill asked. 'Perhaps Radio 1?'

'Sounds reasonable,' Anne said, as she signalled at a junction. 'Let's hear what's on.'

Bill turned on the radio and the sounds of The Rolling Stones immediately belted from the speakers. Hurriedly, he turned it down until Jagger's wailing no longer hurt their ears.

'Bit of a dark horse, our Ruth,' Bill said, tapping along to the beat of *Midnight Rambler*. 'Likes it loud.'

'You'd want to yell a bit after working with those Neanderthals,' Anne said.

'I hope I wasn't anything like that back then.'

'You were better than most,' Anne said, smiling. She placed a hand on his shoulder. 'I loved you for your chivalry then as much as I do now.'

Bill smiled and ducked his head. 'Light's green, by the way.'

'Male chauvinistic pig, telling a woman how to drive,' Anne said primly. She pressed the accelerator and the car jumped forward, before stalling.

'A little too much petrol, dear,' Bill said, mildly.

'Not another word.'

CHAPTER NINE
Rock and Roll Suicide

'CAN'T WE CUT HIM DOWN?' ANNE ASKED, STARING UP at the body twisting slowly back and forth, the rope creaking with every movement.

'No,' Hartigan said harshly. 'Let the daft sod swing a little longer.'

The telephone call had come at six that morning, rousing Anne out of bed under the disapproving glare of Ruth's landlady, Mrs Franklin. Hartigan's voice had sharpened Anne's attention immediately, and she had scribbled hasty notes. A quick wash and change of clothes, and she was in the car and driving back to the station before Bill knew what was happening.

After Bill changed his shirt and socks, an impatient Hartigan bundled them into another car and drove them to the site of the death. A cracked concrete footpath, bracketed by dead weeds, ran parallel with the Crouch End Canal. A putrid smell wafted off the sluggishly moving water, and Anne was sure there were things floating in it that didn't bear scrutiny. Council flats loomed on one side, overlooking the canal and a band of wasteland that wouldn't see development for another two decades. The body hung from a lamppost, the only one along that stretch of footpath whose globe remained intact.

Despite the hour, a small crowd of ghoulish onlookers watched silently, kept back by a pair of officers. Several children played among the legs of the watchers, stopping occasionally to peer up at the body hanging from the lamppost. One of the officers had been partially successful in covering the dead man's face with a cloth. A blood-filled eye glared down at Anne while she contemplated the slowly twisting corpse.

An ambulance arrived. Two white clad men bustled out and retrieved a stretcher from the rear. The crowd parted reluctantly and then reformed to watch with an avidity that turned Anne's stomach. Someone had procured a stepladder, and one of the uniformed officers clambered to the top step and began awkwardly sawing at the thick rope with a switchblade, while the two ambulancemen each held a dangling leg.

The rope parted with a snap. The men holding the body almost dropped it as the onlookers groaned and cooed. After a moment spent disentangling themselves, the ambulancemen manhandled the corpse onto the stretcher.

Anne and Bill came over. Bill tugged aside the cloth, revealing the blackened face of the solicitor, Holcombe.

'Someone's cleaning up their dirty work,' he said.

'Let me have a look.' Anne tugged at Holcombe's collar, revealing the rope cutting deep into his neck. Picking up one of his stiffened hands, she examined the fingernails. 'See, here,' she said to Bill, pointing.

'That's skin?'

'He put up a struggle. Someone out there has a pretty deep scratch on them.'

'Another needle in a haystack,' Bill said, over the rising mutter of the crowd.

'Murdered, was he?' someone yelled in the crowd.

Bill, Anne and the other officers turned, as the ambulancemen wheeled the body away.

'What was that, sir?' Bill asked.

An older man with a wild beard pushed through to

the front of the crowd. His Mackintosh flapped in the rising breeze, revealing trousers shiny at the knees.

'Bloody useless,' he called. Some of the people around him shifted uncomfortably. 'The place is going to ruin, and you stand around doing nothing. These people agree, but they're too gutless to say it.'

'We're investigating a man's death,' Anne said. 'If you have any information, we'd be happy to take a statement.'

'Typical,' the man said. 'Why do we pay taxes just for you to tell us *you'd be happy to take a statement?*' There were murmurs of agreement. 'Was the same during the Great Gas Leak of '69. Up and down the country, the place is going to the dogs, but what do the police do? What's the government doing?' There was a smattering of applause.

'Come on, let's leave Ronald Slim to it,' Hartigan murmured to the others.

'Know him, do you?' Anne asked.

Hartigan gave her a cold look. 'Don't we all? Always been a troublemaker that one. Right, time to go. This could get ugly.'

'That's right. Scurry off to your bolthole,' Mr Slim yelled, as the officers walked through the increasingly restive crowd. The tension had grown palpable. 'People are murdered on our doorstep and you lot can't be bothered to do anything about it. The time's coming when we'll take the matter into our own hands and clean the filth out. That man, Arbuthnot, he knows what needs doing!'

The applause gathered momentum, following them as Anne and Bill clambered into Hartigan's car. Anne remembered that name from last night: Arbuthnot.

'There's a mood about, that's for sure,' Bill said.

'You're not wrong,' Hartigan agreed. He turned the ignition and the engine roared into life.

'What do you mean?' Anne asked.

'The local MP, Arbuthnot, has been stirring the locals up for months. Haven't you seen him on the telly? Man's a fool. Causes more trouble for us than the criminals.'

'Don't watch the telly too much,' Bill said.

'That wife of yours keeping you busy, is she, Harry?' Hartigan said, shaking his head and chuckling. 'Arbuthnot goes on and on about how the Liberal Government is failing the people. The crazy thing is, he's attacking his own side. Says a crisis is brewing and no one in the Cabinet gives a fig. If you ask me, wild talk like that gives others license to cause trouble.'

'I see,' Bill said, sharing a glance with Anne. *Who knew Hartigan kept up with the politics of the day* his raised eyebrows seemed to suggest.

Anne nodded absently, and turned her head to watch the crowd, which was slowly dispersing.

After grabbing a bite to eat at a greasy spoon around the corner from the station, Anne and Bill drove to their first interview for the day. Although the circumstances were different, it felt nice to be working together again. It seemed like an age since she and Bill had 'worked a case', as it were. Their career paths had diverged some time ago, ever since the Fifth Operational Corps and other similar organisations had been merged into a *Unified* Intelligence Taskforce and Bill had gone on to advise the United Nations Security Council.

Anne switched off the engine. Bill, freshly showered and changed at the station, looked through the window. A tree lined street, with well-to-do houses, spoke of the comfortably rich.

'Nice neighbourhood,' he said.

'The file said Perkins was an investment banker. Mainly dealt with Eastern European countries.'

'Hardly the type to have a Sumerian symbol carved into his chest.'

Anne nodded. She glanced at a house across the street. 'Let's go see his wife. She seemed eager to speak with Ruth when I called this morning.'

They climbed out of the car and crossed the street. A young boy rode his Raleigh Chopper, the infamous wheelie bike of old, up and down the street. He stopped, looked at Bill and waved. Bill smiled and waved back. Anne grinned; how very different from the youth of their time. Trust in the police had gone a long way since the '70s – all downhill.

A neatly manicured garden fronted the brick house. A midnight blue Mercedes R107 sat in the driveway, the roadster's paint job immaculate in the sunlight. Bill whistled appreciatively as he examined it in passing and Anne could only shake her head in amusement. They walked up the steps to the front door and Anne pressed the button. A bell clanged distantly. Footsteps approached, and the door opened. An exhausted looking woman greeted them.

'Yes?' she asked, with a trembling voice.

'Mrs Perkins? I'm WDC Ruth Winters. This is my partner, DC Champion. I spoke with you on the telephone?'

'Oh yes.'

Anne noticed how her gaze lingered on Bill longer than felt comfortable, before sliding away. He exchanged a quick glance with Anne, who shrugged.

'Please, do come in. My son, Damien, is upstairs. I'll call him down. I'm sure he is eager to hear how the investigation is proceeding.'

Mrs Perkins ushered them into the reception area. Checkerboard tiles marked the floor. A staircase rose to a wide landing. A small study sat on the immediate left, and a larger, formal dining area on the right. She led them through to a well-appointed kitchen, and beyond that, to a small patio that looked over the extensive rear garden.

'I'll just make some tea, shall I?' she said. She had a distracted air. Anne recognised the signs of shock.

'That would be nice, Mrs Perkins,' Bill said. 'Milk with two sugars. Ruth?'

'Just black, please,' Anne said.

Above them, she could hear someone moving around on the first floor.

'I'll just be a moment then,' Mrs Perkins said, returning to the kitchen.

'She's not coping,' Bill said.

'No, she's not,' Anne agreed. 'I'm not really surprised. Hartigan was the detective who came around for the first interview. Probably treated her like the prime suspect.'

They waited patiently until Mrs Perkins appeared with a tray containing cups and a teapot. Bill rose to help but Mrs Perkins shook her head.

'No, no, Detective. I may have suffered a terrible loss but I'm not a cripple.'

Her face crumpled for a moment and Anne thought she would start weeping. After taking a moment to compose herself, Mrs Perkins poured for both of them.

'What have you found so far?' she asked, setting aside the pot.

'Very little, I'm afraid,' Anne said, taking a sip from her cup. 'But we do think that your husband's death is linked to that of another man.'

'Oh, my goodness.' Mrs Perkins' grip on her cup was so tight that Anne thought it might break in her grasp. She flinched at the sound of heavy feet upstairs.

Anne and Bill exchanged a glance.

'Can you tell us anything about your husband's demeanour in the few weeks up to his death?' Anne asked. She sat her cup down and opened a notebook.

'He was busy with work. He would spend one week of the month on the Continent, meeting with business clients.'

'Did he travel extensively while he was there?' Bill asked.

'Mostly in Berlin. On both sides of the wall,' Mrs Perkins said.

'Were you aware of anyone who was dissatisfied with the advice he gave?' Anne asked.

Mrs Perkins shook her head. 'My husband was deeply conservative about the money he invested. He took great pride in always being able to repay the money entrusted to him to invest on their behalf.'

'So, you're not aware of any disgruntled business investors, then?' Bill asked.

'No. Though…' Mrs Perkins stopped, and looked aside for a moment.

Anne allowed her the moment.

'He did have a meeting with a man, here. A Mr Holcombe.'

Anne and Bill exchanged sharp glances.

'Do you recall what that meeting was about?' Anne asked, trying to keep the excitement from her voice.

Mrs Perkins shook her head. 'Richard would take his meetings in his study. He would always close the doors. Not because he distrusted me,' she added quickly. She allowed herself a smile. 'But he wanted to give his clients the assurance that their financial dealings were safe with him, even from his own wife.'

'An admirable man?' Bill asked.

'Yes.' Mrs Perkins took a tissue from inside her sleeve and dabbed at her eyes. 'We would always go away during the summer, Richard and me. And Damien, when he was a boy. Germany, mainly. Richard had a real love for the country.'

'Richard never told you about the details of this meeting with Holcombe?' Anne made notes as she asked the question.

'Not specifics, no. But it had nothing to do with

investment. Mr Holcombe was a collector. Of war memorabilia.'

'What sort of memorabilia?' Bill asked.

'World War Two. I think it was because Richard was unable to serve. He was deaf in one ear, the poor dear.'

'So, you think Holcombe wanted to buy a piece from your husband?'

'I do. However, Richard was adamant in refusing to part with it.'

'What did he have in his collection?'

Mrs Perkins shook her head, as if she didn't really know. 'Medals, mostly. But also soldiers' diaries, photographs. The largest part of it is on display in his study. But this piece he had stored away.'

'Where?' Anne asked, looking up from her notes.

Mrs Perkins gave Anne a look. It was, sadly, one she'd received many times the first time around. Women like Mrs Perkins didn't think much of women in a position of authority. It was as if they had broken some cardinal rule that said women were only meant to be tied to their husband's side, or, worse, the kitchen sink.

'Richard began his career working for the Bank of Shetland. Right at the end of the war. He kept a safe deposit box. He said the item was far too valuable to keep at home.'

'What was it?'

Mrs Perkins tilted her head for a moment. 'A sword.' She shrugged. 'As I say, I never saw it.'

'And after he refused to sell, did he have any other meetings with Mr Holcombe?'

'No. Richard was quite firm with him. He raised his voice, which I could hear on the other side of the house. Mr Holcombe left, and Richard was in quite a state for the rest of the day. Even snapped at me, which he never did.'

'No other contact about the matter?' Bill asked.

Mrs Perkins started to shake her head, then paused. 'For a week or two afterwards, the phone would ring. Always late in the night, and after I'd gone to bed. Richard would always answer, and he never told me what the calls were. Except...'

'Except?' Anne prompted.

'There's a telephone by our bedside table. I knew it was breaking a trust, but I was concerned. Richard wouldn't tell me who had called. He looked very worried each time he rang off.'

'So, you did listen in on a call?' Bill asked, gently.

'Just the once, you do understand?'

Bill nodded.

'What did you hear?' Anne asked.

Again came the look. 'It was near the end of the call...'

'...tell your boss I'm not interested, for the tenth damned time,' Richard Perkins said. Sweat stood on his brow and he twisted the cord with his free hand. He glanced at the roof, wondering if the telephone had woken his wife again.

'My... boss, as you say, Mr Perkins, is a man most eager to come into possession of the item. Do you understand?'

'I understand a thug's lawyer is bothering me in the dead of night about something I have no intention of selling to anyone. Do you understand me? Never.'

'Perhaps I haven't made myself clear, Mr Perkins. We know about your... service record during the war. People supported the effort in so many different ways, don't you think? Not everyone would want to talk about it, I understand. It would be a pity then if such private dealings were made public.'

Perkins seethed. 'It... it's too dangerous to see the light of day again. I held it. I know.'

There was silence then. Perkins had the sense that a conversation was happening to one side, then Holcombe came back on the line.

'Very well then, Mr Perkins. Your obduracy in this matter is unfortunate. However, we shall vacate the field. If you ever change—'

'I won't!' Perkins snapped and hung up the phone.

'And that was all. Really,' Mrs Perkins said.

The door behind her opened.

'What's he doing here?' Damien Perkins snarled. Young, shaven headed, standing belligerently in the doorway.

Bill felt the full wrath of the boy's hate. He'd seen plenty of examples of racism over the decades, remembered well one drunken night at the local when Samson had attempted to explain just how it felt. He had been in the body of a black man before, quite a few jumps ago, but to face it again, and in the 1970s, was something he could never have prepared himself for.

'Damien, dear. Please calm down. These are detectives investigating what happened to your father.'

Damien's eyes flashed. 'Father would never allow his sort into our house. "Can't trust them," he said. And he was right.'

'I think you should listen to your mother's good advice, son,' Bill said, struggling to keep his voice reasonable.

'As if I'd take notice of the likes of you.' Damien actually sneered at Bill.

'You'll take notice of him if you know what's good for you,' Anne said, rising to her feet. 'Tell me,' she said, deliberately speaking over Damien's spluttered reply. 'Where were you the night your father died?'

Damien's eyes bulged, and he gaped at her as if she'd kicked him in the groin. He looked at his mother, who stared red eyed at him.

'I was out with friends,' he said, with a catch in his voice.

'Names?' Bill asked. 'We'd like to have a chat with them.'

'No,' Damien said sullenly, crossing his arms. 'I don't

think I will.' Confronted, he'd turned into a petulant child. Like all bullies and racists the world over, in Bill's experience.

'Here's what I think,' Anne said. 'There have been reports of racist graffiti appearing on synagogues across this part of London. Jewish gravestones knocked over, too. Anything to do with you, Damien?' The boy went pale when she smiled, but he remained quiet. Anne's smile faded. 'Make sure you get your answer right, because unless I'm very much mistaken, there's paint on your right hand. I imagine if we looked through the garage, for instance, there'd be one or two spray cans matching that colour. Don't you think so, Detective Champion?'

Bill nodded. 'I do indeed, Detective Winters.'

Damien looked appealingly at his mother, who could only look stonily ahead. For a moment, his resistance held, before it collapsed under the weight of his mother's silence. Sullen, Damien gave them several names.

'One more thing, before we go,' Bill said. 'Do you know a Mr Holcombe?'

The flash of recognition on Damien's face vanished as soon as it appeared, but it was there long enough for Bill and Anne to note.

'No. I don't know anyone called that,' Damien said. His fists sat clenched by his side and something of his earlier stubbornness had returned.

'I see,' Anne said, and snapped her notebook shut. 'You can go now. But if we need to speak with you again, we'll make sure to call your mother first.'

Damien nodded curtly then vanished into the house. After a few moments, they heard the front door slam shut.

'I'm so terribly sorry,' Mrs Perkins said miserably to Bill.

'It's all right,' Bill said, feeling anything but.

Anne laid a hand on Mrs Perkins arm. 'You've been

very helpful.'

'Have I? Have I really?' Mrs Perkins blinked rapidly.

'We're a step closer to finding out who killed your husband.'

'He was a good man. Damien… Damien wasn't his fault.' Mrs Perkins shook her head. 'They would argue about money. Richard was always insistent Damien make his own way in the world. They had such a frightful row, just before the meeting with Mr Holcombe. Damien wanted to go away with his friends, and Richard refused to give him any money for the trip. In the end, I gave it to him out of the housekeeping, but Damien… He couldn't forgive his father.' She looked up at them, suddenly terrified. 'You don't think Damien…? No, no. He wouldn't do anything like that. He's such a good boy. It's just those friends of his he mixes with. They've changed him.'

Bill resisted saying anything. Anne must have noticed as she said, 'We'll let ourselves out. Someone from the station will keep you updated. Thank you for the tea.'

Mrs Perkins nodded. Bill's last sight of Mrs Perkins was of her seated at the table with her head in her hands.

'Bloody hell,' he said, once they were back in the open. 'What a family.' He looked back at the house. 'All the money in the world can't hide the cancer behind the pretty façade.'

Anne descended the steps to the driveway and he followed her.

'Do you think Damien could've killed his father over money?'

'Maybe,' Anne said. 'But I don't think his crimes amount to much more than being a dumb racist.'

'You know, he could've been approached by Holcombe to try to convince his father to sell the sword.'

'A boy in need of money might just do that.'

'And get a finder's fee, no doubt.'

'Well, we've got bigger things to worry about,' Anne pointed out. She checked her watch. 'We'd better go. We've that appointment with Alistair's friend, Foley.'

As Bill tucked himself into the passenger seat, he spared the Perkins' house a glance. 'A cancer,' he murmured, as Anne drove away.

They carried on in silence for a while, before Anne glanced at him. 'Do you think we will ever get home?'

Bill remained silent for a moment. 'After 1999 I'd all but given up hope. But, here I am with you.'

Anne nodded. 'Yes. It's just... Seeing Mrs Perkins and her son...'

Bill swallowed. He understood. He'd done his best to not think about it, fearful that to do so would drive him mad. But he knew what Anne was saying. If they never did return to 2011, then they'd never see their own son again. Samuel was twenty-three years old, but he wasn't alone. He was married, first child on the way... There was still plenty of family there for him. Bill knew that even if they never returned home, their son would be fine, but...

He placed a comforting hand on Anne's knee. 'Like we said yesterday, if you-know-who is behind this, why wouldn't we all return home? And, even if we don't... Well, next time we're in the '90s or the early noughties, we'll check in on him.'

'It won't be the same, though,' Anne said with a sigh.

And she was right.

Whatever the Brig was doing in 1973, Bill hoped he had it sorted soon. Then they could all return home. Or at least be one jump closer...

CHAPTER TEN
Super Creeps

EARLY MORNING SUNLIGHT SLANTING THROUGH A RIP IN the blinds woke Alistair. He lay for a moment, confused as to where he was, thinking that maybe he was back in the home, before his memories snapped back into place. He rubbed at his eyes and stifled a groan.

Throwing off the blanket, he rose and went over to the basin. He stared at unfamiliar features in the cracked and blotchy mirror, and wondered what he had done to deserve this.

'Stop moaning, man,' he muttered to himself. How many people actually had a chance to relive their life, solving things that never made sense the first time around? Whoever was behind the Gnome was doing him a great favour. He would, he knew, when he returned to 2011, be able to die in peace. Content and complete.

Outside, he could hear the rising mutter of the awakening streets. Sweeping up the toilet bag, Alistair made his way down the corridor to the bathroom. A few minutes under a niggardly showerhead convinced him the sooner he resolved whatever it was he needed to do with Vaar, the better.

Refreshed somewhat and finding his mood improving with a fresh suit and tie, Alistair made his way down to the breakfast room. Only one other person, a man who resolutely refused to make eye contact, sat at one of the small round tables. Noises and smells from beyond a door indicated the kitchen.

As he sat down, a small Asian woman came out, carrying a steaming pot in one hand, and a heaped plate in the other. She set them down in front of the other diner with an audible thud, then advanced on Alistair with all the determination of a battalion commander.

'Yes...?' Mrs Chin began.

Confused for a moment, Alistair realised she was asking for his order. 'Err. Poached eggs and bacon, please?' he ventured.

'Poached? No poached. Fried. You like fried?'

'Not really,' Alistair said, before hastily amending his answer under her formidable glare. 'Yes,' he affirmed and was grateful when she turned and bustled into the kitchen.

A paper on a nearby stand attracted Alistair's attention. He stood and went over to get it. *Bloody Gangland War* the top of the fold screamed at him in solid black letters.

'Clearly not *The Times*,' Alistair said cheerily to his silently dining fellow. The man stared resolutely into the middle distance, mechanically chewing his food and ignoring him.

Alistair sat and unfolded the paper. The rest of the front page was a small article to one side, dominated by the covered bodies of two slain men, lying in front of the shattered entrance to a building. He spotted the author of the article, and chuckled; Harold Chorley. Well, naturally. At this point the old fellow had finally given up chasing Alistair. Wasn't any point really, when the object of your obsession was the public face of a 'top secret' organisation that everybody knew about. Man had to find something else to chase. Still, good on him for picking his career up after all that business with Sebastian Collins.

Alistair turned his attention to the article and read it

with dawning horror. He opened the third page, where the story continued in all its breathless glory.

The bloody murder of Sammy "the Hammer" Wilberforce brings to an end a reign of terror by one of Britain's most notorious gangland bosses, Chorley wrote.

Alistair had vague memories of hearing something about that, but he'd been too busy dealing with the alien ambassadors to look into it.

For many years, Wilberforce built and maintained a criminal enterprise that successive police commissioners failed to bring down. Wilberforce, who many blame for the death of gangland rival Henry Cooper in 1962, died as he lived.

It is the sheer brutality of the attack, which left five of Wilberforce's men also dead, that has enraged many. Most angered is local M.P., Richard Arbuthnot, who, with this newspaper, has long campaigned for stricter sentencing and a tougher approach to law and order in this country.

"I'm not afraid to say I welcome Wilberforce's death," Arbuthnot told your correspondent as news filtered out about the murders. "His type has been allowed for too long to run rampant. And not just in London. Elsewhere we can see that a failure to impose tougher sentences and allow our police forces to do their job has led to frightful riots and the murder of innocent members of the community. The government, of which I am a part, has to wake up; otherwise, it may find the whole place falling down around their ears."

The Home Secretary was not available for comment.

'I'm sure he wasn't,' Alistair said, shaking his head.

The whole tone of the article bothered him. It smacked of triumphalism, of a cheap and dirty pleasure at the wanton slaughter of men who by rights should've been charged and brought to the dock, not slaughtered like cattle on the killing floor.

So much for Chorley picking up his career. No wonder the man went into ghostwriting memoirs.

Alistair stared for a long moment at the unsmiling

photo of Arbuthnot accompanying the article. He didn't look at all familiar to Alistair.

He paged through the paper, stopping at times to read over what seemed like a fevered campaign to chronicle every law and order outrage the length and breadth of the country. Riots in Liverpool, a hostage drama in Edinburgh, more outrages in Northern Ireland, a serial killer stalking the slums of Manchester, and yet more gangland violence in the other urban centres of Britain.

Fire At Police Station in Crouch End caught his attention. A photo of a fire engine standing in front of the building accompanied the article. A woman and a black man, presumably detectives, standing at the edge of the photograph, caught his attention.

'Here. Eat.' Mrs Chin hove into view, surprising Alistair. She placed another pot of coffee on the table, followed by a plate of eggs and bacon. The edges of the eggs were a crisp brown, and the bacon looked as if it had been drowning in boiling oil for an uncomfortably long time. Yet still Alistair's mouth immediately filled with saliva. He nodded his thanks to Mrs Chin, who turned her back and went straight to the kitchen. Alistair tucked into his breakfast with gusto, while reading the rest of the article.

Police refused to comment about the fire at the Crouch End Police Station yesterday evening. Sources indicate the dead man, Frank Carnarvon, may have had links to the Black Sons Gang. He was being held in custody pending questions about his involvement in the murder of Sammy Wilberforce at the Cock and Bull in Soho. Police are pursuing multiple lines of enquiry and have not ruled out foul play. One of the first female detectives in the MET, Detective Ruth Winters, declined to comment.

He looked up from the paper and saw Max enter the room.

'Let's go,' Max said, after he had a look around. The other diner hurriedly averted his gaze.

'To where?' Alistair asked, bridling at the tone.

'The Big Man has called a meeting.' Max placed his hands on the either side of the table and leaned forward.

'Why does he need me?'

Max flashed a smile that was anything but friendly. 'The Big Man likes to put on a big show. Now get up. He hasn't got all day, and neither do you.'

Max switched the engine off, and it ticked as it began to cool. Through the front window, Alistair saw a decrepit warehouse. He could just make out movement inside the double doors that stood open.

'Vaar's inside?'

'Yeah,' Max said. 'Come on. He doesn't like to wait.'

Outside, standing on the windswept macadam, Alistair glanced at his surroundings. More warehouses stood in a line, hugging the southern bank of the Thames. He knew in a couple of decades, massive development would sweep all of it away, but for now, the area had a menacing atmosphere.

'You are here,' Vaar said, when Alistair walked into the dim interior of the warehouse.

The Dominator stood leaning against a concrete pillar, his face paler than the previous evening. Through gaps in the far wall, Alistair glimpsed the sluggish waters of the Thames.

'I trust you slept well?' Vaar asked.

'There was some excitement last night,' Alistair said, glancing at Max, who ignored him. 'But I managed to fall asleep quickly enough.'

'Yes. Max and I have discussed his activities last night. It will not happen again, unless absolutely necessary.'

'Why are we here?' Alistair asked abruptly.

'I have called a meeting,' Vaar said. He winced, and shifted position.

'The other gang leaders?'

'Of course.' Vaar looked pleased.

'You're not worried they'll try to ambush you?'

'How do you know I am not ambushing them?'

Alistair smiled slightly. 'I think even you wouldn't bring that much trouble down on your head. I think when you have your enemy on the run, you don't stop to admire the scenery. That's what you're doing, isn't it? They're off balance, which means you have them where you want them.' None of this was supposition; Alistair knew Vaar of old, and knew what would come of him in another ten years… Or was it thirteen? Being stuck in a period of history that was full of contradictions wasn't easy, especially when you could see the temporal discontinuities.

'It is a good thing, I think,' said Vaar, giving the first genuine smile Alistair had ever seen him make, 'that you are here to steal for me, and are not in opposition to me. Once we have finished here, you can begin the break in.'

'So, it's tonight, then?'

'Yes.'

'And then you will return my niece to me?'

'Oh yes,' Vaar said. 'I am a man of my word, as the other men invited to this meeting will soon find out.'

Alistair felt his heart beat faster. Back at his rooms, he had the blueprints to the bank stored in his case. The plan, which he had cobbled together in the few hours allowed to him since he had boarded the boat, hovered in his memory. And now, Vaar had him here, standing guard duty. He sensed the Matador's frustration equalled his own.

Minutes ticked by as they waited for the other arrivals. Alistair noted the glasses and an open bottle of scotch sitting on a nearby table, around which sat several chairs. Every minute, he checked the position of Vaar's driver and the guard he had brought with him. They maintained a watch, circling the warehouse, eyes hard, hands hovering near their revolvers. Pigeons ruffled their feathers in the joists. Outside, Alistair heard the slap of water against concrete pilings. A horn sounded; the noise a reminder of how far they were from the hustle and bustle of London. Beneath his feet, he felt a faint rumble, as of the clanking of machinery. Vaar's operation, it seemed, extended beyond simple crimes.

'Max,' Vaar wheezed, his voice loud in the quiet. Out in the open, away from the confines of his headquarters, Alistair thought Vaar looked diminished. Whatever it was that ailed him, it had grown worse in the space of only a few hours.

'Boss?'

'Wait outside for the arrivals.'

'I thought you needed me in here.'

'The Matador will do the job well enough. As will the other men. Today we need cool heads, not trigger-happy fools who cannot help but draw attention.'

Max glared hatefully at Alistair, before nodding curtly and storming through the open double doors.

'I don't think he's happy,' Alistair said.

Vaar's response was a disgusted snort.

To ease his disquiet, Alistair paced around the empty space. He could see where machinery had once stood, the faded patches testament to what had long ago been dragged away for scrap. A set of rusted metal steps disappeared into a sub-basement. When he paused beside the opening, he heard movement; things scurrying about in the darkness. He shuddered and moved on.

He nodded to one of Vaar's men. The guard stared back, his hand resting on the butt of the revolver jammed into his belt. Alistair thought the man had watched far too many Western movies to treat his weapon so cavalier.

'It is good you are here,' Vaar remarked into the silence. Alistair again noted the deathly ashen hue to Vaar's face. Only the fierce, unbending fire in his eyes gave a hint of the banked flames of his personality.

Alistair nodded. The weight of his revolver pressed against his side, and he was glad he had it with him.

'Cool heads are what I require,' Vaar said. 'Although there was a time when I was as, ah, hot-headed as the best of them. But... My situation has changed somewhat.'

A flash of memory and Alistair saw Vaar at the height of his power: at the Dominex plant, four years ago. Blustering, bombastic and as scary as hell. So far from the man that now stood near him.

Regardless, Alistair sensed the potential for violence in the air, and tasted iron in his mouth. The Dominator may not have been at his best, but only a fool would lower their guard around him. And neither the Matador nor Alistair were fools.

A car drove up to the warehouse. Brakes squealed, then multiple doors opened and shut. Alistair heard Max speak and an unfamiliar voice answer.

'You've got a hide, Vaar.' A short man trailing two others stormed into the warehouse.

His echoing footsteps unsettled the pigeons. Some burst into the airy gap below the ceiling, the clatter of their frantic wings loud. White feathers fluttered down as the birds swooped and dove before returning to their perches.

The short man paused, and glared up at the rafters. An unlit cigar jutted out from between clenched teeth. He was short, round faced who radiated barely contained rage. His two men, whose necks had merged with their massive shoulders, kept a wary eye on Alistair and the other guards.

'Freddy Casterton. The self-styled Prince of Soho. It is nice to see you too, Freddy,' Vaar said.

Alistair thought Vaar's levity sounded strained.

'Sammy Wilberforce was my friend. How is killing him good for business? I should shoot you down like a dog.' Casterton seethed.

'You could try,' Vaar said, smiling like a shark. 'Though if the tables were turned, I would not talk about killing you. I would do it.'

Casterton blinked, and laughed uncertainly. Vaar indicated the table with a wave of his hand.

'Pour yourself a drink. I will be raising a toast, soon enough.'

'A toast. To what?'

'Patience, oh Prince,' Vaar said, smiling mockingly.

Casterton's face purpled, and the tension increased. After a moment, he went over to the table and poured himself a drink. Alistair kept an eye on the man's guards, who glared back at him in return.

'The others will be here shortly,' Vaar said. 'All your questions will be answered then. And do not worry, business will be very good.'

Scowling, Casterton tipped back his head and swallowed the scotch. His throat worked, and tears came to his eyes, then he slammed the glass back onto the table.

'At least you brought the good stuff,' he said, almost gasping. He poured another glass, and sipped from it. He looked over the rim of the glass at Alistair and his forehead creased.

'Do I know you?' It took a moment for Alistair to realise Casterton was talking to him.

He looked at Vaar, who looked back.

'I don't think so,' Alistair said. The Matador's memory said otherwise, however.

'Majorca. Three years ago. I've a thing for faces. Especially criminals. You sat at the table next to mine for an hour or two the night after someone cracked the main safe in the diamond market. One of the dealers came in, screaming blue murder and pointing at you. I remember you broke his jaw before you returned to your lobster. Did you do a little break and enter on your holiday?' Casterton smiled unpleasantly.

Alistair shrugged his shoulders. 'I travel,' he said, 'a lot. So maybe yes, maybe no,' he added, emphasising his Spanish accent. Casterton held his gaze and swallowed another mouthful of scotch.

The second arrival made less fuss than Casterton. Tall and lantern jawed, the gang leader strolled into the warehouse with an amused smirk on his face.

'Freddy. Vaar,' he said. He waved his men to one side. 'Not as if they can do anything if you've set a trap, eh, Vaar?' He nodded to Casterton. 'How are you, Freddy?'

'All the better for seeing your long face, Victor,' Casterton said. 'Ever heard the one about the horse who walked into a bar?'

Victor's smile slid from his face. 'No. Never.'

The final guest took longer to arrive, and the tension in the warehouse grew as the men shifted from foot to foot. Alistair noted Vaar holding himself up with a great deal of effort, sweat now rolling down his face. Eventually, a black Jaguar pulled to a stop beside the other vehicles, its heavily tinted windows obscuring the occupants.

Alistair glanced from Casterton, to Victor, to Vaar. A sense of anticipation grew, broken by a car door creaking open.

'Where's that damn Vaar?' An old man, walking with the aid of a stick, stepped out of the back of the Jaguar with some difficulty. One of his guards was on hand to assist, which the old man waved irritably away. His white hair lifted around his head in a halo and his rheumy eyes glittered unpleasantly. Another of the old man's guards stepped out of the driver's side and joined his companion.

'Lester Holt,' Vaar said. With an effort, he stepped away from the concrete pillar. He swayed a little, then indicated the table. 'Help yourself.'

Glaring at Vaar, Holt stumped unsteadily to the table and collapsed into one of the chairs. With his walking stick planted between his feet, he looked around the assembled men.

'When the Big Man calls, everyone jumps.' Holt sneered, shaking his head. 'Pathetic.' He looked at Vaar again. 'At my age, my time is better spent than answering the same question with the same response. You want to buy us out. The answer is still no, no matter the price.'

'Please, Lester,' Vaar said. 'Before we begin, at least have a drink. Matters such as these should be discussed over drinks, surely?'

Holt's mouth compressed into a thin, bloodless line. After a moment, he nodded. When no one else offered to pour, Alistair approached the table and did the honours. Holt smelled like mothballs.

When Alistair withdrew, Vaar took up his own glass, and the others followed.

'We all know each other, yes?'

'Of course we do,' Casterton said.

'Good,' Vaar said. 'So you know I do not mince my words, or my actions, for that matter.'

'Are we here to talk about Wilberforce?' Victor asked. 'Wilberforce was a fool, but what happened to him crossed a line.'

Vaar chuckled, a deep throbbing noise that set Alistair's teeth on edge.

'Something funny?' Casterton snapped.

'Absolutely. You men, who have built your empires on the blood and suffering of others, have suddenly developed a conscience.' Vaar shook his head. 'This is, as it has always been, a business proposition.'

'You mean a takeover,' Holt said. He swallowed a

mouthful of scotch, grimaced and set his glass aside.

'Precisely,' Vaar said. Watching him, Alistair could only imagine the restraint the Dominator was displaying. He knew, without a shadow of a doubt he knew, that if the circumstances were different, Vaar would gladly have shot each man out of hand and taken what he wanted without saying a word.

'I don't know about these two,' Holt said. 'But I intend passing my business on to my son, not some jumped up mystery man who thinks the answer to everything is spilling someone else's blood.' He pushed himself to his feet with some difficulty. 'Is that all? Because like I said, I'm an old man with better things to do with what little time—'

A deep booming noise stopped the conversation and sent pigeons into the air. Despite Vaar's evident exhaustion, the smile that crept across his face was full of sadistic glee. Sensing movement behind him, Alistair pulled his revolver out. The other men followed suit.

'Put those pathetic toys away,' Vaar snarled, something of his old command returning. He turned to Holt. 'When was the last time you saw your son? I imagine a man as debauched as he tends to vanish for days at a time. A dangerous habit.'

Holt opened his mouth to answer, then stopped.

Footsteps rang on the metal stairs leading from the sub-basement. Alistair took a step backward as, out of the shadows, two shapes appeared, carrying a slumped form between them.

Alistair looked at Vaar, who minutely shook his head. Still, he kept his revolver aimed at the approaching figures.

With leaden flesh and rudimentary, if powerful, limbs, they moved with mechanical precision. Eyes glimmered red beneath thick folds of bone. A domed skull sat atop a squat neck that merged with shoulders as broad as an ox. It was only when they approached closer that Alistair saw a symbol carved into the forehead of each creature.

'What the hell are they?' Casterton's cigar drooped from his slack mouth.

'Their creator calls them the Golems of Kyr,' Vaar said. He shrugged, as if the matter of what they were didn't interest him. 'They are the keys to total victory.'

The hair on the back of Alistair's neck rose at Vaar's triumphant words. He was about to open his mouth when Holt spoke.

'Arthur? Is that Arthur?' Holt's voice was suddenly querulous and old.

The figure held between the two creatures hung limp. Dried blood clung to the side of his face like a mask.

'Don't stand there!' Holt shouted at his men, his face going crimson. 'Get him free of those things.'

The two men looked at each other and then at the creatures. One approached directly, while the other circled, looking for an opening. The motionless golems stared straight ahead. Vaar, for his part, looked at the unfolding contest with keen interest.

The first man attempted to grapple with one of the golems. His fingers failed to find purchase on it. The golem's head turned slowly to look at him, then its free hand swung back and threw the guard through the air. He landed in a sprawled heap on the ground some distance away. He struggled to his feet, covered in dust and blood from a scrape down the side of his face. The golem returned to staring blankly ahead.

The other guard leaped at the second golem. His arm went around its throat and pulled tight. The golem appeared unaffected. Its free arm rose mechanically, blunt fingers grabbing the guard by his jacket and pulling him free. He dangled in the air, mouth open wide in surprise, then he was slung away, cannoning into a concrete pillar. He slid to the ground in a broken heap. This golem, too, returned to his former position.

Vaar looked around him with the imperious gaze of a Roman Emperor. All that was missing, Alistair thought with a chill, was a Triumph all the way to the Capitoline Hill.

'Sit down, Lester,' Vaar said, as more hulking figures emerged into the open, faces blank, eyes glittering with barely restrained power. They gathered around Vaar, a grim praetorian guard.

Vaar's face was grave, but the light in his eyes spoke of victory. 'Sit down, so we can discuss terms of surrender.' He looked at the others, and grinned. '*All* your terms of surrender.'

CHAPTER ELEVEN
Sorrow

LATER THAT MORNING, BILL AND ANNE FOUND themselves inside the solid grandeur of the Imperial War Museum. On one of the upper levels, they were ushered into an inner office by a secretary, who announced them, then left.

A man in a suit looked up from his desk. 'So, detectives from Crouch End Station, how can I help you?'

'We're investigating the recent murders of two men,' Anne said.

'I'm not sure what information the Imperial War Museum can furnish you with,' Foley said, looking puzzled. 'Our mission here is remembrance, not murder.' He essayed a smile, then thought better of it.

'There's evidence of a link between both men.'

'What sort of link?' Foley asked. 'Did they serve in the British military?'

'It's a bit obscure,' Bill said, trying not to look too embarrassed. 'It seems that whoever killed them had an interest in the occult. Sumerian, to be specific. With the possibility of Nazi involvement.'

Foley stared at them for a moment before he broke into laughter. 'This is some sort of game, isn't it? I didn't ask to see your warrant cards when you arrived, but perhaps I should? I am a busy man, so if you've finished...?'

'We've not,' Anne said. 'This is deadly serious.' She

glanced at Bill. 'I'm told you were the man for the job. Recommended by Brigadier Lethbridge-Stewart, in fact. If you aren't the man he said you are, would you mind pointing us in the direction of someone who is?'

Foley looked at Bill as if seeking help. Bill shrugged his shoulders. *Can't help you, mate* the gesture indicated.

'Nazi occult. Sumerians, of all the... It's ridiculous of course,' Foley muttered, as if he was the only person in the room. He straightened a file on his desk, then looked up. He seemed to come to a decision. 'I suppose you've heard of the Thule Society?'

'We've heard of it,' Anne said, cautiously. 'Not that we have much contact with that sort of thing in our line of work, obviously,' she added quickly. Bit hard to explain why two CID officers had such knowledge.

'Glad to see there's still some respect for history in your generation.' Foley shook his head. 'The Annenerbe sprung from the remains of the Thule Society; a secret society devoted to the mystical history of Germany and other claptrap. After Hitler shut them down, a few of its members joined Himmler's circle. With Himmler's enthusiastic embrace of the occult, they built the Annenerbe.'

Anne's eyes brightened. 'We've definitely heard of the Annenerbe. Spear of Destiny, runic magic, expeditions to Tibet. Even underground bases in the Antarctic.'

Foley shook his head. 'Like I said,' he said sourly. 'Claptrap.' Pausing, he looked shrewdly across his desk at them. 'Do you have a case that involves something to do with the organisation?'

Bill gave his best professional smile. 'We'd like to be more specific, Mr Foley, but we can't give out the particulars. We are here to find out if you can point us in the direction of some expert help.'

Foley drummed his fingers on the desk, then slapped

his palm down. 'I might just have the man you're after.' He rose from his chair and turned to a row of filing cabinets. Several Third Reich propaganda posters hung from the walls.

'Is that entirely appropriate?' Bill asked, knowing he should keep to the matter at hand, but bridling at the blatant display.

Foley looked up from a file and smiled humourlessly. 'When their loathsome history is hidden away between the covers of a book, it's easy to forget what they did. Not so easy when their imagery is front and centre.' He shook his head as he rifled through the file.

Placing the folder aside, he found another in the back of the cabinet. Leafing through it, he pulled a page free and handed it to Bill. 'Professor Pyotr Mazurski. Survivor of the 1944 Wrzici Massacre in Poland. He has as a degree in theology and wrote his PHD on the Nazi's obsession with the occult. Which means he's also an expert on the Annenerbe. And he lives in London.'

Foley was about to put the file aside, when something occurred to him. From the back of the folder, he pulled out another page and handed it to Bill.

'Colonel Paul von Werner,' Bill said, looking up from the page. 'What's the connection?'

'Mazurski testified at von Werner's trial *in absentia*. It was his testimony about the Wrzici Massacre that got von Werner a death sentence.'

'There's a question mark next to his date of death,' Anne said, taking the paper off Bill.

'Like a lot of men of his ilk,' Foley said, 'von Werner was happy to trample civilisation while the tide was with them, then ran like a rat when the Reich began to topple.'

'Tell us about Wrzici,' Bill said.

Foley didn't immediately respond, a cloud sweeping across his face. 'A terrible business. Most of the inhabitants were machine-gunned and the village razed to the ground.'

'Most?'

'Yes, Mazurski and his five-year-old daughter escaped. His wife didn't. He's a tough old bird, as you'll no doubt find out. He'll outlive us all. He gave me some assistance last year with research for the Human Rights Conference at the Hague.'

'Well then,' Anne said. 'The professor indeed seems like the man for the job.'

'Good,' Foley said, turning back to his cabinets. 'Let me get Mazurski's address. I have it in a file somewhere.'

Anne parked the car. She released the steering wheel and flexed her hands. 'Power steering. Who knew how much of a godsend it would be? This is like trying to steer a brick.'

Bill grinned as he checked his watch. 'Right on time.'

Anne tapped an imaginary hat brim. 'Right you are, guv. That'll be a fiver, thanks.'

'A fiver? I would've made it to Land's End on a fiver. Plus a pint and some chips out of the change.'

'Cost of livin', guv,' Anne said, and smiled briefly. 'Come on then, let's go see what the professor has to say.'

Outside, the air was chilly despite a clear sky. A breeze shivered the orange and golden leaves in the elms that marched up and down both sides of the street. The distant rumble of traffic drifted to them, but other than the sound of children playing in a backyard, the street was empty.

Dignified terrace houses lined the street. Most were one or two storeys, each with a set of steps leading up to the front door. Anne and Bill briskly climbed to a black painted door. Bill knocked.

Footsteps echoed down a long hall. The door opened with a light creak, revealing a woman.

Watch out for this one, Bill thought, at the frosty gaze

that greeted them. She wore a cardigan over a white shirt, with a plaid skirt to her knees. She had her dark blonde hair pulled back in a tight bun.

'DC Champion and WDC Winter. Crouch End Police Station,' Bill said. 'We called earlier today.'

'Identification, please,' she said crisply, with the faintest hint of an accent.

Smiling tightly, Bill pulled out his identification, as did Anne. The woman glanced carefully at both, before nodding. Some of the stiffness left, and she stepped back, inviting them in.

'Thank you, Ms Mazurski,' Bill said as they stepped into the cool dimness of the hallway.

'The formality of men when they see a beautiful woman never ceases to amaze me. Don't you think, Detective Winters?'

'Absolutely,' Anne said, a mischievous smile playing on her lips.

'I wasn't...' Bill began, before Ms Mazurski cut him off.

'You're saying I'm not a beautiful woman?' She quirked an eyebrow, and laughed throatily.

'I fear I've walked into a trap,' Bill said, looking between Anne and Mazurski.

'It's your head in the noose, Harry,' Anne said, before composing herself. 'We're here to speak with your father.'

'Yes. Detective Champion mentioned something about the war when he called. I counselled my father not to speak to you.'

Useful, Bill thought. *Always nice to have an obstruction immediately placed before you.*

'Why?' Anne asked.

'For some, the war never ended.'

'Your father is one of those people?' Bill asked as gently as he could.

'Yes.'

Anne reached out a hand, and gently touched the other woman's elbow. 'We're not here to cause distress,' she said. 'But we are on urgent business and your father is our best hope.'

'To catch a killer, perhaps?' Miss Mazurski asked, eyes narrowing.

Anne nodded.

Ms Mazurski considered them for a moment. 'Please, call me Magda.' She reached out a hand and first Anne, then Bill, shook it. Magda indicated the far end of the corridor with a nod of her head. 'Please, he is at the end of the house.'

Passing down a long crimson rug chased in gold thread, Bill glanced into the rooms on either side of the corridor. Dark shelving lined most, heaving with countless books. Others were crammed with the bric-a-brac of a lifetime's travel and study. Bill had a sense of glimpsing inside the mind of Mazurski; a labyrinthine place full of secret knowledge and shared joys and sorrows.

Bill slowed to look at a portrait hanging in a room otherwise jammed with books. The seated woman in the painting stared boldly from the canvas. He noticed scorch marks around the edges, and the frame was newer than the painting itself. There was much of Magda in the woman's face.

'Your mother?' Bill asked.

'Yes.'

'A fine woman,' he said, glancing at Magda.

'From what my father has said, the finest.' Magda raised a finger. 'I warn you that he is easily taxed. I have only agreed to let you see him because Mr Foley vouched for you.'

'Very well.'

Magda led them into a sunroom overlooking a well-tended garden. Several high-backed chairs sat around a number of low, book covered tables. Seated in a chair, wrapped in thick blankets, an old man dozed, an open book lying in his lap.

'Father,' Magda called softly. 'Our visitors are here.'

Eyes blinked open at once, instantly alert. Bill, then Anne, shook the old man's hand, which was thin, dry and cold. The old man coughed, making a wet sound that made Bill wince.

'Professor Mazurski, thank you for agreeing to speak to us,' he said.

Mazurski waved a hand. Magda sat in the chair next to him, while Bill and Anne settled into chairs across from them.

'You have a wonderful place,' Anne remarked.

'I confess it is my sanctuary from a world increasingly sliding into chaos.'

'Father,' Magda chided him.

'They are the police,' he said, with some vigour. 'They know what the world outside is like, even if you refuse to see it.'

'I see it, Father, just not with your apocalyptic view.

'You should,' Mazurski said, peevishly.

Bill glanced at Anne and smiled slightly, reminded of her and Professor Travers back in the day. Or, he realised, only a few years ago…

'I think we're a little off track here,' Anne said, an all too knowing tone in her voice.

'The problem with you young people is that you are far too direct in your conversation,' Professor Mazurski said. 'Given my age, it should be I who cuts so quickly to the heart of the matter, don't you think?' He shook his head.

Another look passed between Bill and Anne. *Yes, so Edward Travers.*

'Tell me,' Mazurski continued. 'What brings two

detectives to my door?'

'We're pursuing parallel investigations, Professor, which we believe are linked,' Anne said.

'Who?' Magda said.

'Two men. One named Richard Perkins, the other Frank Carnarvon.'

'Carnarvon?' Mazurski's eyes narrowed.

'Yes,' Bill said, jumping on the recognition. 'A man with links to organised crime. He was involved in a number of deaths yesterday. He died in custody last night.'

'I saw something in this morning's papers,' Mazurski said, his eyes narrowing again. 'Did he burn to death?'

'Yes... and no,' Bill said, after a moment.

Mazurski clapped his hands like a delighted child on Christmas Day. He looked over at his daughter. 'The common conception of the police, my dear, is they are unimaginative clods. And yet here we have two who have presented us with a conundrum.'

'I'm sure they're delighted by your analysis, Father,' Magda said drily.

'Ah, my dear. You were much more entertaining when you were a child.' Mazurski looked shrewdly at his guests. 'And what of this Mr Perkins? Did he perhaps die and yet not die?'

'That's why we're here to see you, Professor,' Bill said. From a folder, he slipped out a photograph of Perkins' corpse, and handed it to Mazurski.

The colour drained from the old man's face. The lines around his mouth deepened and his eyes narrowed.

'You recognise the symbol?' Anne asked, leaning forward eagerly.

'I recognise the man *and* the symbol,' Mazurski said, tapping the photo with a finger. 'He was born Arthur Seaton. The man bearing that named vanished in 1945.'

'And re-emerged as Richard Perkins,' Anne said. 'We

know he was in finance. He had offices in the City. What do you know about him that we should?'

Mazurski considered. 'Britain in the 1930s was a hotbed of Nazi sympathisers, almost exclusively in the upper classes. Historians call them the Cliveden Set. Traitors, I think, is a far better way to describe them.'

'Seaton was a follower of Oscar Mosley,' Magda said, taking the photograph from her father who settled back in his chair. She stared at the image for a moment, then laid it face down on the folder.

'What about the symbol?' Anne asked. 'You said you recognised it.'

'Yes.' Mazurski pursed his lips. 'The closest approximation for it is traitor. Apt, don't you think? Carving this symbol into the dead person was thought to ensure they would never reach Paradise.'

'Who would want him dead?' Bill asked. 'He had no known criminal associates, no political affiliations. I've never seen a cleaner record than his.'

'And that should sound alarm bells,' Magda said. 'Do you honestly think a man can go through life without even a parking ticket? You English, with your faith in laws and justice.' She shook her head.

'My daughter's cynicism is justified, Detective Champion,' Mazurski said. 'I was on a war crimes panel in the 1960s. Seaton engaged in low-level activity designed to undermine Britain's war effort. His fascist sympathies during the war were unmistakeable. Nothing came of our recommendations. I doubt the report even exists anymore.'

There was silence for a moment, then a thought occurred to Mazurski.

'You said you were pursuing parallel investigations. What else links Seaton with Carnarvon?'

Anne looked at Bill, who nodded. 'We came across this, last night.'

From an envelope, she took the charred fragment found in Carnarvon's fist and handed it to Magda. She put on her glasses to study the surviving symbols on the tiny piece of paper, then handed it with a trembling hand to her father. Mazurski stared, shook his head with a mutter of frustration, and used a magnifying glass to look at the symbols. He closed his eyes.

'You must understand my field is primarily in the occult,' he said, handing the scrap back to Anne.

'Debunking?' Bill asked.

Mazurski shook his head. 'In a way. Suppressing, I think, is how you would describe it.'

'Suppressing indicates a certain belief. Do you believe?'

'You are a strange man, Detective Champion,' Mazurski said, looking at Bill as if for the first time. 'There are few today who believe in the powers of darkness.'

'We live in strange times, Professor,' Bill said. 'Science alone can explain the mysteries of the universe, though explaining them doesn't necessarily make them less frightening.'

Some of Mazurski's earlier humour returned. 'Perhaps the police aren't a mixture of time servers and plodders after all.' He looked at Anne. 'Do you share your partner's expansive world view?'

'Yes,' Anne said. She glanced at Bill. 'We've both had experiences well outside what anyone would consider normal. I hardly know what normal is anymore, to be frank.' She pointed to the scrap of paper. 'What are the odds that the same symbol appears on a corpse and this piece of paper?'

'Not the sort I would place money on,' Mazurski said.

'It's to do with Wrzici, isn't it?' Bill asked bluntly, and felt Anne's glare burn into him. 'Sorry,' he mumbled.

'You can't think my father a suspect,' Magda said, outraged.

'I confess to having not left the house in weeks,' Mazurski said, smiling tiredly. 'Magda wouldn't allow it, especially after that recent virulent flu outbreak. Strange that, don't you think? The military seemed involved in dealing with the issue.'

Bill cleared his throat. 'We don't suspect you, Professor.'

'But you do have a suspect?' Magda asked.

'We do,' Anne replied.

'And Father can assist you?'

Bill nodded.

'How?'

'We're tracking a murderer. Someone who uses occult symbols. Maybe only as a calling card, like the Zodiac killer in America. Perhaps for something much, much darker.'

'Oh, definitely darker,' Mazurski said.

Bill glanced at Anne, who leaned forward and spoke gently, using the same tone she used to use on her father. 'Telling us what happened in August '44 will be of great help. If you don't mind, of course.'

'War,' Mazurski said bleakly. He tilted his head back and closed eyes.

'Fear and horror,' Magda said and Bill saw in her face a little of the five-year-old she had once been.

'Perpetrated by whom?' Anne asked, although she already knew from their earlier conversation with Foley.

'Paul von Werner,' Mazurski said, his eyes distant, voice barely a whisper.

'The Devil himself,' Magda said.

'Yes, the Devil himself,' her father agreed. He looked first at Bill, then Anne. 'Are you sure you need to hear this?'

Anne nodded softly. 'We do.'

Mazurski shook his head. 'Very well then...'

CHAPTER TWELVE
Conversation Place

'I MET VON WERNER ONCE, BEFORE THE WAR. AT A conference, of all places,' Professor Mazurski began. 'He was obsessed with the Sumerians. Had spent time in Mesopotamia, digging into the ruins there. He knew of my research, and sought me out.'

Anne felt her heart go out to the old man, and for a moment she saw her father sitting there. Tired and frail; the final image she had of him before he went off to Tibet... Almost four years ago, and yet, for her, over forty. And still she remembered it as clear as day.

'We exchanged some letters, but then the war came and communication was impossible. By then, I thought the man was obsessed to the point of madness.' Mazurski's voice fell away, then he glanced at his visitors. 'We fled Warsaw early in the war, to my family's home village. Von Werner tracked us there.'

'Why did he want you?' Bill asked.

'Knowledge.' Mazurski sighed. 'The knowledge only I had.'

'What sort of knowledge would lead a man to murder your compatriots and burn your village down?'

Mazurski shrugged, then coughed, a prolonged fit that left him gasping. Magda attended him, looking angrily at Bill, until the professor relaxed back into his chair. His breath whistled like a steaming kettle.

'Why are you both here, really?' Mazurski asked. 'I

am simply an old man.'

Feeling an intuition, Anne leaned forward. 'Describe von Werner.'

Mazurski swallowed. 'Black hair, pale, scarred face. They say he was badly wounded when a mortar round landed near him on the Eastern Front in 1942. He began using a wolf-headed cane...'

Taking an envelope from a folder, Anne removed a sheaf of photographs and laid them on the table. Mazurski looked warily at them. In the end, his daughter picked them up for him. Anne watched Magda shiver as she leafed through the grainy images, then pause on one. With a trembling hand, Magda handed the photograph to her father.

'Where was this taken?' he asked, eyes fixed on the image.

'Surveillance team. In Soho,' Bill said. 'Not ten miles from here. It seems he has an association with a criminal organisation known as the Black Sons. Is the name familiar to you?'

Mazurski and his daughter exchanged a glance.

'When was it taken?' Magda asked. Her face was like wax.

'Less than forty-eight hours ago. It's him, isn't it?' Anne asked, leaning forward. 'Von Werner?'

Magda exchanged a glance with her father. He nodded, minutely.

'Yes.' Magda sighed, almost sobbing. She grimaced, trying to control her emotions. Her eyes were red, but she stared defiantly at the image.

'I'm sorry this is hard for you,' Anne said.

Mazurski passed a trembling hand over his face. Magda leaned over him, but he waved her off. 'You tell them.'

'Several members of the Nazi High Command were fervent believers in the occult,' Magda explained. 'Hitler wasn't, but then he would never have considered anyone or anything more powerful than he. Hess did, but his flight to Scotland saw occult practitioners within the Reich purged. Himmler was a believer. Given his power and influence, he was allowed to continue his interest in it.

'He created an elite unit within the Annenerbe, who styled themselves the Order of the Black Sun. Castle Tuetenborg in Prussia was their headquarters, until it was evacuated in early 1945. Many were captured and shot by the Soviets. Some... simply disappeared.'

'Black Sun,' Bill said softly.

'Black *Sons*.' It was, sadly, beginning to make some sense to Anne. Her mind flicked back to Schädengeist, the first Nazi she'd met. Nothing good ever came of Nazis in the UK.

'And von Werner was a member?' Bill asked, turning back to Mazurski.

'According to the lists I have seen, von Werner remained the highest ranking member of the Order whose whereabouts haven't been confirmed.' Mazurski glanced down at the photographs scattered across the table. When he looked back up, there was a new determination in his eyes. 'He is your link in your investigation. The use of these symbols matches his obsession with Sumerian magic. Whether he is working for himself, or this organisation, that is for you to discover.'

'What's he doing in London?' Anne wondered.

'He had relatives in England,' Mazurski explained. 'Before the war. They changed their surname at the outbreak, and never reverted. There were rumours of a family estate a couple of hours drive south east of London...'

'He's been hiding in plain sight all this time?' Bill was incredulous.

'Any more surprising than Schädengeist?' Anne asked.

'Suppose not.' Bill looked back at Mazurski and prompted the old man for an answer.

'Seaton... or Richard Perkins, as you call him, is your answer to that. I mentioned the Cliveden Set. There are rumours that Churchill survived an assassination attempt, by a man wielding a sword, of all things, on the same day Hitler committed suicide. Such a thing could only have been attempted with sympathetic elements within the British Establishment.'

'Sword?' Bill asked, exchanging a glance with Anne.

Mazurski nodded. 'Only rumours, though.'

'The novelty of it,' Bill said, attempting a smile that felt like a grimace.

'And after the war,' Magda added, cutting into the conversation, 'a man with connections like von Werner could hide in plain sight easily.'

'And what did they get in return for protecting him?' Bill asked. 'They must have realised harbouring a known war criminal would've completely discredited them.'

'Power,' Mazurski said, as if the answer was obvious. 'Or the promise of it. The Empire may be gone, but Britain retains global influence. There are sections of the Establishment who think it could yet again rule the world. For decades, they have yearned to snatch back the reins of power that fell to the Americans. Being the honest broker at peace conferences with the Chinese isn't enough. They want their seat back at the table. Possibly von Werner has stumbled across such a way.'

'There have long been rumours that Arthur Seaton was in some way linked with Hess' arrival in Britain,' Magda said. 'Though how Seaton knew is a secret he took to the grave with him.'

'And Carnarvon?' Bill asked.

'You were there,' Mazurski said. 'What did you see?'

'Carnarvon was the only living witness to this gangland massacre. He meets with a solicitor, who we strongly believe is the legal front man for the head of the Black Sons.'

'And Sumerian magic kills him?' Magda asked.

'A dry run, I think some would call it,' Mazurski said. 'At Nuremberg, there was a separate trial for members of the Annenerbe. To a man, they testified that von Werner was a fervent believer in the occult.'

'So, he uses this magic to punish someone considered a traitor?' Anne nodded to herself, putting the pieces together. 'But why now?'

'Look at both men,' Mazurski said. 'Carnarvon was on the brink of betraying his boss. Seaton had lived a quiet life for the last thirty years. Yet, clearly, he had something this boss wanted, and refused to give up. Something that related back to the war? Something that related to Hess? Something a powerful criminal might want.'

'That's a leap in the dark,' Anne said.

'What else do we have?' Bill asked. He glanced at Mazurski. 'Von Werner wanted knowledge from you during the war. You and your daughter escape. He flees to Britain at the end of the war, remains hidden, and only re-emerges now. And you think he may've been linked to Perkins... I mean, Seaton?'

'In temperament only, I think. A man like von Werner doesn't shed his beliefs like a snake does its skin. During the war, Seaton was a functionary, a willing accomplice, but his beliefs were not as vile as von Werner's. After the war, it appears he made a comfortable life for himself. Why jeopardise that? I think he was content to remain hidden, and not have anything to do with men like von Werner.'

Anne brushed her hands over her trousers. 'The link is von Werner. Find him, and we find out how and why

Perkins and Carnarvon died.'

'Maybe,' Mazurski said. 'A man like von Werner is a tool. Find the carpenter, and you will find the man behind all of it.' With that, the professor sat back in his chair, exhausted.

Taking the cue, Anne began to gather up the documents. 'Thank you for your time, Professor, Miss Mazurski.'

'Will you capture him?' Mazurski asked. With his grey face and whistling breath, he seemed close to death. Magda attended anxiously to him.

'We'll do our best,' Anne said. She reached down and held the old man's hand, which felt very, very cold. 'We'll do our best.'

The weather had turned. Clouds milled low overhead, and a cold drizzle swept the buildings around them.

'Will we catch him?' Bill asked, turning up his collar.

'Von Werner? We owe it to them, don't you think?'

'I think Perkins was killed because he refused to sell the sword to Holcombe, who had to be representing the Big Man. We have a confirmed visual on von Werner in the vicinity of where we believe the Big Man is headquartered.'

'That sounds right,' Anne said. 'This sword must be worth a great deal for all the effort that's gone into finding it. So, if von Werner is after it… then he must be doing so for Vaar.' She chewed on a thumbnail, deep in thought. 'We could visit the bank. Have a look at this sword and see if there's anything unusual about it.'

'What did Perkins' wife say; the Bank of Shetland?'

'She did. We need an address.'

Bill went to reach into his pocket for his mobile phone, and stopped. '1973,' he said, with a smile. 'For a moment there, being with you again made me forget. No mobile phones, no Google.'

'Only the phone book.'

'Right. It's back to the station, then.'

'Where the hell have you two been?'

Anne and Bill stopped in the entrance to the squad room. An acrid smell, legacy of the previous night's inferno, lingered.

Hartigan stood at Champion's desk, the telephone receiver cradled on his shoulder.

'Gathering evidence,' Anne said. 'Who's on the phone?'

'Surveillance got a hit in Soho,' Hartigan said. He put the phone to his ear, listened for a moment, then signed frantically for a pen. Anne rummaged through the desk, found one and tossed it to Hartigan, who commenced scribbling notes on a pad. 'What road are you on? We'll be in radio contact in five minutes. Stay on them.'

Hartigan slammed down the phone, his eyes alight with excitement. 'The Big Man is on the move,' he called, and half a dozen heads instantly turned in his direction.

'How?' Bill asked.

'One of Lester Holt's guys was seen speaking with a known associate of the Big Man. We've got a car tailing him at the moment. Reckons they're heading to the London Docks.' He signalled to the other detectives who began to make their way out.

'Not likely, love,' one of the detectives said to Anne as he walked past her desk. 'Best you keep the home fires burning, while the men do the real work.'

'Get stuffed, Pete,' Anne said, as she pulled on her jacket.

'Might be time to give it a rest, Pete,' Hartigan said, surprising Anne and Bill. He looked at the other detectives. 'Come on, move it. We've got a raid to conduct.'

'What makes you so sure anything is happening?'

Anne asked.

'What else could it be other than a meeting? Holt's a curmudgeon. The only reason he would agree to a meet would be to save his hide. The Big Man is taking them down one by one. Holt would want to be first in line to get something sorted. I reckon we might be onto a winner with this one.'

Anne wasn't so convinced. 'You're building a pretty big case on very shaky foundations. The Big Man has been quiet all year, and now you think he's just going to show up?'

'You might be surprised, Ruth,' Hartigan said. 'Me and you are more alike than you think. We both want the same thing.'

'What's that, then?'

'The Big Man in handcuffs in front of a judge. This is too good an opportunity to pass up. Now, are you coming or not?'

Anne looked at Hartigan, trying to find an angle that involved him humiliating Ruth.

'Look, I know I've been a bit of a sod to you —'

'A bit? Really, Tom?'

'All right. A lot. But we're on the same team here, you, me and Harry.'

'If that's the case,' Anne shot back, 'how about treating me like I'm on the team, and not the bloody bootstudder?'

Hartigan surprised them both by breaking into laughter. 'Bootstudder? She's a funny one, Harry. Of course we're on the same team. Now, are you coming or not?'

Hartigan didn't wait for a response; he left the room with the rest of the team. Anne held back and looked at Bill.

'What do you think?'

'I think we can't *not* go.'

'No.' Anne narrowed her eyes. 'We can't. Let's do it then, let's go meet the Big Man.'

Bill followed Anne out. 'A London gangster. We've dealt with much worse.'

Anne smiled, but she didn't look back at Bill. 'Haven't we just? Easy-peasy.'

CHAPTER THIRTEEN
Heroes

SWEAT TRICKLED DOWN BILL'S NECK AND INTO HIS collar. He squirmed, his hip bumping up against Anne's. He smiled an apology.

'You're saying surveillance couldn't get inside the site?' Bill asked, peering through a slot at several vehicles parked beside a derelict warehouse.

'I'm saying surveillance had no idea this site existed,' Hartigan said. He shifted, the suspension in the van rocking from side to side. 'We're lucky they decided to follow the car and call it in.'

'Here comes another one,' said a detective, looking through a pair of binoculars. In the space of fifteen minutes, a number of cars had arrived, disgorging their occupants into the warehouse.

'Casterton, Victor Transom and Lester blinking Holt now,' Hartigan said, shaking his head. 'We should scoop them all up, just on general principle.'

'Our focus is on the Big Man. He's the head of the snake,' Bill said. He sat beside the radio receiver, the faint crackle of static soothing in the tension-filled van.'

'We should just arrest him,' Hartigan said.

Bill turned to him and smiled. 'For once, Tom, I agree with you. But let's not remount the D-Day landings, yeah? Let's wait for the others to leave, then we can scoop up the Big Man and his men. Less risk and we all get to go home tonight in one piece.'

Hartigan nodded, smiling. 'Sure thing, Harry.' He turned to Anne. 'Since when did Champion start making so much sense?'

Despite herself, Anne smiled. Bill tried to look hurt then broke into a smile.

'They're leaving,' a detective with a pair of binoculars said.

Three vehicles performed a tight circle in the parking area and left, kicking dust into the air.

'Let's go in,' Bill said, knocking on the metal partition separating the rear from the driver's cabin. The engine started up, and the van rolled forward, picking up speed as it turned into the parking area. 'Block that entrance.'

The van came to a jolting stop. Hartigan pushed open the rear doors, and half a dozen detectives emerged.

'No one move!' Bill called as he entered the warehouse.

A handful of men stood in the middle of the empty space, a table containing a bottle and empty glasses nearby. One of the men, the swarthy fellow with the moustache that Bill and Anne had spotted earlier in the photograph, looked startled to see them. The others, evidently guards, moved to stand beside a hulking figure.

'Oh my...' Anne turned to Bill, who stood there, his body tense. 'Bill,' she whispered, careful to hide her voice amid the clattering echo of footsteps, 'it's Director Vaar.'

'What the hell is he doing here?' Bill asked through gritted teeth.

'He's the Big Man.'

'Apt.'

'Did we know he became a gangster?' Anne asked.

Bill wasn't sure. He remembered Vaar had disappeared off their radar for a few years after... He shook his head. No, he shouldn't think about that. It was a long time ago. He had to let it be.

Anne touched Bill lightly on the arm. 'Are you okay?'

Bill wasn't sure. He had found a way to process and move on from what had happened back in September 1970. But the memory of it... Forty years on and still it often haunted his dreams.

He took a deep breath. 'I'll be fine,' he said, equally quiet. 'I'm not here to indulge my whims and desires. What would Harry Champion do?' he asked, forcing a smile.

Anne nodded. 'Exactly. Play the part we've been given.'

Anne watched Vaar closely, mindful of her husband beside her. Vaar seemed to be amused to see the police. He rubbed his hands as the detectives gathered in a tight semi-circle. Hartigan looked like he desperately wanted to use the shotgun cradled in his arms.

'How can I help you, officers?' Vaar asked.

'We'd like you to come down to the station for some questioning,' Bill said, his voice surprisingly calm.

'Of course,' Vaar said. 'I am more than happy to assist the local authorities. Though, truth be told, I am unsure exactly how I can help you.'

'Oh, I bet,' Anne said, keeping in step with Bill. 'You've probably heard about the murder of Sammy Wilberforce.'

'Wilberforce?' Vaar's brow furrowed, a truly terrifying sight. 'I saw his name in the papers. Never met him, of course. Why would I? I am a businessman.'

'I see,' Anne said. 'Regardless, we'd like to speak with you, and your men, about your whereabouts at the time of the murders.'

'Of course,' Vaar said. He spread his arms. 'My men will drive me to your police station.'

'Funny,' Hartigan said, swapping the shotgun from one hand to another. 'You'll get in the van and I'll drive your car.'

Vaar stared hard at Hartigan for a moment, then nodded. Hartigan signalled to a couple of the detectives, who quickly patted the men down. They produced a number of revolvers. Hartigan smiled.

'London is a dangerous city,' Vaar said. 'My men need them for protection.'

'Really?' Hartigan said. 'What sort of business are you in that requires armed guards?'

Vaar remained silent.

'You'll have no need for protection, seeing as how we're the police,' Bill said.

'I am sure.' Vaar signalled to his men as if he was still in control of the situation, and they moved towards the van.

For Bill it was a strange return journey to Crouch End. First of all, it was being in the proximity of Director Vaar – or Dominic Vaar, as he still called himself. Nobody else, bar Anne, was aware they had an alien in their midst. They all saw him as a simple London gangster, a particularly nasty one certainly, but a gangster nonetheless, and so there was the expected jibes and displays of bravado from the other detectives. They had no idea, none at all, of what he was capable. Bill knew, all too well.

But despite all that, he found his attention drawn to the swarthy looking man. Early forties, by the look of him. Hair trimmed in the style of the day. A neat, precise moustache over a mouth of Latin sensuousness. Bill's attention was drawn to the hands; smooth and unlined, nails immaculate. These were the hands of a man used to delicate work. Not those of a thug, who did his business with his fists. But if he wasn't an enforcer, what was he?

There was something else about the man that was off. His body language, even in the cramped van, was at odds with his surroundings. He kept looking around the van, sizing everything up, calculating. But not in the way one would expect from a gangster's associate. There was something... familiar about the look in his eyes, about the way he moved.

Bill was probably reaching, but for the first time since leaving 2011, he and Anne had arrived in proximity to each other. The odds of the Brig doing so, too... Well, they had to be good, right?

Bill nudged Anne, and told her quietly to engage the man in conversation. This she did, and Bill listened. Listened to the man's poor excuse for a Spanish accent, as if it wasn't natural for him. And the words he used... They didn't quite fit.

'Pity we don't have Google,' Bill said, trying out a theory. The man tried to hide his reaction, but he almost snapped his head around to look at Bill. So, he continued; 'All we'd need is facial recognition software to find out your true identity.'

Hartigan gave Bill a look. He shook his head, mumbled something about foolish darkie talk, and the detective next to him laughed. But Bill ignored it. He nodded softly towards Anne, who leaned closer to him.

'You don't think...?' she asked in a whisper.

'Let's see.' Bill spoke directly at the Spaniard. 'Let me guess, your name ain't gonna be anything as simple as Owain or James, is it? Something like Gore, maybe?'

The man regarded Bill carefully, and a slight tug of a smile played at his mouth. 'Maybe it's Ormond,' he said, and looked at Anne. 'Or Goff.'

Gore, Ormond, Goff. Three names, all with one thing in common. Each was the name of their individual maternal families. It was all the confirmation Bill needed.

Sir Alistair Lethbridge-Stewart was in 1973 with them.

*

They arrived in the Crouch End Station car park half an hour later. Vaar stepped out, shot his jacket sleeves, smoothed back his hair, and waited expectantly.

'Hartigan,' Bill said. 'You can take our... guest to interview room one. You and Hoskins can interview him.' Hartigan shot Bill a look of surprise, but nodded. 'Jessop, Flowers. Take these goons to interview room two. Winters and me will have a lovely little chat about paellas with our Spanish friend here, in what's left of three.'

There were murmurs of agreement. They ascended the stairs from the parking garage and trooped into a corridor. Once there, they were split and ushered into their respective interview rooms.

'Done a spot of redecorating,' Alistair observed, looking with interest at the fire damage marking the floor and walls. 'I must confess, I don't like it.' He turned around, his face broadening into a grin as Bill closed the door firmly behind him.

'About time, Alistair,' Anne said, and hugged him.

Bill came up and took Alistair's hand. 'So many questions,' he said. 'Much to catch up on. Little time, though. But one thing I've wanted to say since leaving 1969, thanks for rescuing me from the Yeti. I know it was a long time ago for you, but...'

'Rescuing...?'

'In Tooting Bec. I tried to tell you, but, well, who's gonna listen to a boy?'

Alistair's brow crinkled, then he smiled. 'Good Lord, you were Jonathan James?' He laughed. 'Then you're welcome, and it was *me*, by the way. Not just my contemporary self of '69.'

Anne blinked. 'What? You ended up in your 1969 self?'

'Yes. Turns out I was responsible for getting myself to London all this time. Only I didn't realise the first time around.'

'Then it was you who...' Now Anne laughed, and Bill exchanged a look with Alistair. 'We bumped into each other. I ended up in the body of a woman called Rachel Ashcroft, and you... Well, accosted me. I was blonde then. You sent soldiers after me.'

'I...' Alistair thought for a moment, and shook his head. 'It seems vaguely familiar, but unfortunately I've been through a lot since we left 1969.'

'And you were in your own body?' Bill pursed his lips. 'That hasn't happened to me or Anne, we've only ever ended up in a stranger's body. Wonder why?'

For the next few minutes, they compared notes, not unlike Bill and Anne had done when they first met up in the present. Anne explained her theory of why they were travelling through time, and Alistair explained he too had come to that conclusion.

'Although I'm still not sure who is behind the Gnome, but whoever it is, this person seems to be doing me a favour.'

Bill nudged Anne. 'You tell him.'

She was about to do so when Bill raised a hand.

'First things first.' He took out Alistair's confiscated revolver and handed it back to him. 'You never know,' he explained.

Alistair nodded his thanks and slipped it into his jacket. 'Now then; tell me what?'

Anne explained what Bill had learned, and the circular inscriptions on the base of the Gnome.

'Bless my soul,' Alistair said. 'I should probably have guessed it was the Doc–' He cleared his throat and looked around the interview room. 'Right, well, since we're here and clearly our paths have converged, then we should probably discuss where we go from here. Our hosts have roles to play, and we need to make sure they succeed. And find out why I'm here. Something to do with Vaar, of course. Finally uncover what he was doing when he disappeared, perhaps?'

Bill nodded. 'Agreed, although I doubt it's that simple.'

'No, doesn't seem likely. Well then, let's get started.'

The three of them spent the next hour comparing their experiences since arriving yesterday.

'We know he's been after the sword for some time,' Bill said in conclusion. 'Bribery, then violence. He can't want it for the money. Perhaps it's some sort of relic? Something tied up with Anne's Sumerian magic? After what happened with Sebastian Collins we thought he went into hiding... But three years later, here he is.'

'I think he's sick,' Alistair said.

A searing image of 1970 rushed to Bill's mind. 'No arguments there.'

Alistair looked at Bill, and nodded slowly. 'Of course, I did wonder how you'd feel about all this...' He placed a hand on Bill's shoulder. 'It's been no picnic for me either, Bill. I haven't forgotten his hand in...' Alistair stopped. 'Sally,' he managed, his voice choked.

Bill hadn't forgotten that either. 'Anne is right, though, this isn't about revenge. We've already taken care of that. Or will, I suppose, technically speaking.'

'Quite right. We're not here to change the past. It'd be too late anyway. Sally's been gone for almost three years by this point.'

Anne waited a moment, then asked, 'You said Vaar is sick?'

Alistair nodded. 'Yes. He's not as robust as he was in 1970. He's using creatures he called golems, too. Ugly, powerful brutes. But I don't understand how an artefact stored in a bank vault could be of any use to him. It's just a sword.'

'We've got letters that kill people, and golems roaming London,' Anne said. 'His desperation for the sword indicates he needs it badly.' She rubbed her chin.

'Tell me more about these golems. Describe them.'

Alistair went over his description again. When he came to the symbol carved in their foreheads, Anne stopped him.

'Did it look something like this?' she asked, pulling a page from her file.

Alistair shook his head. 'No. However, it appears to be from the same alphabet.'

'And von Werner,' Bill said. 'You're definite its him?'

Alistair nodded.

Anne paced around the room. 'If Perkins was a Nazi sympathiser and von Werner has been hiding in England all this time, what are the odds they're somehow connected, even if tangentially?'

'I've never been one for coincidences, Anne,' Alistair said. 'And these travels have done nothing to dissuade me of that notion.'

Bill remembered the first time Alistair had said that to him. So long ago. Like Alistair, Bill had seen too much since to believe in coincidences either. There were always patterns though, even if they couldn't see them at first.

'We know Holcombe worked as a solicitor for Vaar,' he said. 'He offered money to Perkins for the sword.'

'So, the sword is the key,' Alistair said.

'What do we do if you do manage to steal it?'

'Keep it out of Vaar's hands,' Alistair said. 'He can't be allowed to have it.'

'We must find out what the sword can do,' Anne said. 'Didn't Professor Mazurski say there was an attempt on Churchill's life at the end of the war?'

'Mazurski?' Alistair asked.

'Occult researcher,' Bill explained. 'He escaped von Werner during the war.'

'Foley would know,' Anne said.

The name caught Alistair by surprise. 'Foley? James Foley? From the Imperial War Museum? Frosty Foley.

Now there's a fella.'

'Frosty Foley?' Anne asked with a smile.

'You had to be, ah… there, to understand,' Alistair said. He coughed. 'Good man.'

A story for another time, Bill realised, promising himself to ask when they returned home. And, for the first time in ages, he honestly believed they would. He turned to Anne.

'Will you go to speak to Foley again?'

'What about you?'

Bill couldn't help but smile. 'I thought that I could, maybe, help the Brig here.'

'Of course you did. The old team back together.' The tone was teasing, but Bill could tell Anne was mildly annoyed. 'Fine, I'll visit Mr Foley this afternoon. What do you two boys intend to do?'

'I've got access to all the Matador's memories and skills,' Alistair explained.

'His memories?' Bill asked.

'A trick I learned a while back.'

'We occasionally get a sense of trace memories.'

'Maybe it's different for you because you're the one being guided by the Gnome?' Anne pondered.

'Perhaps,' Alistair said. 'Either way, the point is, the Matador put together this plan on the fly. It needs two people to execute, not one, so your help will be greatly appreciated, Bill. I've got the blueprints memorised and I know of a way into the vault that won't trip any alarms. I'll have to gather my equipment from where I'm lodging. You'll have to supply a motor, though.'

'A motor? My God, you've gone all *Sweeney*,' Anne said, breaking into laughter.

'It pays to adapt.'

Once Anne had stopped laughing, with an apology to Alistair, Bill said, 'We've got a couple of *motors* impounded downstairs. One of them is a van. It should do.'

'What's the timeframe?' Anne asked.

'Four or five hours,' Alistair said. 'The thermite lance I have is a prototype. It should work, but the Matador has never used it before.'

'And afterwards. Assuming you succeed?'

'We'll need to ditch the van somewhere, and transfer cars.' Alistair looked at Anne. 'You have access to one, don't you?'

Anne nodded. 'I have to visit Foley this afternoon. With some luck, I'll be meeting with someone else. Afterwards, I can keep an eye out for you boys at the Bank of Shetland.'

'What do we do with it when we get the sword?' Bill asked.

There came a knock on the door. They all exchanged glances, and Alistair moved to the corner of the room, taking up a position that was equally nonchalant and defensive. Anne affected an aggressive stance, as if she was being interrupted in her questioning.

Bill crossed to the door and opened it.

'Cut him loose,' Hartigan growled. In the corridor, detectives led Vaar's guards from their interview room. Vaar loomed over them, a half-mocking smile playing on his lips.

'All right, you,' Bill said, turning to Alistair, 'get out.'

Bill and Anne followed Hartigan and the other detectives as Vaar and his men left via the main entrance. Vaar climbed into his Rolls Royce. The remaining members clambered into another vehicle parked behind. The little convoy turned into the street and disappeared into the distance.

'Well, that was a waste of time,' Hartigan said, when they had all reassembled back in the station.

'Not really,' Anne said.

'How's that?' Hartigan asked.

'The Big Man's led a charmed life up until now. He'll think twice knowing we're on to him.'

'On to him?' Hartigan shook his head in disbelief. 'The Big Man is a stone-cold killer. If he gets his way, he'll be running the underworld before the end of the year.'

'We know him now,' Anne said. 'We'll tail him and put the clamps on his business. Wherever his men are, we will be. He won't be able to step outside his hole in the ground without one of us standing next to him. Like Holt or any of those other cockroaches, we have them where we want them. The Big Man will trip up, just you watch.'

'She's a feisty one,' Hartigan said, smiling at Bill.

'You don't have to tell me.'

'You two are hilarious,' Anne said. She pulled on her jacket.

'Where are you going?' Hartigan said.

'To see a man about a mouse,' Anne said, as she swept from the room.

Bill shrugged at Hartigan, hiding his smirk. How easy Anne stepped into Ruth's shoes.

'Well, I'm off to the horses,' Hartigan said. He checked his watch. 'If I hurry, I should be able to make the second race.' He hesitated, then looked back at Bill. 'What about you, Harry? Want to come along? You must need a drink, after today.'

Bill thought furiously for a moment. He shook his head. 'Sheila will have my guts for garters if I don't keep the house clean. I'll have a kip, then the carpets need vacuuming. See you Monday,' he said, walking out of the office.

'Carpets? Vacuuming? Blimey,' Hartigan said, then went over his desk to find the form guide.

CHAPTER FOURTEEN
Heathen

'You're back,' Foley said. His lack of enthusiasm was palpable.

'I am.'

Without waiting for an invitation, Anne took a seat at his desk. Foley closed a folder and sat back, watching Anne with narrowed eyes.

'How can I help you, WDC Winters?' His words were a shade warmer than a rebuke.

Anne smiled. She admired the work Foley did, but she would enjoy more duelling with him.

'My partner and I spoke with Professor Mazurski.'

Foley raised an eyebrow. 'Really? How is the old bird?'

'Ailing,' Anne said, shaking her head. 'Still possesses a great drive and intellect. His daughter is much the same.'

'Magda?' Foley smiled. 'Did you know I took her to dinner once?' He said it as if he were admitting to standing naked in a den of lions. 'Demanded that I split the bill. There's Women's Lib and then there's plain manners.' He tried to feign indignation and mostly succeeded.

'I think you should count yourself lucky you came out ahead, Mr Foley,' Anne said. 'Most men wouldn't.'

'Quite.' Foley rubbed the thumb and index finger on each hand, as if to marshal his thoughts. Outside, a lorry drove by, the driver apparently anxious to grind his way through all the gears seemingly at once. 'Was the professor of any help in your investigation?'

Anne nodded. 'A great help. He provided context we were lacking. But…'

'But…?'

Anne leaned forward in her chair. 'Background information will only get our investigation so far.'

Foley leaned back in his chair. 'You need something more concrete?' He smiled once more.

'Indeed.' Anne took out a notebook and pen. 'How extensive are your records?'

'Regarding what topic in particular?' Foley looked intrigued, no doubt thinking that his Saturday might be something more exciting than shuffling pages around his desk.

'Attempts on the life of Winston Churchill.'

'It's all a bit moot now, don't you think?'

Anne stared at Foley, trying to work out if he was trying to be funny. She decided, on balance, he probably wasn't.

'Quite,' she said. 'I understand there was an attempt on Churchill's life the same day Hitler committed suicide.'

Foley quirked an eyebrow. 'Really?'

Now he was interested. Anne smiled. 'Absolutely.'

Steepling his fingers, Foley stared at the ceiling for a long moment. Then, leaping to his feet, he walked over to a filing cabinet. 'You must realise the Official Secrets Act is often an impediment in these matters,' he said, pulling out a drawer. 'Men and women who might otherwise chronicle their experiences of being near the seat of power stay silent for the remainder of their lives.'

'But you have something?' Anne watched Foley rifle through the drawer.

He pulled out a buff folder and brought it to the desk. 'We do. You have to understand the Imperial War Museum's mission is to memorialise the sacrifices and service of those who served.' He opened the file, looked at a summary page for a moment, then leafed through the papers.

Anne tried to contain her impatience. 'So, you do have a record of attempts on Churchill's life?'

'We do. We have records of four reported attempts. Not all were made public. For instance, on April 30th, 1945...'

Anne leaned forward. 'Did the attempt involve someone wielding a sword?'

Foley stared at her as if she had grown antlers. 'A sword? What, like a cavalry sabre? A falchion? A cutlass, perchance?' He shook his head, smiling. 'Really, Detective Winters, is this some sort of joke?'

'It's no sort of joke, I assure you. Did the attacker use a sword?'

Foley stared at Anne for a moment and, apparently convinced she wasn't joking, looked down and continued to page through the report. After a few minutes, he found a stapled section, typed on paper that had turned brown in the intervening years. He scanned the first page, turned to the next, then stopped.

'Good lord!' he said, eyebrows raised in surprise. 'Here it is in black and white. Its described as looking like a Roman gladius.'

He handed the report to Anne, who roved over the neat rows of typed testimony. When she finished it, she looked up, puzzled.

'Why not simply shoot Churchill?'

Foley shrugged. 'Looking back, the Reich operated more as a series of personal fiefdoms for some of the most grotesquely odd individuals ever to get their hands on the levers of power. If Hitler, or Himmler, or Goring, or anyone else of that mad bunch, ordered their men to kill Churchill with a rusty old sword, then those orders were followed without question.'

'The whole thing is insane,' Anne murmured. 'This

name; Martin Renfield. Is he still alive?'

'I'd have to call up his service record.'

'I'm happy to wait,' Anne said, settling back in her chair.

'I can see that.' Foley looked at the work piled up on his desk. Sighing, he leaned over and pressed the intercom. 'Mrs Franwell? I need the service record for a Martin Renfield from 1945.'

'What was his battalion, Mr Foley?'

'His battalion?' Foley peered at the file in front of him. 'Fifth Lancashire.' He paused, frowning. 'Seconded from it in August 1944. Make it quick, please, Mrs Franwell. My guest will be leaving shortly.'

'Something's bothering you?' Anne asked.

'What, apart from the fact that I'm not getting my actual work done?'

Anne smiled, and waited.

Foley sighed. 'Yes, as a matter of fact, something is bothering me.'

'Out with it, then. Neither of us will be satisfied otherwise.'

He eyed her with distaste, clearly not used to being addressed in such a manner by a woman. 'It says Renfield was transferred from the Fifth Lancashire. It doesn't say where he was transferred to.'

'That's unusual?'

'Yes. And no.'

'Well, which is it?'

'Files this old are often incomplete. It's perhaps no surprise in this instance. The war had ended, and people had other things on their mind than recording every detail. Still… There's simply no information about Renfield in the Armed Forces until he returned to the Fifth Lancashire in the '50s.'

There came a knock on the door.

'Come in,' Foley called.

A woman in her mid-thirties wearing a skirt Anne thought a trifle short even for 1973 entered, and handed Foley a manila folder. She peered down her nose at Anne, turned on her heel, and left the room.

'The jealous type, I take it,' Anne said drily.

Foley coughed, and went a little red. 'I'm sure I don't know what you're talking about, Detective.'

'Oh, I'm absolutely sure,' Anne said, smiling broadly. 'Now, about Renfield's last address...'

On the last afternoon of April 1943, Martin Renfield, latterly of the Home-Army Fourth Operational Corps, roared across Westminster Bridge on his Triumph. The engine rattled and coughed and sputtered on the last dregs of petrol in the tank. He willed it on, conscious of time trickling through his hands like sand.

The Palace of Westminster loomed on his left. Barrage balloons dotted the sky, their ungainly bulk twisting lazily on thick metal cables tethered to wagons themselves bolted to the ground. Aeroplanes crisscrossed overhead, distinctive livery lit in the pale sunlight. Concrete cubes, waist high on a man, dotted Westminster Bridge, a distant reminder of the invasion across the Channel that had never come.

People walking on both sides of the bridge turned to stare at Renfield as he zoomed by. Big Ben rang out to mark the quarter hour, sending a flock of pigeons into the air. They circled, swooped low towards the street, before spiralling up to land again on the crenulation and stone fretwork.

'Half their luck,' Renfield muttered. He shook his head, trying to dislodge the memories of the basement beneath the half-bombed house off Waterloo Road.

Ahead, a tight knot of bodies dissolved as people scattered in panic. Shots rang out, and above the blat of his engine, Renfield heard screaming.

Approaching the roadblock at a thundering roar, he saw two bodies crumpled in the road. A tight group of men sprinted around the corner of the Treasury Building's looming bulk. Swearing, Renfield gunned the throttle and swerved past the roadblock and roared after them.

Careening along Great George Street, he passed the statues dotting Parliament Square Garden. They stared blindly at him as he passed an abandoned milk cart standing in the centre of the road. A figure slumped over the wheel told him all he needed to know.

The Triumph sputtered and gasped and died as it approached House Guards Road. Instinctively, Renfield relaxed his grip on the handlebars and, as the motorcycle's momentum slowed, he kicked his left leg over the empty tank, jumped off, and hit the ground running. The motorcycle described a lazy arc across the road before crashing into the gutter.

Revolver in hand, Renfield paused briefly at the corner and ducked his head around for a look.

He caught a brief glimpse of black clad men entering the building at a run. Gunfire punctuated the afternoon again, and a short scream slashed the air. Renfield muttered a brief, earnest prayer, then ran towards the steps leading into the building.

No sooner had he entered than a shot whistled by his ear. Firing blindly, Renfield dove over the body of a guard through a door into an empty room. He had an image of a white-faced man standing at the end of the corridor, pistol levelled.

Renfield took a deep, shuddering breath. His eyes fell on the empty, blood-splashed face of the guard lying just inside the entrance to the building. Impulsively, he closed the staring, glassy eyes, his fingers trembling at the rapidly fading warmth of the dead soldier's face.

'Here we go,' he muttered, then hurried down the corridor, skirting the edge of the wall.

He caught glimpses of men and women huddled in rooms on either side, shocked at the sudden violence. One of the public servants, a short balding man with pebble thick glasses, made to join him, but Renfield motioned him back.

Renfield heard more gunfire from the stairwell. Breaking into a run, he skidded to a halt on the landing.

A startled face stared up at him. As cold blue eyes locked with Renfield's own, instinct took control. Aiming and firing,

Renfield felt the pistol's recoil jolt up his arm. The man groaned and fell back, clutching his shirt, suddenly sodden with blood. Bounding down the stairs two at a time, Renfield leaped over the dying man and proceeded down the stairs.

Sounds of a struggle came to Renfield. He cannoned into two men wrestling in a doorway. One, a young man dressed in the uniform of the Home Guard, clutched the shoulders of a taller figure who had his hands locked around his throat. Renfield raised his pistol and smashed the butt of it into the back of the German's skull. Bone crunched, and his grip abruptly loosened. The body slumped against the wall, and the guard collapsed to his knees, sucking in great gasps of air.

'Where's the PM?' Renfield shouted. The guard, his face slowly changing from purple to red, looked blankly at Renfield. 'Churchill, damn it. Where is he?'

The guard raised a shaking hand and pointed. 'Two levels down,' he croaked.

Renfield ran down the long corridor. A sobbing woman knelt beside the body of a man lying in the corridor. His surprised face stared blindly at the low ceiling. Then Renfield saw a figure appear at the end of the corridor and fired at him.

A stabbing pain burst in his left shoulder. A red haze descended as Renfield staggered into the wall, leaving a long smear of blood. The German fired again, and this time Renfield managed to half fall, half roll into an open doorway. Somehow, he kept his revolver level, and fired, the loud report deafening in the corridor's close confines.

The German howled as his shattered fibula gave way beneath him. His pistol clattered to the ground and he clutched his leg. Renfield, his face set, stood and walked to the German, who looked up at him with bleak, wintry eyes.

'Sorry, mate,' Renfield said, and shot the German in the face.

A commotion from downstairs drew his attention. He looked at his left hand and saw blood patter from the sleeve onto the floor. Renfield gritted his teeth to keep down a scream as he tucked his arm inside his jacket. The bullet grated inside the shoulder joint. He blinked back tears and made for the stairs.

He caught a glimpse of a figure staring up at him from two levels down. Renfield fired. The figure screamed and flung himself aside. Back to the wall, Renfield cautiously descended the stairwell.

When he reached the bottom, he saw a pair of doors at the end of the corridor. A light flickered overhead, sending his shadow sprawling along the walls. He saw the man he had shot crawling away, leaving a trail of blood behind him. Renfield strode up to him and kicked him onto his back. Blood pulsed from a wound in his neck. Eyes wide with shock, the German reached blindly for the abandoned Walther PPK. Scooping up the pistol, Renfield jammed it into his belt. He left the German to bleed to death, then pivoted and kicked open the doors.

The doors slammed open, revealing a room crowded with men pointing and shouting at two figures struggling beneath a map of the world pinned to the wall. One, his pugnacious features unmistakable, fought to shake off the iron grip of the remaining German. The German, his face twisted in a grimace, held the blade of a Roman gladius against Churchill's throat.

The sheer incongruity of the blade struck Renfield immediately. Even as he raised his revolver, he had a brief moment to wonder why in the mechanised world of twentieth century warfare the German assassin had chosen to arm himself with a sword. His finger tightened on the trigger as his gaze locked with the blade's dull edge. There was something... wrong with the weapon.

He felt bile rise in his throat even as the weapon called to his mind distant battlefields, where men fought and shrieked and died, a mad pell-mell of heaving bodies pressed together, unable to squirm away from stabbing blades and falling arrows, death on all sides as the blade drank blood and lives with equal abandon.

Shouted words came to him through the fog in his mind.

'Shoot him, damn it!' Churchill yelled.

Renfield locked eyes with the German, whose mouth curved into a smile. Renfield saw the blade press tight against Churchill's throat; saw a bead of blood trickle into his collar. The world narrowed around him, and for the briefest of moments, there was only Renfield and the German, whose arm muscles bunched as he moved to saw the blade back and forth.

'*Wotan ist tot!*' the German cried out in triumph.

Renfield fired.

The German's head snapped back. His hand opened convulsively, and the gladius fell. Whatever evil glamour it radiated faded away and it was simply an old piece of iron lying at Churchill's feet.

The German reeled back several steps, hands clasped in a futile effort to stop the blood spurting from the ruins of his eye. Then he collapsed dead on the floor.

A ringing silence filled Renfield's head. Men with wide eyes and white faces stared in shock. The smell of blood and gun smoke filled his nostrils and his visions swam. Behind him, Renfield heard the clatter of booted feet. He half turned, then abruptly his legs gave out. He fell to his knees, then his side, his revolver slipping from his fingers.

He lay on the cold floor staring at the gladius as men swarmed around him. His vision turned grey for a moment and when it cleared, the gladius had vanished.

He opened his mouth to call out to someone to find the weapon, but Churchill's unmistakeable growl interrupted.

'Cut myself worse shaving. Someone get a medic down here. That man's bleeding to death.'

Then Renfield heard no more as he fell into darkness.

Shadows crept across the road as Anne parked in front of Renfield's modest flat on the outskirts of London. Stepping from her car, she could distantly hear the cheering of a football game coming from the park several streets away. She closed her eyes for a moment, and allowed herself a moment to enjoy the sheer ordinariness of the sounds, then opened them and went up to Renfield's front door and knocked.

'Been expecting you,' Renfield said, as he ushered her into the house.

'That's right,' Anne said. 'Mr Foley called for me a little while ago.'

'Not that,' Renfield said, leading her into the kitchen.

'I've been waiting since the end of the war for someone to talk to me about what I saw.'

Anne paused, momentarily nonplussed. Renfield looked intently at her. 'What did you see?' she asked.

'What did I see?' Renfield echoed. He busied himself at the sink, taking two cups from a cupboard and setting a kettle on the stove.

His kitchen overlooked a tidy garden. Anne saw no evidence of a feminine touch in the house, other than a photo of a rather severe looking woman who she strongly suspected was Renfield's mother. The kettle began to whistle, and Renfield set about collecting cups and milk and sugar.

'What does the file say?' he asked, handing Anne a cup of tea.

She nodded her thanks as Renfield joined her at the table with his cup of coffee.

'You don't remember being interviewed?'

'I do,' he said, his eyes distant for a moment. 'But I was in hospital after they dug a bullet out of me. Morphine is wonderful for the pain, but it plays with the memory.'

Anne stared at Renfield over the top of her teacup. She had been surprised that Renfield's file mentioned both her father and Eileen Younghusband (or rather, le Croissette, as she had been back then) in connection with him. But she supposed she shouldn't have been. Over the decades, Anne had learned much about the role the Fourth Operational Corps had played during the war.

'I very much doubt that the sort of man the Fourth Operational Corps entrusts with the task of protecting Winston Churchill from Nazi assassins is the sort of man given to forgetting.'

'I see,' Renfield said, setting down his cup. 'Why would a police woman, even a detective, have such a high regard for the Home-Army Fourth Operational Corps?

Or indeed have any real knowledge of it? To you it shouldn't be much more than a minor name in my story.'

Anne considered her answer. None she could give would help, or be believed. So a half-truth would do. 'I have... connections, Mr Renfield. My Uncle Ben used to know Professor Edward Travers.'

Renfield turned his head and looked out of the window into his garden. His lips quirked and then he looked back at Anne. 'Detective Winters. May I call you Ruth? I've had a lifetime of addressing people by their titles and I'm heartily sick of it.'

'Only if you let me call you Martin,' Anne said.

'Done,' Martin said, smiling for the first time. 'What did I see?' he said again, tapping his fingers on the table. 'I saw four German fanatics attempt to kill Churchill, with a sword. A Roman gladius no less.'

'Tell me about the gladius.'

Martin raised an eyebrow. 'Not the question I was expecting.'

'What were you expecting?'

'What was it like to save Churchill's life?'

'I imagine it gave you a great deal of satisfaction,' Anne said. 'But I'm more interested in the sword.'

'The gladius.' Abruptly, Martin stood and walked over to the sink. He gripped the counter's edge and Anne saw the knuckles of each hand go white. Without turning, he spoke. 'Evil is a real thing, Ruth.' His voice sounded strained. 'That... gladius the German wielded. I can't begin to describe it other than to say it was evil.' He turned and looked at Anne. 'You must think me a little around the bend, to talk about a piece of metal like that.'

Anne shook her head. 'Do you know why they wanted to kill Churchill with a gladius? I imagine they were armed.'

'Definitely. I was shot by one.' Martin's hand strayed to his shoulder before he dropped it by his side. 'There was a ritualistic element to the whole endeavour. Their focus was on killing Churchill. They wanted their man right beside him. It seemed to me then, and now, that killing Churchill was a means to an end.' He shook his head. *'Wotan ist tot*. That's what he said, just before I shot him. It's always stayed with me.'

'Wotan...' She was reminded of the incident at the then-Post Office Tower in 1966, and the mad computer there. Named after... 'Wotan was an old Germanic deity. God is dead?'

'Bloody krauts and their mysticism,' Martin said. 'I'm convinced they regarded Churchill as some sort of sacrifice.'

'A sacrifice.' Anne turned her cup around in her hand. 'You said the gladius was evil. How did you arrive at that conclusion?'

'To look at it was to know,' Martin said simply. 'It had an aura about it, an aura that made me sick to the pit of my stomach. You could feel the weight of its age. There was a hunger about it, a hunger that only blood could sate. It sounds melodramatic, I know, but I was there.'

'You speak as if it were alive.'

'Maybe. Some places are haunted,' Martin said, clearly groping for an example that would convey his meaning. 'That sword. It was haunted. I've heard rumour that Hess stole the gladius and flew with it to Scotland in the '40s. If you want to know about it, he'd be the one. Good luck getting into Spandau, though.' He took a deep, shuddering breath, then exhaled, as if doing so would remove the stain of the memory from him. 'So tell me, what is your real interest in the gladius? It went missing during the struggle. I've long suspected the Germans had someone inside the War Cabinet Bunker who spirited it away after the attack. One of ours, who was really one of theirs.' He shook his head in disgust.

'An inside job?'

'Of course. No one wants to talk about it now, but there were people in Britain who welcomed Hitler's rise. Mosley and his ilk.' Martin almost spat out the name.

'The Cliveden Set,' Anne said, realisation dawning.

'You've heard of them?' Martin sounded impressed. 'I thought they'd been whitewashed from history.'

'History doesn't forget, Martin,' Anne said, gently. 'It only averts its gaze for a while.'

'Well I bloody well wish someone would listen to me about them.' Martin shook his head. 'They still meet, did you know that? Bloody gits still get together and celebrate. It's disgraceful.'

'You keep tabs on them?'

'Too right. I've watched them prosper. Watched them assume positions of power. Damned parasites escaped with barely a slap on the wrist.'

'So, you know where they meet?' Anne felt her heart beat a little faster.

'Aylesbury. Right on London's doorstep. Its disgusting.' Martin paused. 'There's actually a meeting tonight. Some sort of soiree.' His frustration was palpable. 'I can hardly credit it, but I've heard there's even an escaped Nazi addressing them.'

Von Werner. It had to be.

'How would I get an invite?' Anne asked.

CHAPTER FIFTEEN
Black Tie White Noise

ANNE STOOD IN THE ENTRANCE OF *THE BLACK PRINCE* and scanned the main bar. A lone barman leaned over a newspaper. As a concession to the season, a forlorn looking Christmas tree no taller than the bottle of Johnny Walker stood on a shelf, covered in threadbare tinsel. A black and white television was tuned to the BBC's coverage of the races at Aintree. A fog of cigarette smoke hung over the dozen or so men sitting or standing at the bar. Over the bar itself hung a portrait of the Black Prince, standing on a battlefield in his plate armour while French knights fled in disarray. And sitting directly beneath the portrait was Tom Hartigan.

'How did you know I was here, darling?' he asked, recovering from his surprise at seeing Anne.

'I'm a detective, Tom, or had you forgotten? I know how to collect facts. Plus,' she said, in an effort to reduce the sting, 'you're a creature of habit. You've spoken more than once about your Saturday afternoons at *The Black Prince*.' She didn't know if it was true, but it seemed a likely conclusion.

'Fair enough,' Hartigan said grudgingly. He took a sip from his beer and wiped his mouth with the back of his hand. 'So how can I help you?'

'I need for you to come out with me tonight.'

Hartigan stared at her in astonishment for a moment, then he broke into laughter. 'That's a good one, Ruth.

You want me to go out on a date with you?'

Anne raised her eyebrows. 'Not a date,' she said firmly. 'It's really more an assignment. It's to do with the Big Man.'

Hartigan's humour faded. 'How's that?'

'Harry and I believe that Dominic Vaar is tied up with two other men. A fellow by the name of Paul von Werner. And a politician, Charles Arbuthnot.'

'I've heard of the last bloke, but not this Werner fellow. What links do they have?'

Anne took a deep breath. On her drive to the pub, this was the part of the conversation she had most dreaded. From her bag, she pulled out a folder. 'We both know that Vaar is in the process of consolidating his power in London's underworld. I think the trucking company he recently purchased indicates he has national plans. Von Werner... Well, Harry and I have intelligence that he is a former Nazi.'

Hartigan stared at her. Anne hoped he was digesting the information, and not simply preparing a disbelieving retort.

'A Nazi,' he said. He took another sip from his beer. 'In London. Conspiring with a crime boss. How good is your intelligence?'

'You believe me?' Anne asked, eyes widening in surprise.

'I didn't say anything of the sort. But you're a good detective, Ruth. And I've never heard you talk nonsense about an investigation. You've talked nonsense about a whole lot of other things, granted, but not about any investigation we've worked on together. What proof do you have? And what about Arbuthnot?'

'Well...' Anne moved to flip open the folder when she saw the BBC ident flash onto the television screen. A news presenter appeared, looking slightly flustered. The picture was split into two, and the second half held a still photograph of Arbuthnot. 'Turn that up!' Anne snapped at the barman, pointing at the television.

He looked at her, then at Hartigan, who nodded. The barman reached over and turned up the television.

'...has announced his intention to challenge the Prime Minister for leadership of the ruling party. He did so as he announced his resignation from the Cabinet. This report has just come in.'

'In a bombshell announcement just half an hour ago,' said the anodyne voiceover, 'former minister Charles Arbuthnot made the announcement from his offices at Westminster.'

A shot then appeared of a florid looking man sitting at a large desk. On the edges of the screen, the press could be seen jostling for position, waiting impatiently for Arbuthnot to finish.

'It's my sorry duty to announce that I can no longer remain a member of the Cabinet,' Arbuthnot said. 'As many of you know, I have long stood up for law and order in this country, often in the face of derision from my ministerial colleagues. But the facts are the facts and no amount of handwringing can deny it. This country faces a breakdown of control. Crime is rampant. We saw more rioting overnight, in Liverpool, Manchester and Exeter. And what is the Prime Minister's response? Merely to shrug his shoulders and promise more police on the street. Well, enough is enough! If we remain on the same path, then the very unity of our Kingdom will come undone.'

'What do you ascribe these riots to?' a journalist off camera asked.

Arbuthnot smiled. 'It is no secret that this Liberal Government, like its predecessor before it, has maintained an open door policy for immigration into Britain. What does that lead to? Ghettos. Where the main language is not English, but a polyglot babble. And within those areas, crime festers and spreads, like a disease. No, if the cancer is not cut out, we will fall. Britain for the British, that will be my rallying cry. I have the numbers. Prime Minister Thorpe should do the gracious thing and step aside.'

'Number Ten has been approached for comment,' the presenter said. 'We will bring it to air as soon as we have it. And now, back to Aintree…'

'Nothing's changed,' Anne said, shaking her head in disbelief.

Hartigan looked at her in puzzlement, his eyebrows pulled together. 'He might have a point,' he said, raising a hand to forestall Anne's anger. 'I'm not saying he's right about immigration. You've been down to some of those estates. Crammed together, like sardines. If we're going to have immigration, the government should make sure they're not closed off in enclaves. Let them live with the rest of us. That's the only way we're going to get to know one another. Otherwise, the Charles Arbuthnots of the world will be proven right.'

Anne looked at Hartigan with astonishment.

'Didn't think I thought that, did you, Ruth?'

Anne shook her head, a smile playing on her lips. 'You've got me there, Tom. I may even end up liking you, if you keep talking sense like that.'

Hartigan chuckled, a raspy sound that wasn't entirely unpleasant. He pointed to the folder. 'We were talking about proof. What have you got?'

Anne pulled out a photograph. 'That's von Werner,' she said, pointing to a surveillance shot. 'I've got contacts in the MOD who confirm that a German by that name was a member of the Nazi Party, and who remains on the run.' She turned over another page, revealing a grainy photo. 'That's Dominic Vaar. And that man next to him is Arbuthnot.'

'When were these taken?'

'They just came in this morning. Some sort of mix up at the lab. Taken a week ago at a club in Soho. They look very chummy, don't you think?'

'He's a politician,' Hartigan said. 'They want to be friends with everyone.' He didn't sound convinced by his own words.

'Friends with a known crime boss? Come on, Tom, Arbuthnot is as bent as Vaar.'

'He made a few good points. Crime *is* on the rise.'

'Do you want a racist running the show? You heard what he said. He's pinning the blame on migrants. That sort of talk only leads to trouble.'

'Britain for the British, that's what I heard,' Hartigan said, stubbornly.

'You don't really believe that, Tom,' Anne said. She tilted her head. 'You work with Harry. Would you want him deported simply because of the colour of his skin?'

'Of course not,' Hartigan blustered. He rubbed his neck and looked down at the photograph. 'This was taken last week, at a party both men attended?'

Anne nodded.

'Could be a coincidence.'

'You and I have been in the game too long to believe in coincidences, Tom.'

He stared at her. 'You don't like me much, do you? Don't be shy.' He folded his arms and smiled.

Anne's instinct was to lie, to protect Ruth from any kind of fallout after she left, but something told her that Ruth would be more than honest about how she felt. She shrugged. 'No. I don't. You're a bloody good copper, but as a bloke…'

'Funny. That's what my ex-wife used to say.' He glanced down at the photograph, then called the barman over. 'Hand us the phone, Terry. I need to make a call.' The barman nodded and lifted a telephone from beneath the bar and sat it in front of Hartigan.

'Who're you calling?' Anne asked as Hartigan dialled.

'Got a mate in MI5. He owes me a favour.' He held up a finger before Anne had a chance to ask another question. 'Gary?' he said into the receiver. 'Tom Hartigan. Don't be like that, mate. C'mon. I just need to know... Look, I got you out of that spot of bother with the dancer who unaccountably speaks fluent Russian, didn't I? So you owe me, yes? Good. I want whatever information you have on Charles Arbuthnot. Yes, the politician. You don't need to know. You've got ten minutes.'

Hartigan put his hand over the speaker, and looked over at the barman. 'Terry, what's the number?'

After he relayed it, Hartigan hung up the phone.

'Friend of yours, I take it?' Anne asked, drily.

'Went to school together. How he ever ended up at MI5 is beyond me. Defence of the Realm, my arse.' Hartigan looked at his glass, which stood empty. He signalled to the barman, then looked at Anne. 'What do you fancy?'

'Scotch, neat,' Anne said.

Hartigan picked up the phone after the first ring.

'Right,' he said after a short exchange, laying down his pen. 'Be a good lad, Gary, and stick to local girls, all right?' He rang off. For a moment, while Anne waited impatiently, he stared at the hastily scribbled notes across his newspaper. 'He's bent. There's no doubt about it. Got some large gambling debts, which have been covered by Vaar.'

'So Vaar has him under his thumb?'

'Yeah. But...'

'What?'

'There's something else. Something... odd. Gary gave me a rundown of what Arbuthnot gets up to outside of Westminster. Attends these parties. Down in Buckinghamshire.'

'Aylesbury?'

'Yeah,' Hartigan said, surprised. 'How did you know?'

'Sources, Tom. Sources. Did your friend say what sort of parties?'

'Gary mentioned the Cliveden Set. Some sort of club. Funny. He didn't want to go into too many details.'

Anne felt a chill run up her back. 'You're sure that's what he said?'

'I just spoke to him about it. I'm not deaf, Ruth. Is there something I should know?'

'That's the second time today I've heard someone mention the Cliveden Set. What else did your friend Gary say?'

'He said Arbuthnot is out of London this weekend. Attending another meeting.'

Anne straightened. 'It must be the same meeting.'

'Meeting? What are you talking about?'

'Von Werner and Arbuthnot are making an appearance together. Tonight, and if I'm right, they won't be alone. This may be our only opportunity to find out what it is they're planning.' Anne's eyes narrowed as she sized Hartigan up. 'Like I said earlier, me and you are going out tonight.'

They drove through the evening twilight, the engine rumbling softly in the background. Stars began to appear over an undulating landscape of hills and fields.

'Such a pretty place,' Anne said absently as she looked out of the window. Swaying trees lined either side of the road, black against the gathering night. Behind them, the glow of city lights gathered strength. Another time and she would have easily stopped to paint it – alas, all this astral projection through time didn't seem to allow for such luxuries.

'Is it?' Hartigan grunted, steering smoothly around a bend.

'You've the heart of a bricklayer, did you know that, Tom?'

'At least bricklaying's useful,' Hartigan said. 'Last time I checked, not too many homes built by poets.'

Anne smiled in spite of herself. Hartigan glanced at her.

'Tell me one more time what you hope to achieve tonight,' Hartigan said.

'Information.'

Hartigan paused at a lonely intersection, and peered at a sign that pointed both ways, the writing black in the chancy light.

'We have pretty strong circumstantial evidence of a link between Arbuthnot and Vaar,' Anne continued. 'This is our best opportunity to find out more.'

'How does Werner fit in, though? I'm still trying to get my head around why an ex-Nazi, if he is one, would get involved with these two.'

Anne knew she had stretched her luck mentioning von Werner. She was convinced that Hartigan would turn around if she started talking about Sumerian magic and cursed swords.

'That's a bit shaky, I agree. But if you've been on the run for almost thirty years, the only connections you're going to make are criminal. Von Werner is sticking to form.'

Hartigan nodded. Over a far hill, the soft glow of lights lit drifting clouds. He glanced across at her, his forehead furrowed.

'Out with it, Tom,' Anne said, sighing.

'How do I know this isn't some wild goose chase you've cooked up to embarrass me in front of the inspector?'

Anne almost laughed. She'd met his sort so often in her career. Always threatened by women of equal standing. Wasn't intentional, just a result of his limited upbringing. She wished she could say things had improved in the four decades since, but she'd be lying. In small increments, maybe, but for most women 2011 wasn't a whole lot different. She often wondered if it ever would be.

'If you get into trouble, so do I,' she told him. 'I'm the woman putting her career on the line. You blokes skate by without much more than a slap on the wrist. Keep that in mind.'

Pines pressed up against the macadam for a few miles, blocking out the sky except for a narrow band of sprinkled stars directly overhead. Anne began to feel claustrophobic. The road twisted and climbed and soon they were on the summit of a low hill. Looking down, set against gathering shadows, they could see the black bulk of a house. Lights illuminated a driveway packed with cars. Figures moved near the entrance.

'Ready?' Anne asked.

'Run me through your plan again.'

'You're Major Arthur Harrington and I'm your blushing bride, Hilda. Thanks to my godfather, we were invited to our first meeting with these monstrous traitors just before our wedding. No one here will know us, as my godfather is on the Continent.'

'Right,' Hartigan said. He tugged at his shirt collar, then looked across at Anne. 'I'll deny it if you mention it back at the station, but I did rather well in drama at school.' Anne saw a flush spread up his neck. 'After all,' he said, as he coasted the car down the hill and onto the gravel drive, 'it can't be too hard to play the part of an empty-headed fascist sympathiser with a pig ignorant wife.'

Hartigan smiled broadly as Anne, despite herself, broke into laughter.

Hartigan dropped the keys into the hand of a tall,

thuggish looking man with thick shoulders and cropped blond hair. He went around the side and opened the door for Anne. Pulling her coat tight, she nodded haughtily to the valet.

'Scratch it and we'll peel the hide from your flesh.' Anne's voice was icy and full of arrogance. The man stared at her. Turning, she slipped her arm through the crook of Hartigan's elbow. 'The help,' she said, loud enough for those walking nearby. 'They need to know their place, my dear.'

Hartigan harrumphed and suppressed a smile. Together they crossed the driveway, towards the main entrance.

'What does that lorry say?' Anne asked. A delivery van stood in the shadows on the far side of the building. She felt a chill steal over her.

'L-A-N... Landry's? Landry's Trucking. That's...'

'The company Vaar recently bought.'

'You don't think he's here?' Hartigan asked.

'I don't know,' Anne said as they joined the end of a short queue of people. 'Keep your eyes peeled, okay?'

CHAPTER SIXTEEN
Rebel Rebel

'READY?' ALISTAIR ASKED, CHECKING THE REAR-VIEW mirror. The road, lit by streetlights, was empty in both directions.

'I can't believe I'm saying it, but yes,' Bill said. 'I am ready to spend my Saturday evening breaking into a City of London bank. I think the millennials call this ticking off a bucket list item.'

Alistair chuckled as he wound down his window and inserted the card into the reader. The reader beeped and he retrieved the card. The roller shutter rattled into its housing. Alistair drove into the building and the shutter descended back into place.

'Where'd you get the card?' Bill asked.

'Vaar's desperate to get this sword,' Alistair said, as he carefully drove down the circular ramp. 'He's thrown so much money at this, it was only a matter of time before one of the cleaning staff in this building agreed to hand over their card and look the other way. On the positive side, at least Vaar didn't break his legs.'

Bill laughed, a dry, ironic sound that brought a smile to Alistair's face.

'It's very strange,' Alistair said, looking at Bill.

'What is?'

'Different voice, but the inflections are all yours, as are your mannerisms. But it's not…you.'

'I keep thinking the same about Anne. I've accepted

it in myself now, got used to it, kind of. But when you *meet* someone you know, and see them in another person...' Bill shook his head. 'Strange isn't the half of it.'

'Still, it's a relief to be around someone I can trust.'

'Agreed. Months out there on our own....' He glanced out the window as Alistair drove. 'What did Vaar say, after we released everyone?'

'Not much. He seemed pensive. It's possible he was suspicious. Even if he was, I think he's in far too deep to back out. He's clearly desperate to get that sword.'

'It can't just be the sword he's after, can it? He's been on Earth for a good five years now; he tried to play the nuclear game. Failed. Then all that business with Collins. Again, failed. What happened to him between then and...' Bill paused, and Alistair knew what he was thinking of. The damage the Dominator had wrought when they last met. 'It has to be more than some sword.'

Alistair snorted. 'Either way, there is something more bubbling in the background.' He grinned, and glanced at Bill. 'Glad you offered to come along?'

'There's no sense me tagging along with Anne. She's capable enough to keep out of trouble. This is a better use of our resources.' Bill rubbed his jaw and shot Alistair a glance. 'Run the plan by me again. How exactly are we getting into the bank?'

'Just like I told Vaar last night after you released me, the blueprints show me the way, but a good thief, like a good magician, never reveals his secrets.'

'Did he go for that explanation?'

Alistair shook his head with a smile. 'What do you think?'

'Tell me how you will do it,' Vaar demanded.

'How?' Alistair smiled. 'A magician doesn't reveal his tricks.' He set down his glass.

Vaar sat opposite him, picking absently through a pile of steaming vegetables. A part of Alistair was amused to see that the marooned galactic conqueror was a vegetarian. Looking deathly ill, Vaar had been in a bad mood since his release, though nothing had come of the police questioning.

'You are not a magician,' Vaar rumbled. 'And I have your niece's life in my hands.' He paused, peering at Alistair from under his heavy eyebrows.

'You do,' Alistair said. He felt disgusted that he had to tamp down his natural instincts about Vaar, but there were larger factors at play. 'Accessing the vault is the easy part. The buildings in that area date back over a hundred years. There are tunnels and other access points long forgotten. Really, the only modern part of the structure is the interior of the vault itself.'

'And accessing the vault?' Vaar considered a piece of asparagus for a moment before crunching it to pulp between his teeth.

'Once I'm in the neighbouring building, there is a shared set of pipes designed for flood mitigation. London, after all, is built on a flood plain.'

'Good.' Vaar set his fork aside and wiped his mouth with a napkin. 'And once you are inside?'

'Once we're inside,' Alistair muttered as he shook his head free of the memory. He turned to look at Bill. 'Well, we'll see what happens then. The grating should be in the corner.'

He retrieved the case, while Bill took out a pair of balaclavas from his satchel, and handed one to Alistair. Both men pulled them over their heads. Sliding the van door shut, Alistair switched on a torch and shone it into the corner of the basement car park. A black grating glinted in the light.

'That's it,' he said. 'Let's see how badly rusted it is.'

Thankfully, it proved to be relatively rust free. Working methodically, Bill scored out the rust around the rim of the grating. Tucking the tool away, he stepped to one side of the grate and, with Alistair, he lifted the grate out of its slot and placed it to one side.

Alistair's torch revealed a set of rungs set into the wall. Playing the torch into the depths revealed the pipe to be around fifteen feet deep. Unfolding the blueprints, he pointed to a spot on the thick paper.

'Here we are,' he said to Bill, then began to trace a finger, following the pipe as it ran underneath where they stood to the bank building next door. 'How far do you think that is?'

'Thirty yards, if the scale is right. Long way to go in the dark.'

'We've been through much worse, Major,' Alistair said, using Bill's contemporary rank.

Bill smiled grimly. 'Yes, Brigadier, we have, sir.'

Alistair chuckled. 'Ah, those were the days, eh?'

'They were. Unfortunately, at this point in time we didn't have many opportunities working together, what with me in charge of 1 Battalion up in Stirling and you…'

'Playing the part of the sardonic and bemused military officer.'

'Often out of your depth.'

'Quite. The Doctor found out eventually, of course, many years after I left military service. I could never decide if he was disappointed or proud about my skill in deception.'

'Probably both,' Bill said.

'Anyway, let's get this over with. You need a torch,' he said, and searched in a pocket for the second torch. 'Always be prepared.' He handed it to Bill.

Replacing the blueprints in a plastic pouch, Alistair clamped his torch between his teeth. Easing himself into the hole, with the case gripped in one hand, he began carefully descending.

Halfway down, Alistair glanced up and saw Bill looking down, his eyes wide beneath the balaclava. Bill nodded encouragement.

After a minute or two, Alistair had the impression the descent was taking longer than it should. Dank air, thick with mould, moved slowly around him. In the tight confines, his breathing grew loud in his ears. Cobwebs clung to him, and more than once, he saw a glittering insect scurry away from the light.

Was the Matador claustrophobic? Alistair knew he wasn't. He'd literally been in tighter spots. So the odd feelings had to come from the Matador…

Just as claustrophobia began to overcome him, his feet found the bottom of the pipe. Heaving a sigh of relief, Alistair set the case down on the crumbling brickwork. He looked around. The pipe ran east and west. The ceiling hung low. For a moment, the image of tens of thousands of gallons of water tumbling from above and rushing in a torrent down the central concrete channel filled his mind.

'Only a fool would want to be down here,' he said to himself, the sound of the Matador's voice distorted by the narrow space. No comfort there.

'What was that?' Bill asked, as he stepped off the last rung.

'The sooner we get out of here and into the bank the happier I'll be,' Alistair said. 'I think the Matador suffers from claustrophobia. A surprise to both of us.'

He pointed his torch down the other end of the pipe. The light vanished in the darkness, but there was enough to show where the pipe connected to the next building. The blueprints indicated that a series of similar pipes ran under all the buildings above, letting out into the Thames. Shuddering at the idea of being down here alone with a faltering torch, Alistair stepped aside to give Bill some space.

'Part one achieved,' Bill said, shining his torch around the narrow space with great interest. 'Imagine it. All this engineering in an era where a strong back and a shovel were the most modern equipment available.'

Alistair indicated with his torch a row of crimson eyes glaring at them from the other side of the pipe. 'I prefer to concern myself with the here and now.'

Following the light, Bill chuckled uneasily. 'Ah, your favourite creature.'

'Yes, never liked them since that business with the Yeti in New York.'

Bill stamped his foot, and the rats scattered, their sleek, black bodies glistening wetly in the light. Chittering squeaks filled the air, the sound like shattering glass.

Alistair and Bill followed the fading sound into the darkness.

'You can almost feel the weight of all that concrete above us,' Bill said as they paused at a junction.

Alistair ignored the comment, and consulted the blueprints. He glanced up from them, the light of Bill's torch casting shadows over his face. He waved at the brickwork. 'What is it our American cousins say? All this is a walk in the park?'

'A walk in the pipe, I think you mean,' Bill said, smiling briefly.

'Very droll, Bill.' He tapped a section of the blueprints. 'We'll be up top soon enough.'

Another set of metal rungs were revealed a few minutes later. Alistair wiped sweat from his face and peered up. Crosshatched metal bars appeared in the torchlight.

'I'll go first,' he said and started up the rungs.

Reaching the top, Alistair set his shoulder against the grating and pushed. It didn't budge. Gritting his teeth, he tried again, pushing harder and harder until he collapsed against the wall, breathing hard. Unease trickled down his spine.

'How's it going up there?' Bill called.

'Damn thing's rusted in place.' Holding up his torch, Alistair ran his nail around the seam. Flakes of rust rained down on him. Shaking his head, he looked at Bill. 'We're in a spot of bother,' he said and then his eyes alighted on the case. 'Though I think I have the key.'

Climbing back down, Alistair indicated the case with his torch.

Bill smiled broadly. 'Maybe we're using a hammer to crack a walnut?'

'Maybe. But right now, we're operating with limited options.' Kneeling, Alistair opened the latches and lifted the lid. The lance, with its trio of heavy-duty power packs, sat inside foam moulding.

Bill whistled. 'Looks like the Matador has sunk some serious money into this.'

'It's an early prototype. The police are lucky this is the only one to enter the market. Imagine the havoc someone like Vaar could wreak. Help me get it out.'

Together, the two men lifted the lance and the power packs free, and carefully set them down on the ground. Bill watched as Alistair connected the multi-colour leads into the power pack.

'Hopefully these power packs have some legs, or we'll be in trouble in the vault,' Alistair said, looking up at Bill.

From a pocket in the case, Alistair removed a pair of welder's goggles, which he slipped over his eyes. He then took out a pair of gloves, heavily woven with asbestos, and pulled them on.

'EU-OSHA would have kittens,' he said, grinning at Bill.

'Lucky they don't exist yet, then.'

Standing, Alistair clipped the connected power pack to his belt. Balancing the lance on his shoulder, he slowly climbed the ladder one-handed until he reached the grating. After checking to make sure Bill had stepped back into the safety of the pipe, Alistair set himself in place with the tip of the lance held against the underside of the grating.

The next ten minutes were fraught. Igniting the lance, Alistair, even with the goggles, felt like he was staring straight into the heart of the sun. Aware of the risks of molten metal splashing down on him, he clung awkwardly to a rung with one hand and started on the far side of the grate.

The power pack quickly grew hot. The power thrummed through his arm as the lance discharged energy in a focussed beam. The metal lath turned red in a blaze of sparks, then white as it softened like cooked spaghetti. Shimmering pieces of molten metal fell into the darkness, and roiling smoke filled the narrow confines. After about five minutes, Alistair stopped to allow the smoke to clear.

'How's it looking?' Bill called softly from beneath.

'Good,' Alistair said, feeling anything but. His face felt tight, as if he'd spent an unprotected afternoon on the beach at the height of summer. The skin beneath the pocket holding the power pack felt scalded and he could well imagine the blister that would form. Silently apologising to the Matador, he flicked the switch and the lance burst into life once more.

Finally, as the power pack began to fail, Alistair shoved the badly damaged grating free. It bent up and over, the metal swiftly cooling, allowing the grating to stand upright.

'I'm coming down,' he called. Sweat streaked his soot-marked face. Bill helped him down, and took hold of the lance.

'That's hot.' Bill grimaced as he lowered the lance back into the case.

Alistair tossed the empty power pack into the

darkness. He stretched, and his back cracked in several places.

'At least we know it works.' He checked his watch and was surprised to see it was well past midnight. 'We'd best get moving.'

The lowest level of the bank was much the same as the building next door. A garage of rough concrete floors, and walls dotted with pillars supporting the ceiling. There were no vehicles, just an echoing expanse hemmed by shadows.

'Blueprints were right,' Alistair murmured, scanning the upper sections of the walls. 'No security cameras down here.'

'If we're successful tonight, I'm sure that will change.'

'At least we'll be responsible for an innovation,' Alistair said drily.

He shone his torch on the far wall, revealing a lift with an access door just beside it.

'We're going to use the stairs, aren't we?' Bill asked.

'It's almost like we've worked together before,' Alistair said. 'The guards on station will be alerted if the lifts are used outside normal bank hours. It's the tradesman's entrance for us.' He pushed open the door and started up the stairs.

Their footsteps echoed softly as they ascended. At each landing, they paused to listen at the access door. The bank, unnervingly, was as silent as the grave.

'It's a bit like being on night patrol,' Bill murmured.

On the next level, the access door had *Safe Deposit Access* stencilled on it. Bill set down the case, while Alistair checked the door. It opened silently on well-oiled hinges. Alistair produced a small mirror from a pocket. Holding it through the gap at an angle, he first checked both ends of the corridor. He handed Bill the mirror, who repeated the same manoeuvres.

'Security cameras,' he whispered, handing the mirror back to Alistair, who nodded. 'I trust the Matador has something else up his sleeve to deal with them?'

'Remarkably resourceful.' Alistair knelt and opened the case. He produced a small square device dominated by several buttons and a black screen.

'Let's hope the Matador's eagerness to be an early adopter of new technology doesn't let us down,' Bill said.

'I think you'd like him.' Alistair pushed several buttons in a particular sequence.

'How so?' Bill leaned in close for a look at the device.

'Can't say I approve of his profession, but I do have a liking for someone who has honed their craft until it becomes second nature. The Matador is also something of an electronics genius, and I think you know I have an appreciation of those who can conjure an intergalactic communications device out of some bailing wire and a colander.'

Alistair jabbed a button, and a low-pitched whine came from the device. He nodded in satisfaction and glanced at Bill. 'Why should the Doctor have all the fun, eh?'

'I suppose,' Bill said. 'What is that thing, anyway?'

'This? It blocks transmissions.' Alistair flicked a switch on the side of the device and the crackle of static filled the air. 'Sends out something called a sine wave, I believe. It gets us into the safety deposit vault room undetected. Just wait.'

The sine wave appeared on the screen, the line rising and falling in an endless wave. The hiss of static rose and fell with the line. Slowly, Alistair twisted the dial.

The sine wave moved frantically, the smooth rise and fall giving way to a jagged movement. The static worsened, buzzing like a hive of enraged hornets. Bill winced and covered her ears. After a few more seconds, Alistair turned the dial the other way, and the sine wave reverted to its former pattern. The painful sound of the static fell to a low crackle.

'Here we go,' Alistair said.

CHAPTER SEVENTEEN
Let's Dance

'LADIES AND GENTLEMEN, TONIGHT'S GUEST OF honour has arrived. If you would follow me, proceedings will begin apace.'

Anne and Hartigan joined the rear of the excited crowd as they moved from the parlour into a much larger room. The lights had been turned low, and a podium set up at one end. A massive painting of a man in uniform riding a rearing horse with the flames of a battle behind looked down over them.

'Suitably martial,' Hartigan murmured, looking around.

Anne thought he was looking for the exits. A good idea. She, too, memorised them. Waiters stood at intervals around the walls. The conversation grew until it was almost a shout when the lights rose and the man who had led them in emerged from the shadows beside the podium.

Johnson, an entrepreneur in the plastics industry whom they'd spoken to in the parlour, reappeared with a freshened glass and planted himself beside Hartigan. Johnson was positively vibrating with anticipation.

'I've heard talk that the guest of honour hasn't been seen in almost twenty years.'

'Is that so?' Hartigan said. He glanced at Anne, who raised an eyebrow.

'This country needs men like him to speak the truth

about the sorry mess our leaders have dragged us into. Truth to power, that's what we need!'

'I may have to kill this idiot,' Hartigan whispered to Anne. 'Any chance you could lend me a hand?'

Anne chuckled, a throaty sound that caught the attention of those nearby. She raised her glass in salute and smiled icily at them.

The man at the front of the room clapped his hands together. 'Thank you for attending tonight. It is a regrettable fact that we have to hide our true allegiances amongst a sea of indifference and degeneracy. But our guest tonight... Well, I will let him tell you of the high hopes he has for the future. Please, welcome Paul von Werner.'

A man emerged from a side door and strode confidently towards the podium amid rapturous applause. He stood there, basking in it for a moment, before raising both hands and calming the crowd.

'My friends, it is such a pleasure to be amongst polite society once again.' This drew laughter from the audience, and a hiss of anger from Anne.

'Don't give the game away,' Hartigan said in her ear. He smiled at Johnson and nodded. Johnson raised his glass in salute and turned back to the front, his eyes shining with excitement. 'They'll tear us apart if our covers are blown.'

'My time here is necessarily short, but I do bring with me great news,' von Werner continued. Anne noted the faintest hint of a German accent. 'For too long, as you have all been aware, this great nation has been in the thrall of a disgraceful class who, even now, threaten to betray us all in the name of equal rights.' A discordant murmur rose at this. 'You are right to be angry, my friends, for there is no doubt that given a few more short years, the great legacy of this nation will be washed away by a tide of filth that must not be allowed to enter!'

The murmurs rose in angry agreement. Anne shifted uncomfortably, feeling like she was witness to the birth of a new age of Nuremberg rallies. Von Werner let the angry noise run for a few moments, then raised one hand.

'There was once a man, my friends, who saw to the truth at the heart of our world. Who saw it, and grasped for it, and was betrayed by his natural allies, here in these great isles. Instead of standing shoulder to shoulder with him against the red tide of lunacy from the East, they stabbed him and his great and glittering armies in the back. And what have they achieved in return? The Americans encamped here, whispering lies in the ears of your leaders. Europe divided as the Red Bear growls at the gates.'

There were shouts from the crowd.

'Fortunately, there are like-minded individuals such as yourselves scattered across these isles who see as you see, who understand the worm gnawing at the roots of all that is strong and right.' He paused, and the audience seemed to lean in towards him. 'I can tell you, my friends, that the time draws near, very near indeed, to the moment when we no longer have to skulk in the shadows, cloaking our true thoughts and wishes. A time is coming, of fire and blood, when we will cleanse this great nation once and for all and reclaim our true place as leaders of the world!'

Silence, a long, pregnant silence, which shattered when the audience broke into rapturous applause. Von Werner basked in the adulation for a moment, his scarred face beaming.

'I think I'm going to be ill,' Anne said. Johnson, his face lit with drunken glee, pounded Hartigan on the back, and it was clear that even Hartigan was squirming inside.

Von Werner called for quiet.

'Friends, I thank you. Know that I am just the herald of this new age. Your tribune is here, amongst us. A man who knows the true, beating heart of this great nation. A man who, given the opportunity, will give voice to the silent majority who cry out for real leadership. Friends, I give you Charles Arbuthnot.'

Arbuthnot bounded into the room and stood next to von Werner, soaking up the cheers and applause.

'I want to thank you,' he said, when the cheering had quieted. 'I want to thank you for that wonderful reception. My friend is right. For too long, Britain has fallen behind, fallen behind nations that have no right to be ahead of us. There are traitors in Westminster, men and women who think that our glorious past is an embarrassment, who believe that where we have sunk is our natural state. Even worse, they have abandoned the tenets that made Britain great. Law and order. Respect for our culture, our language, our race!'

'Shame!' someone cried from the audience.

'And damnable it is,' Arbuthnot said, pumping his fist to emphasise his words. 'But what should we do about it, eh? It is one thing to gather, as we do tonight, and mutter into our drinks about how bad things have become. That is too easy. It is cowardly.' His voice sunk, and the room grew quiet, hanging on his words. Anne sensed the ominous atmosphere running through the crowd. 'It is time for a new direction, friends. A new direction, to those sunlit pastures that damned fool Churchill promised us but failed to deliver. I stand before you, my friends, and pin the blame for our present impasse on the leader of my party, the Prime Minister of this country. Jeremy Thorpe,' he said, his voice full of sarcasm. 'Good old *Jeremy*.'

People started to laugh.

'And well might you laugh. Our dear old Prime Minister has to go. As you know, today I resigned from the Cabinet. Before I left London, I stood in his office and told him I intend on challenging him for the leadership of the Liberal Party. He agreed to call a meeting of the party on Monday morning.'

A stunned silence followed, then the applause and cheering swelled as men and women mobbed Arbuthnot.

'But there is more, my friends,' he said after the cheering had subsided. 'Shakespeare had it right when he wrote that there are more things in heaven and Earth than are dreamt of in our philosophy.'

'Horatio,' Anne whispered. 'Everyone forgets to mention Horatio.'

A puzzled silence fell across the room. Arbuthnot's smile broadened. He turned to von Werner, who watched the proceedings from the side of the room, and signalled to him.

Von Werner nodded. Anne felt a deep sense of unease when the German closed his eyes for a moment, his lips moving silently. When he opened his eyes again, they gleamed in triumph.

A deep tremor ran through the room. Heavy footsteps approached as von Werner moved to one side. Squat, heavy shapes moved into the light. The crowd fell back, in awed silence. A woman cried out, which was quickly hushed.

'A cause needs an army, my friends,' Arbuthnot said. He stood beside the nearest golem, and even though he stood taller than it, its squat frame radiated size and an overpowering strength. 'In the days and weeks ahead, as we begin our work, we will have need of creatures such as this. And mark my words, when our work is done, we will retain our hold on power with the aid of these creatures. Our time is near, our cause is just, and the blood of traitors will wash away their sins!'

The cheering that followed dwarfed any that came before. Once again, Arbuthnot was mobbed, as were the golems, which stood silent and stoic under the prodding of the guests gathered around them.

'Let's get out of here,' Hartigan said. He took Anne by the hand and led her towards the nearest door, where a waiter stood. 'My wife, she is not feeling well. Is there a room I can take her to recover?'

The waiter, his eyes bright with fervour, nodded and pointed perfunctorily towards a door across the corridor. Hurriedly, Hartigan and Anne made their way towards it.

They entered a small sitting room. A connecting door led into another room.

'He's planning a coup,' Anne said. 'With those things.'

'What are they?' Hartigan asked, eyes wild. He had just entered a world he was not prepared for. Anne could sympathise, remembering the feeling all too well.

'Golems. Did you see the symbol carved into their foreheads?'

'How in... Where did they come from?'

'Von Werner and Vaar. It has to be. They've been dabbling in very dark things.'

'What do you mean, dark things?'

Anne looked at him a moment. She had to find a way to ground him. He was out of his depth, and struck her as the kind of man who would more likely drown than learn to swim.

'Do you trust me, Tom?' He gave no response, so Anne ploughed on. 'I know it's hard, but trust me when I say von Werner has tapped into powers beyond the understanding of science.'

Shakily exhaling, Tom nodded. 'So, these are going to be their shock troops?'

'I think so. You've seen the news. Arbuthnot has been campaigning on law and order for months. Imagine if those things were unleashed across Britain.'

'The trucking company, Landry's...'

'Yes,' Anne said. 'That's why Vaar bought it. To move those things into key positions. They'll strike within days.

He's challenging the PM Monday morning. The situation in the country is bad enough as it is, but if there is a collapse of law and order because these things are rioting through the streets of Britain… Arbuthnot would win in a canter.'

'Arbuthnot as Prime Minister,' Hartigan said, finally finding something his mind could grasp.

'Can you imagine? A new Reich here, in Britain.' Anne paused a moment, to let it sink in. 'For all his bluster, Arbuthnot would be little more than a puppet, manipulated by von Werner and Vaar.'

'We need to tell the authorities,' Hartigan said.

'That's us, Tom. Who would believe us? Inspector Pearson? He's probably hip deep with this lot, if the motley crew out there is anything to go by.'

'So what the hell do we do?'

'Take a deep breath.'

At first it seemed like Hartigan was going to rage against her; the anger burned in his eyes. It wasn't really directed at her, but rather his inability to accept what he'd seen in the hall. The golems. Getting angry at a woman talking down to him was easier. But, surprising Anne, he managed to tamp that down and did as suggested. He took a deep breath.

Anne nodded. 'Good. Now, we follow Arbuthnot back to London, and arrest him.'

The anger and confusion surfaced again. 'Have you gone raving mad? He's a bloody MP, for God's sake!'

Anne shook her head, keeping her voice calm. 'Doesn't matter. You arrest him, and sit on him at Crouch End Station.'

'Me? What the hell are you —?'

Anne raised her hand for quiet. They heard voices on the other side of the connecting door. Anne beckoned Hartigan over and they gathered next to the door.

'Get the creatures back into the lorry and have them

driven back to London,' said the voice on the other side of the door. 'Yes, tonight. We need them in place tomorrow night. That buffoon Arbuthnot will need all the help he can get to sway the vote on Monday.'

'That's von Werner,' Hartigan whispered.

Anne nodded.

'Me? I'll return to London. Dominic Vaar has his man at the bank even as we speak. The gladius is in my reach. And the beauty of it is all the hard work will be done by that degenerate Spaniard.'

Harsh laughter followed. It faded, and they heard a door closing softly.

'Alistair,' Anne said, then shushed Hartigan before he could query the name. 'Von Werner's going back to London. I think I know where he's going to be, why he was so cocky on stage.'

'Where's that?'

'The Bank of Shetland.'

'The Bank of...' Hartigan shook his head. 'Why would he go there?'

'Because he wants something from a safety deposit box.'

'How do you...?' Hartigan shook his head. Anne suppressed a smile. 'No. Don't tell me. I swear, Ruth, it's like you're a different person.' He ran a hand through his hair and looked around. 'All right then. We—'

The door swung open.

'What the devil is going on here?'

Anne froze. It was Johnson. He held a drink in his hand and his face was red and sweaty. Music drifted down the corridor.

'Took the wrong turn,' Hartigan said, moving rapidly towards Johnson, who had yet to recover from his surprise. 'A very stirring speech, don't you think?'

Before Johnson could respond, Hartigan closed with him. Anne heard a thud, and Johnson doubled over.

Hartigan deftly took his glass from his hand before Johnson could drop it.

'Shut the door, quick.' Hartigan set the drink aside and dragged Johnson to a chair.

Anne closed the door gently, and turned to the two men. Hartigan dropped Johnson into a chair. Rapidly, he had the man's tie off, which he stuffed into his mouth. Anne removed two curtain ties and brought them over. In a minute, they had Johnson bound foot and wrist.

'We can't leave him in the open,' Anne said.

Hartigan nodded, and looked around the room. He spotted a door off to one side. 'Let's see what's in there.'

An airless cupboard presented itself. Lined with shelves, it was musty with the books packed inside.

'This will have to do,' Anne said.

Dragging Johnson across the floor, Hartigan shoved him into the back of the cupboard. Johnson stared up at them, his eyes bulging with fear.

'You're going to have a nice, restful nap,' Hartigan said, smiling grimly. 'You'll probably wake up with a headache.' Before Anne could react, Hartigan punched Johnson in the head, knocking him out. 'Not quite the end to the night this little traitor expected, I reckon.' Hartigan flexed his hand.

'Was that necessary?' Anne asked.

'Yes,' Hartigan said. 'It's not enough to keep him in there. He'd just start banging on the walls and attract attention. We'll need as much distance between us and them when we head back to London.'

'So, you're in?'

'I wanted to be a copper since I was a teenager. I don't think I've done as much good in the last ten years as I've done in the last two days. Yeah, I'm in.'

For the first time Hartigan smiled genuinely. Anne returned it, and was alarmed when Hartigan leaned forward and planted a kiss on her lips.

'Wanted to do that for months,' he said, stepping back.

Anne wanted to slap him, tell him she was a married woman and how dare he, but then she thought of Ruth. She forced a smile.

'Tell you what, keep your hands to yourself for the rest of the investigation and you can take me out to dinner.'

Hartigan's look of stunned surprise amused her.

'Come on,' she said, walking over to the door. 'We have to go.'

CHAPTER EIGHTEEN
Drive-In Saturday

ALISTAIR LOOKED AT THE CAMERAS, THEIR BLACK EYES staring menacingly back at him. He turned, motioning to Bill. 'They're dead,' he said. 'Long enough for us to get in at least.'

Bill didn't need to be told twice. Picking up the case, he joined Alistair in the corridor, where they hurried to the door leading into the Safe Deposits.

'It's locked,' Bill said.

'Not for long.'

From yet another pocket, Alistair removed a narrow leather wallet. Opening it, he took out two thin metal implements. Inserting both into the lock, he manipulated them until they both heard the tumblers click. Alistair opened the door and ushered Bill inside. He closed the door just as the lights on the exterior cameras returned to life.

'Wait,' Alistair said, holding a finger to his lips.

Bill leaned against the door, and heard the low murmur of voices coming from the other side.

'See, they're working,' a voice said.

'They weren't two minutes ago,' said another, frustrated voice.

'Probably a glitch on the board.'

'We both saw it.'

'We both saw something.'

The door handle rattled, and Bill and Alistair took a

step back.

'See, nothing to worry about. If it makes you happy, write it up and tell Vince when he comes on shift tomorrow. They'll get a technician in to examine the board if you're that worried.'

The two men moved away. Bill and Alistair waited until their footsteps retreated to silence.

Bill exhaled in relief. 'This is almost as bad as being a spy,' he said, turning, to find Alistair had vanished.

Bill looked around, then noticed Alistair standing behind the security screen separating the booth from the entrance. His torch played over the counter, and he produced a set of keys.

'How did you get in there?' Bill said through the grill.

'Guards leave the door open for the cleaner, is the best I can come up with.' Alistair shrugged. 'Their laziness gets us one step closer to the vault.' Emerging from the booth, he swiftly went through the keys on the ring until he found the one that unlocked the door leading into the vault area.

Together, they entered a rectangular shaped antechamber, with one vault door painted red. Bill went up to it and ran his hands over the large, central wheel. Beneath it was a large copper coloured dial, notched around the circumference.

Alistair began setting up the lance. With Bill's help, he positioned it so the tip of it rested a hand's span to the left of the dial.

'You better tell me how this works,' Bill said.

'It's relatively simple,' Alistair said, as he busied himself with connecting one of the two remaining power packs. 'We could spend the rest of our lives trying to guess the combination.' He paused for a moment, looking critically at the lance, before nudging it slightly.

'No one likes a grandstander, sir,' Bill said, impatiently.

'Allow an expert his moment in the sun. It's okay for you, Bill, you haven't got around to retiring. Worst mistake I ever made,' Alistair said.

'Surely all this travel through time makes up for it a bit? A chance to relive your youth, in a manner of speaking.'

Alistair raised an eyebrow. 'Literally, too, in some cases. And yes, it helps.' He nodded to the vault door. 'Anyway, in the absence of a supercomputer crunching the numbers, we drill through until we hit the tumblers within.'

'And once you've reached the tumblers?'

'Through the hole, I'll manually align each tumbler until the opening sequence is complete.'

'And *et voila*, we'll be in?'

'Precisely.' Alistair checked his watch. 'We'll have to be quick. It's after one already. Best not be around when the sun rises.'

Flicking a switch on the side of the lance produced an intense beam of light. Alistair twisted a dial, widening the focus and broadening the beam. He stepped back and settled in to wait.

Bill spent the next two hours alternating between bouts of boredom and high tension. The lance worked silently, its brilliant beam emitting waves of heat. Occasionally, Alistair would approach, goggles in place, ensuring the beam remained in alignment. Bill found himself in a seemingly endless orbit around the lance, moving out to the entrance of the Safe Deposit area, listening intently at the door for anyone approaching, before returning to stand impatiently beside the lance.

A warning beep sometime later brought Alistair hurrying over to the lance. The beam's intensity had dimmed, reducing the flow of molten metal.

'How far to go?' Bill asked, as his former commander

swapped out the drained power pack.

He clipped cabling into the remaining pack and jammed the bundle into the lance's canopy. Patting his pockets, Alistair pulled out a jeweller's loupe. He peered into the hole. 'More than half way. Maybe,' he said, looking up.

'Maybe,' Bill said. 'Might as well try to reach for the moon if this next pack runs out before we reach the tumblers.'

'We'll have to trust to the Matador's planning.' Alistair replaced the jeweller's loupe and switched the lance back on. The intensity of the beam lit up the room, casting their shadows against the far wall. 'Relax, Bill,' Alistair said. 'We'll get there.'

'Sorry.' Bill stood staring at the vault with hands on hips. 'I'm worried about this lead Anne's following up.'

'Her instincts are sound. I'm sure she'll be fine. Anne was never a pushover, which is exactly why you married her, remember?' Alistair smiled, briefly. 'If she does come across von Werner, heaven help him.'

The next hour dragged. Bill anxiously watched the lance. Smoke drifted up to the vents, and he was silently glad the modern mania for smoke detectors had yet to eventuate.

A high-pitched beeping noise came from the lance. Alistair swiftly crossed the room and checked the primitive display on the side of the device. He nodded, satisfied.

'Has it finished?' Bill asked, as Alistair dragged the lance aside.

He removed a long metal probe from the case. 'It appears so. The Matador did his research on this type of vault. He pre-set the lance to cut out when it reached a certain depth.' He held up the probe. 'This will be tricky. Grab a torch and shine a light, will you?'

Alistair positioned himself in front of the hole. The metal that had dribbled from the hole had ceased its flowing, and only a mild warmth came from it. He popped in the jeweller's loupe and waited for Bill.

'Ready?' Bill asked, clicking on the torch and holding it over Alistair's shoulder.

Alistair grunted and inserted the probe. He bent forward, the jeweller's loupe jammed into his eye socket. Metal scraped on metal as he twisted the probe.

Bill heard a faint click, followed by another. Then there were several minutes of silence, only broken by Alistair's frustrated muttering and the scrape of metal. Bill wiped sweat from his forehead.

'Keep that light steady!' Alistair snapped.

Bill tightened his grip on the torch. He checked his watch, and swore silently. Then he heard a click.

'Got it!' Alistair withdrew the probe and discarded it. 'Come on,' he said, gripping the wheel. 'Let's see what's in Aladdin's Cave.'

The wheel spun on well-greased bearings. When it stopped, Alistair grabbed the metal bar and pulled it to the left. Bolts clanked and the vault door shifted outward an inch or two. A tiny breeze flowed through the gap. Together, the two men hauled the vault door open, revealing the shadowy interior. Deposit boxes lined both walls. Several benches of brushed metal sat in the centre of the room.

Bill played the light across the ceiling. 'No cameras,' he said.

'Privacy,' Alistair said. 'I doubt, unlike Switzerland, there is any Nazi gold stored here, but I imagine English sensibilities would be shocked to see cameras spying on the great and good as they fawn over their treasures.'

'Not to mention Inland Revenue,' Bill said. He placed a foot up on the sill of the door.

Alistair grabbed his shoulder and pointed to the floor.

'Pressure sensors,' he said.

'You sure?'

'Absolutely. They've made a concession to privacy, but certainly not to security. Step in there and we'll have half the MET on our doorstep within five minutes. I'm sure they'd love to hear the explanations one of their black detectives would have for his presence here.'

Yes, that would be fun. Bill smiled ruefully. 'I suppose the Matador has planned for this?'

'Oh yes. What are your climbing skills like?'

Alistair opened a drawer in the case, revealing a number of stacked rectangular metal plates. He removed two and showed them to Bill. On each, one side was covered in rubber, while one edge projected out a couple of inches.

'I can't begin to imagine what they're for,' Bill said, as Alistair hefted a metal plate in each hand.

He smiled and indicated the floor inside the vault. 'The sensors under the carpet are disabled during visiting hours. When the bank is closed, anything heavier than a few pounds sets the alarm board blaring here and at New Scotland Yard.'

Bill nodded. He looked inside the vault while Alistair piled the plates next to the door. Hundreds of deposit boxes lined the walls. A thin seam ran around all of them, a repeating pattern that triggered a thought. He glanced at the plates again, and realisation dawned.

'The edge slides into the seams,' Bill said, shaking his head in admiration. 'This Matador fella's ingenious.'

'He is,' Alistair said. He joined Bill at the open vault. He took out his torch and played the light across a wall. 'There,' he said, training the light half way down the left-hand wall. 'Number one-eight-one.'

'The sword is in there?'

'Yes.'

'Wouldn't it just be better to walk away and deprive

Vaar of having it?'

'I can't. Vaar is holding the Matador's niece hostage,' Alistair said, heavily.

This was news to Bill. 'Didn't think to mention it before? Kind of important.'

'Yes, and I'm not sure why I didn't mention it.' Alistair frowned a moment. 'I think the Matador prevented me. He's not in control, but he's... an *influence*, you might say.'

Only once in his temporal travels had Bill experienced that, and then it had been due to the formidable will of the host.

'Anyway,' Alistair continued, 'the Matador has to play along, for now. And, to be honest, I'm keen to see this sword. Professional interest. Come on, let's see if these plates work.'

Bill sighed, and let his old boss get to work.

Alistair began by inserting the first metal plate into a seam just inside the vault entrance. The thinner edge slid in with a faint shriek of metal. He rested a foot on it, testing its strength. Much to Bill's surprise the plate didn't flex under Alistair's weight. 'Right then, Bill, ready?'

Bill nodded. Planting his feet, he gripped Alistair by the fabric of his belt. Alistair transferred his full weight onto the plate. He stood there, one foot dangling in the air, nose pressed against a safety deposit box.

'Any movement?' Bill asked, his features tense.

'None,' Alistair said, tightly. Sweat stood out on his forehead.

'Can I let go?'

'I think so.'

'You think so?'

'If you don't, we'll look bloody stupid when the guards come in to unlock the place.'

Bill managed a smile. Heart pounding, he released

Alistair and stepped back. 'Still all right?'

'So far so good,' Alistair said. 'Hand me the other plate.'

Bill passed across the other plate. Alistair took it, swapping it from his left hand to the right. He slowly lowered himself. As Bill watched, agonised, Alistair reached out and slipped the plate into a seam. Bill checked his watch.

'We've got an hour,' he said, his voice low and urgent.

'Plenty of time,' Alistair said, as he wiped the palms of his hands on his trousers. Sweat ran down his face. 'Here we go,' he said.

Rising to his full height, he placed as much of his left foot as he could on the plate. Satisfied it was secure, he slowly lifted his right leg until the foot hung in mid-air, then he stretched it out and placed it on the plate.

'If Doris could see me now,' he muttered to himself. Face pressed against the wall, Alistair gave Bill a wink. 'You need to relax.' He turned his head so he was facing away. 'Easy as p —'

His left hand slipped loose from its damp grip on the wall. In a flash, his body began to lean away from the wall. Bill watched in horror as Alistair teetered backwards. He saw one hand slap the wall as the other flailed for balance. There was a moment when he thought his friend would fall backwards onto the carpet. Instead, slowly, Alistair regained his balance. Leaning against the wall, he panted heavily.

'Not something I'd recommend doing again,' Bill said, trying to ease the tension.

'No, neither would I.' Alistair closed his eyes for a long moment, and when they reopened, Bill saw renewed determination.

Over the course of the next fifteen minutes, Alistair made his slow way across the wall. He found a rhythm – step, brace, pull free a plate, swap it in his hands, lean and insert, then step again. Finally, he came within arms' reach of the deposit box.

'Number one-eight-one?' Bill called out.

Nodding, Alistair reached into a pocket and removed a small metal object. Round barrelled, with slots cut into the leading edge, he leaned across and inserted it into the lock. He straightened, pulled out another key and performed the same manoeuvre.

'Had these made in Barcelona,' he said, almost conversationally. 'Well, the Matador did, obviously. Not me. Damn rush job, so fingers crossed, eh?' He licked his lips. Awkwardly, and with infinite care, he leaned over, grabbed a key in each hand while pressing his left shoulder against the wall, and turned them.

Bill heard the locks disengage with a distant thunk. He breathed a sigh of relief when he saw the small rectangular door pop open.

'Can you get the box out?'

'Should do,' Alistair said.

He took the keys from each lock and pocketed them. He pulled the door wider, revealing a box fitting snugly into the gap. A latch hung from the exposed end. From his jacket, he removed a strap with a clip at either end. Dragging out the box with some effort, he lifted it free and attached a clip to the latch, then the other clip to his belt. Carefully, Alistair began the laborious process of returning to the vault entrance.

There were one or two chancy moments, but eventually he stepped off the plate and back into the room. He lifted the strap off his shoulders and set the box onto a bench, where he and Bill both stared at it.

'Are we going to open it?' Bill asked.

'If we've gone through all that only to find out the box is empty after we've fled the scene of the crime, I'll go spare.'

Without ceremony, Alistair lifted the lid, setting it

back on its hinge. A musty smell filled the air, as if a long-held breath had finally had the chance to be released. Inside, both men could see a piece of canvas, stiffened and yellow with age, sitting within the cavity.

'We should unwrap it,' Bill said, without much conviction.

'I don't... Perhaps later.'

Bill shivered. 'You can feel it, can't you?'

'Yes.'

Bill nodded. 'As soon as you opened it, I felt...'

'Sick?'

'Yeah. And uneasy. Like it's radiating... something.'

Both men stood at the bench, staring into the box. The sound of the clock on the wall ticking away the morning brought Alistair back to his senses.

'We have to check now, before we leave,' he said.

Hesitantly, he touched the material. A heavy object shifted beneath. He winced at the sudden spike of pain behind his eyes.

'What is it?' Bill asked.

'There's something wrong about this sword.' Alistair set his mouth in a firm line and he pulled at the canvas.

The doorknob rattled. The distant jingle of keys drifted to them. Both men looked at each other and glanced at the clock.

'They're early,' Bill whispered.

'Wait beside the door,' Alistair said. 'And put your balaclava back on.' He felt his gaze irresistibly drawn to the box.

'What if they enter?' Bill asked.

'You know what to do.'

Hesitating a moment, Bill broke away and walked over to the door. Alistair, frantic, pulled at the canvas. The jingling of the keys grew urgent. The door opened just as he lifted away the last fold of fabric.

Alistair heard a thud and then a weak cry. He turned,

the sword held in one hand, and saw Bill grappling with a figure. They stopped, and Bill stared at Alistair, fear and concern in his eyes.

A red haze descended across Alistair's vision and he felt his heart surging in his chest as the sound of a thousand shouting men slammed into him. A thousand hammers smashed into a thousand anvils, and the shouts became screams of agony and despair. Over it all hung a dark, hungry presence. Through the red mist Alistair looked at the man who had been fighting with Bill, and a terrible bloodlust fell over him.

He cried out and charged forward.

CHAPTER NINETEEN
Battle for Britain

'BRIGADIER! FOR GOD'S SAKE, YOU'LL KILL HIM!'

Alistair shook his head. He held something heavy in one hand, so heavy the muscles in his shoulder shrieked. He heard the roar of battle in his ears, men fighting and screaming and dying. In the distance, he could see a man standing in the centre of a huge tumult, wielding a sword that glowed impossibly black. Men attacked the figure, and died beneath the terrible blade.

Turning, the man looked directly at him, and Alistair saw that he wore his own face. The shock of the image jolted him, and the haze lifted.

Looking down, he saw his free hand wrapped around a man's throat. Alistair released him, and felt a spasm in his right hand. His fingers loosened, and the sword hit the floor with an echoing thud.

He looked at Bill, who was staring at him.

'What the hell was that about?' he asked, his voice raised and hoarse.

Alistair shook his head and mumbled meaningless words. He stumbled back to the discarded piece of canvas. Picking it up with trembling fingers, he wrapped it around the sword, careful not to touch it. It took several efforts, but when he had it securely bundled up, he rose to his feet and returned to Bill's side. The guard he had tried to strangle, groaned.

'Time to go,' Alistair said, his voice cracking.

Together, both men left the Safe Deposit area and entered the corridor. All around them, alarms burst into life.

'The stairs!' Bill yelled.

Still in a daze, Alistair watched as Bill crashed open the nearest access door. Someone behind shouted at them. Alistair felt Bill's hand grab his arm, and he allowed himself to be led through the door and down the stairs. At the next landing, the two men went through a door into a corridor.

'I'm all right, Bill,' Alistair said.

The fit that had overwhelmed him had gone, and though he still felt shaky, strength returned to his limbs. Bill opened his mouth to say something when a pair of guards came around the corner at the far end of the corridor.

Breaking into a run, Alistair led the way down the corridor with Bill at his heels. They emerged onto a gallery overlooking the ground floor. A marble staircase on the opposite side led down, and Alistair caught a glimpse of the front doors.

'We can't get to the van,' Bill said, panting heavily.

'We'll take our chances outside,' Alistair said. They both heard the sounds of pursuit closing in on them. 'Get that pack open.'

Swiftly, Bill pulled open the drawstrings and removed a pair of canisters from inside the pack.

'Tear gas?' he said, reading the symbol.

'Just the ticket,' Alistair said. He took a canister from Bill. 'Ready?'

Bill nodded. Both men pulled free the pins.

'On three,' Alistair said.

'One.'

'Two.'

'Three!' both men exclaimed in unison.

Alistair rolled away from the pillar and came to his

feet, tossing his canister at the approaching guards. It trailed a streamer of smoke, which suddenly blossomed into a billowing cloud. Bill tossed his canister, where it bounced and rolled before gas erupted from it. As the guards grabbed their throats and reeled away, coughing, Alistair and Bill rapidly descended the stairs to the ground floor. They made for the stationary revolving doors.

'Hit the button!' Alistair said.

Bill dashed over and hit the green button. With a grinding whine, the revolving doors started up. Behind them, more guards appeared. First Bill, then Alistair, burst into the street and the early morning light. Casting a desperate glance over his shoulder, Alistair pulled a screwdriver from a pocket and jammed it at the base of the revolving doors. By some miracle, the handle snagged under the bottom edge, and the door juddered to a halt.

On the other side, the pursuing guards pounded on the glass, before breaking away and making for the side exit.

'Which way?' Bill asked, standing in the middle of the street.

Before Alistair could respond, doors opened on a car further up the street. A number of men, armed with shotguns, leaped out and advanced towards them. Glancing back, Alistair saw the guards clatter down the steps towards them.

'Back,' he said, clutching the canvas wrapped weapon to his chest.

'Do not move!' boomed an accented voice.

Alistair saw the pale hair, the heavily scarred face. The man limped towards them, his wolf-headed cane snarling in the light. Around him, the armed men lifted their weapons.

'I don't think so,' Alistair muttered. He drew his revolver and opened fire.

One of the gunmen spun around, clutching his shoulder. His shotgun clattered to the ground.

Immediately bullets and shotgun blasts sang through the air. Alistair and Bill huddled behind a parked car, which was rapidly being peppered with shots. Shattered glass fell into the street. A shop mannequin spun through the air, its head blown away.

'They've got us pinned down!' Bill shouted over the cacophony.

There came a sudden shriek of tyres. Alistair spun around and saw a car speeding towards them from the south. The car slewed around in a wide circle, smoke boiling from the tyres as they shrieked across the macadam, the sound almost drowning out the gunfire and bank alarms. The passenger door flew open.

'Get in!' Anne yelled.

Alistair and Bill ran for the car. Bill fell into the front seat, and Alistair spent precious seconds wrestling with the back passenger door before he was able to dive in. Gunfire rattled around them, sparking off the roof as Anne slammed the car into gear and sped away. A bullet starred the back window and lodged itself in the ceiling. Then Anne took the nearest corner at high speed, and the shootout vanished from view.

Bill manoeuvred himself into a better position, and looked over at Anne. She grinned at him, and he was reminded of why he had first fallen for her all those years ago. Even now, with the face of a stranger, he saw the fire that had drawn him in like a moth.

'You're welcome,' she said through gritted teeth as she ignored the red light at a junction and flew through it. Car horns blared. She glanced at Bill, then at Alistair's reflection in the rear-view mirror.

'You knew they were coming?' Alistair asked.

Bill glanced back; Alistair cradled the canvas-wrapped weapon in his arms protectively. No, Bill corrected, possessively. He didn't like the effect it was having on the Brig.

'Yes,' Anne said. 'Hartigan and I discovered von Werner is planning a coup, no doubt with Vaar, and Arbuthnot as his puppet.'

Bill said nothing about Anne bringing Hartigan in. She probably had a good reason. 'And where's Hartigan now?'

'Minding Arbuthnot.'

'Minding him? How is he...? Did he *arrest* Arbuthnot?'

Anne grinned again. 'Been quite a night for all of us,' she said, not taking her eyes off the road. 'Hartigan has him under lock and key down the station. The fool is screaming bloody murder, but Tom managed to dig up some old parking tickets.'

'That won't stop them,' Alistair said from behind.

Bill looked at him. His friend's borrowed face looked drawn and pale.

'No,' Anne said. 'That's why we have to do something about that gladius.' She looked at Alistair in the rear-view mirror. 'You can't hand it over to Vaar.'

'Not that simple, Anne,' Bill said.

'It will cost the life of the Matador's niece,' Alistair explained. 'Vaar has her.'

They crossed the Thames and headed southeast.

'So where are we going with it?' Bill asked, gripping the dashboard with one hand.

'Spandau Prison,' Anne said.

'Spandau?' Bill looked across at her incredulously. 'What the hell for?'

'Von Werner,' Alistair muttered, and Bill turned to him. 'Himmler. Hess.' Alistair sat back heavily.

Bill glanced from him to his wife, confused. 'Am I missing something?'

'Hess is the last remaining High Command Nazi in custody,' Anne explained. 'His knowledge of the occult is renowned. If anyone knows what to do with this gladius, it'll be him.'

Bill, looking dazed, simply nodded. 'Where were you all night?'

'I spoke with a fellow named Renfield,' Anne said, slowing as a panda car raced passed, its siren howling in the early morning air. Watching it disappear from the rear-view mirror, she slammed the accelerator to the floor.

'Martin Renfield?' Alistair asked.

'You know him?' Anne glanced at the rear-view mirror in surprise.

'By reputation. One of Kinsella's men during the war.' Alistair shook his head. 'Someone not afraid to get his hands dirty.'

'So he told me. He also provided information that led me to von Werner. That's where Tom and I discovered that all three are as thick as thieves.' She hesitated a moment, then went on. 'We even got to see some golems up close.'

'Bet Hartigan took that well,' Bill said, imagining his reaction.

'As well as could be expected.' Anne looked at her side mirror. 'Anyway, enough chit-chat,' she said. 'I've got three pandas on my tail.'

Anne pushed the car to its limit, the engine revving higher and higher as she worked her way up the gears.

'Watch out!' Bill yelled.

The car veered to the left, almost mounting the kerb. Several early morning pedestrians scattered, and a man came off his bike. He lay stunned in the gutter as they rounded a bend in a screech of tyres.

'Stop the car,' Alistair said.

'What?' Anne frantically dodged through traffic. The braying of multiple car horns filled the air, and more pedestrians scattered in panic as Anne drove through an intersection.

'You're going to kill someone if you keep this up!' Alistair shouted. 'Stop the damn car!'

Bill looked back, still not liking the way the Brig clung to the gladius. He swallowed. 'Anne, stop the car.'

Not happy, but clearly sensing the urgency, Anne found a spot and did as asked. As soon as the car stopped, Alistair opened the back door and jumped out. Police sirens closed in on them.

'Keep the engine running!' he shouted, wincing in pain.

Bill went to open the door, but the Brig shook his head. He stepped into the street. A car drove around him, and the few pedestrians gawked as he unfurled the canvas wrapping with a flourish. A red-tinged light bloomed overhead. Holding the sword aloft, Alistair almost stumbled, but he stood straight, cocking his head as if he could hear voices.

'Put down the weapon!' a voice yelled.

Bill looked through the rear window, watching with mounting horror as police emerged from their panda cars, arms out, trying to calm down the Brig.

'Get back!' Alistair shouted. 'I'm not responsible for what this thing can do.'

Unwillingly, he took a step forward. The light intensified. Shadows unfurled before him, billowing like smoke from a raging bonfire. Bill and Anne looked at each other in astonishment, then turned their attention back to Alistair.

Dimly, Alistair saw the police begin to fall back, their faces transfixed by a vision he somehow knew came from the sword. In moments, the police and other bystanders were in headlong retreat, some of them screaming.

Abruptly, between one breath and the next, the

streetscape dissolved and from the mist emerged a strange landscape of hills and open fields, filled with contending men. Shouts filled the air, and screams, and the distant throb of drums. Horses streamed past, their saddles empty, blood and foam thick on their flanks. A figure, near naked and covered in strange blue symbols, ran howling into the mob. A dark-skinned legionnaire wielding a short sword cut it down. The legionnaire turned and stared at Alistair for a long moment, before he turned and disappeared into the howling morass of men, tearing and clawing and stabbing at each other.

'Alistair!'

A voice shouted in his ear. Dully, Alistair shook his head and the landscape dissolved.

'Come on!' It was a strange black man, pulling at his sleeve. 'We have to go!'

Alistair's head felt like it was stuffed with cotton. He was sure he knew the chap, so he allowed himself to be helped into a car. He realised who the black man was. It was Bill. Of course it was!

Once he had him inside, Bill slammed the door shut. Alistair saw his old friend look around, then disappear behind the car. Distant sounds of tyres bursting drifted down the empty street. With an effort, Alistair glanced through the rear window and saw Bill returning. Behind him stood the police cars, with deflated tyres. In his hand, Bill held a screwdriver, which he absently replaced in his overalls. He got in the front and Anne drove away, leaving the chaotic scene behind them.

Bill reached to take the sword.

'Don't,' Alistair said, struggling to speak. 'It's too... Too dangerous.'

With an effort, he wrapped it in the canvas sheet. When he finished, he sat back, exhausted.

'What happened back there?' Anne asked, driving more sedately now they had escaped the scene.

'Something that proves that whatever else happens, you're right. Vaar cannot be allowed to get his hands on this thing.' Alistair slumped back in the seat.

'What do we do now, then?' Bill asked.

CHAPTER TWENTY
New Killer Star

'IMBER,' BILL SAID, LOOKING OUT AT THE village in the early morning light; how different it looked from his own time.

St Giles' Church loomed out of the mist, its dirty limestone walls pockmarked and streaked with grime. Bill felt himself relax when he saw it; he had spent time inside the building while off duty and had admired the remains of the medieval paintings that lingered on the old walls.

Other buildings emerged, though in worse condition. During and after the war, when the inhabitants had been forced off their land and out of their homes, the village had been used for combat training. Teams of soldiers had engaged in street fighting, while artillery had reduced many of the buildings, some family homes, to rubble. A few years ago, relative time, troops stationed at the local MOD base had started living in the village, and now it housed over a hundred military families, most of them seconded to the Fifth Operational Corps. By Bill's own time, though, thirty-eight years hence, the Fifth hadn't operated out of Imber since 2005. One of his last duties as commander of the Fifth was to ensure that Imber was returned to the civilian population. Since then the village had been built up again, with civilians returning there once more.

'Imber,' Alistair echoed him. He looked tired.

Once they were free of pursuit, Anne had left them so she could return to the station and Hartigan. She hoped to make it there before Inspector Pearson, who was due in around 6am. Bill and the Brig had 'borrowed' a vehicle and began their way north, out of London. They had driven through the dawning of the new day, wary of other vehicles on the road. The gladius sat in the back of the car, a reminder of their ordeal, and the urgency of their task.

The signs of civilisation vanished when they entered Salisbury Plain, the thinly populated rolling hills and desolate plains a reminder that even in the densely populated British Isles, there were still places where the hand of man had but lightly touched the land.

'Are you sure this will work?' Bill asked, returning his attention to Alistair. 'How are you going to convince Douglas to give two complete strangers help?'

'When desperate, improvise,' Alistair said, managing a tired smile. 'Dougie will be simple enough; the main trick is to convince Major Younghusband, so we can actually contact Douglas up in the Madhouse.'

A sign appeared out of the mist, in MOD livery.

'Last chance to stop,' Bill said, watching the sign disappear in the side mirror. 'You don't think they'd really shoot us?'

'Ever ignored a direct order?' Alistair asked. Bill shook his head. 'Neither will they.' He pointed at the guard station where two men, armed with rifles, emerged.

Smoothly, as if they had drilled for this their entire careers, one of them took aim at the vehicle, while his partner waited in the middle of the road, one hand held up.

'Good discipline,' Bill commented.

'It's why I seconded Younghusband from Intelligence. Knew he would be a good fit for the Fifth. Keeps his house in order.' Alistair applied the brake and shifted down the gears. He wound down the window as the soldier approached. His partner never wavered in his stance, and Bill had the uncomfortable sensation that came with having a rifle aimed at him.

'Lost, are we?' the soldier asked.

'Oh no,' Alistair said, brightly. 'We know exactly where we are.'

The soldier looked momentarily disconcerted, before recovering his composure. 'And where is that, then?'

'The Loony Bin,' Alistair said. He smiled as the soldier started. 'Now be a good fellow and get me Major Younghusband.'

'Clever,' Bill said as they were marched into a room inside the facility.

The guards hadn't waited around to question them further. As soon as Alistair had made mention of Loony Bin, they were ordered from the car. Alistair had been relieved of his revolver, and the gladius, and they were escorted through the gates and into the warren of rooms, corridors and chambers.

One of the soldiers took up position by the door while the other went in search of Major Younghusband.

'What do you think?' Alistair said as he sank into a chair.

'About what?' Bill joined him in the other chair.

'Whether that chap's uniform is up to standard. There's fraying at the cuff of his trousers and one of his buttons is ready to fall off.'

'Oh, I see.' Bill leaned forward to study the man at the door. The soldier coloured, but kept his composure.

'I'm sure Younghusband has had to deal with worse,' Alistair said. He turned to Bill, whispering loud enough for the guard to hear. 'Though I wouldn't want to cross him, not after he hears what we have to say.'

At that moment, the door swung open. The guard stepped aside. To their surprise, not one, but two uniformed men walked in. Major Derek Younghusband, and another, more senior officer. It was an old impulse, but still strong; Bill rose to salute, while Alistair remained sitting.

'Dougie,' he said.

Brigadier Walter Douglas, the second commander of the Fifth Operational Corps. It was like looking at a photograph brought to life. Bill hadn't seen his old commanding officer like this in years – at the prime of his life, the steel in his eyes. A far cry from the man who had been crippled in his old age by a terrorist attack.

Douglas frowned at Alistair, and Bill could only imagine how it had to feel to have these two strange men before him, one demonstrating a familiarity that he simply shouldn't have.

'You can leave, Private,' Younghusband said, flicking the soldier a glance. 'And make sure that button is properly secured before I see you again, you hear?'

The private went bright red, saluted, turned on his heel and left the room, closing the door behind them.

The four men glanced at each other, before Douglas cleared his throat.

'Ordinarily I wouldn't let my breakfast be interrupted in this manner, but since I was visiting, and we have two civilians talking quite openly about the Loony Bin, well, you can imagine my interest. And,' he continued, looking at Alistair, 'one who appears to know me. Who are you?'

Alistair stood and offered his hand. 'Brigadier Sir Alistair Lethbridge-Stewart, and this is Brigadier William Bishop.'

Bill looked at him in surprise.

'Really? *Brigadier* Bishop? And, sorry if I misheard you, but you did say *Sir* Alistair Lethbridge-Stewart?' Douglas turned to Younghusband. 'I've left my kippers to listen to someone spouting names they have no right to know. Evidently they need to do better research, but I have to admit I'm intrigued. Intrigued enough to know why a complete stranger would claim to be one of the best soldiers I know, and how a black man could possibly be *Major* Bill Bishop.'

'Wenley Moor,' Alistair said without preamble. Younghusband flinched, while Douglas fixed Alistair with a grim stare. 'I expressed my doubts to you about my actions after I ordered the caves sealed. You told me the greater good demanded I do what I did. You remember, Dougie, don't you? Just you and me, in your office in the Madhouse. It can't have been more than two weeks ago.'

'That's imposs—' Douglas closed his mouth with a snap, then shook his head. 'If there is one thing I've learned in the last four years...'

'Is that nothing is impossible.' Alistair raised an eyebrow. 'A far cry from your point of view when we were up in Edinburgh supervising the refurbishment of the old Longbow facility, I seem to recall.'

Douglas stared at them, hard. 'All right. Let's go to the major's office, I feel more secure there. And when we get to it, you can explain to both of us why you're here.'

Alistair stood. 'Good, I knew you'd believe me, Dougie.'

'Well, I never quite said that, did I?'

Alistair stopped before Douglas and looked him in the eye. 'No, but I know you. After all we've been through since Sandhurst... Well, you know it's me in here.'

Douglas considered, glancing at Bill and then Younghusband. 'Yes,' he said slowly, 'I rather think it is.'

Younghusband's office was Spartan in its neatness. A chair, a desk with a blotter and intercom sitting on it. A bookcase sat to one side, with thick volumes tidily arranged. Only a copy of yesterday's *Times* marred the room's clean lines. Bill saw the front page and nudged Alistair, as Douglas settled into the chair behind the desk, with Younghusband standing by his shoulder.

Riots from John o Groats to Land's End! the headline thundered. Ignoring Douglas for a moment, Alistair read from the opening paragraph.

'Riots across Britain. There are reports of heavily armoured figures leading the charge against police. It is understood that the army may be called out if rioting continues.'

'Is that true?' Bill asked.

'It's under consideration,' Douglas said. 'I've received word from Fugglestone, and the Fifth stands ready to support UNIT and the regulars. Once the leadership vote is out of the way, whoever leads the government will have to decide very quickly.'

'Vaar,' Alistair said, glancing at Bill.

'Vaar?' Younghusband looked to Douglas, who simply stared.

'That's what I said, Major. Late of Dominex Industries, originally commander of the Dominator War Fleet. Responsible for the death of Sally,' Alistair added, pointedly looking at Douglas.

Something slipped on Dougie's face. Alistair resisted smiling. They'd know each other since before Sandhurst; they'd passed out together, served together. Dougie was even Kate's godfather.

'Sally... Penny still visits her grave every month.'

'I know. I remember.'

Dougie shook his head. 'This is insane. You're supposed to be at Space Control, aren't you? And you,' he said, looking at Bill, 'are on leave. With Anne. First anniversary.'

'We are,' Bill said.

'Dougie, it's a very long story, and one I can't tell you.' Alistair leaned towards the desk. 'All you need to know is we're from 2011, and we are here to deal with Vaar.'

'Okay, tell me more. Vaar disappeared off the grid years ago.'

'Yes,' Bill said. 'And he's currently running a criminal gang in Soho.'

'Soho?' Younghusband repeated.

'Better than that,' Alistair said, with the ghost of a smile. 'He recruited me... Well, the fellow you currently see, to steal something on his behalf.'

'That sword,' Douglas said.

'A gladius,' Alistair said.

Douglas pressed a button on the intercom. 'Hawthorn? Tell Private Judkin to bring me that sword they took from these two men.' He leaned back and the men waited.

After a few minutes, there was a knock at the door, which swung open. A uniformed man carried in the canvas-wrapped gladius. He looked ill at ease holding it, and hurriedly placed it on the desk before retreating to the outer room.

'I suppose you're going to tell me that this gladius is at the centre of all this hubbub down in London?' Douglas asked.

'And across the country,' Alistair said. He placed his hands on the desk and leaned forward. 'We need your help, Dougie.'

'To do what?' Younghusband asked.

Alistair smiled. This was the bit they'd really have trouble swallowing. 'We need to get to Spandau Prison and speak with Rudolf Hess.'

'Bloody Pearson,' Hartigan said, standing on the steps of the police station. Early morning light swept over them.

'Bloody Pearson,' Anne said, standing with Hartigan

as they watched the car drive away.

Inspector Pearson had arrived fifteen minutes before Anne. Hartigan had managed to keep the other officers away from Arbuthnot, who had spent most of the night angrily proclaiming his innocence. Anne had been surprised when she returned to the station to find Arbuthnot still there; but not for much longer. She'd walked in to find Inspector Pearson and Hartigan sparring over Arbuthnot's temporary incarceration.

'Parking tickets!' Pearson said, shaking his head. Spots of crimson rode high on his cheeks. 'This is a Minister of the Crown you've got locked up here for parking tickets, Tom.'

'Former Minister,' Hartigan said.

'Don't be splitting hairs with me!' Pearson snapped. 'I want him released, I want him released now.'

'You're one of them, aren't you?'

Pearson's eyes narrowed. 'What are you talking about?'

'The Cliveden Set. A fancier way of saying traitors, I reckon.'

Blood drained from Pearson's face. He stepped close, until he was barely an inch away from Hartigan. 'I can make your career disappear like this!' he snarled, snapping his fingers.

'Really?' Hartigan said. 'I can make *you* disappear like this,' he said, snapping his fingers in reply.

Anne couldn't believe it. Hartigan had a certain edge to him, she knew that, and clearly wasn't a man who always played by the book, but to threaten a superior so blatantly. Despite herself, Anne found herself warming to Hartigan. She didn't want to see him risking his career.

'Tom,' Anne said, stepping in and surprising both men, neither of whom had evidently noticed her arrival. 'Enough. Let Arbuthnot go.'

Hartigan turned on Anne, a look of astonishment on his face. 'If we let Arbuthnot go then—'

Anne shook her head. 'We've got bigger fish to fry. Trust me.'

Hartigan stared at her for a moment, then nodded. With a glare at Pearson, Hartigan stormed out of the room and down the corridor to the interview rooms. Anne followed him. He unlocked the door to interview room one.

Arbuthnot charged out, eyes wide in outrage. 'This won't stand, do you understand? I'll have your job.'

'That will do, Charles,' Pearson said smoothly, approaching behind Anne. He took Arbuthnot by the arm. 'I'll deal with the disciplinary matters. You've got a meeting to attend.'

And with that, followed by Anne and Hartigan, the two men had left the station.

'Now what?' Hartigan asked. 'How do we stop them now?'

This was the hard bit. She hoped she was right, but unfortunately there was little chance that either Bill or Alistair could contact her once they arrived at the Loony Bin. 'Harry has gone to West Berlin.'

'West Berlin? What the hell is he doing there?'

'Getting answers,' Anne said. She looked at Hartigan. 'You'll have to trust me, Tom. There are bigger things going on than simply a challenge to a prime minister.'

'You're telling me. I've got reports on my desk of a dozen riots across the country, and that's just last night.'

'It's all of a piece,' Anne said. 'Look, I'll fill you in, but only after I get a change of clothes.'

'Fill me in?' Hartigan called, as Anne hurried to the locker room. 'Where are we going?'

'Westminster,' she called over her shoulder. 'We're going to stop a coup.'

*

They made good time through the West Berlin traffic. Dougie had arranged for them to be picked up and driven directly to Spandau. Alistair was suitably impressed with the strings his old friend had pulled, but he knew he shouldn't be. It wasn't without reason that Alistair had brought Dougie into the Fifth Operational Corps at the beginning. He couldn't have asked for a better successor.

Finally, they arrived. The gatehouse materialised in the lights of their car. It stopped at a checkpoint manned by several British soldiers. Major Younghusband showed them his ID, and together with Alistair, Bill and their driver, they waited as the soldiers carefully examined the undercarriage of the car using mirrors on long probes, and checked the boot. German shepherds snuffled around the tyres. After a few minutes, one of the soldiers signalled to the man on the barricade, which rose.

Younghusband nodded to the driver, and the car moved into a short tunnel formed by two stubby towers. They parked next to a jeep being loaded by soldiers. Several lorries, their canvas backing lifted forward, were stacked with boxes.

They all climbed out of the car. The driver left them, and Alistair and Bill allowed Younghusband to lead the way. They walked up to a gatehouse and were buzzed inside. A corporal and a lieutenant waited for them.

'Sorry, Major, if you don't mind,' the lieutenant said.
'By all means.'

The three men suffered the attention in silence until the corporal finished.

'Best check the bag,' the lieutenant said.

'That won't be necessary, Lieutenant,' Younghusband said. 'Orders from Major General Hamilton.' He produced a letter of authorisation. 'The bag contains an historical artefact which these gentlemen are the legal custodians of. We need your... guest to verify its authenticity.'

Alistair forced himself to keep quiet. They couldn't be real orders from Hamilton; Dougie hadn't the time to get such authorisation, and besides, how could he have convinced the old man to authorise this anyway? No, it seemed more likely Dougie had forged the orders. It was a risk, but not one beneath Dougie. Alistair glanced at Bill, who smartly kept his eyes on the ground.

The lieutenant perused the orders, then snapped a salute. 'Very good, Major. If you'll pass through these doors, Major Hollister is waiting for you.'

'Damned inconsiderate timing,' Hollister said, as soon as the door closed behind them. 'What with the Soviets ready to take over. They'll break out the thumbscrews if they discover I've snuck visitors in to see him.' He planted his hands on his hips and shook his head. 'Come on then, let's get this over with.'

Hollister led them down more corridors. At intervals, they passed through internal checkpoints, manned by bored looking soldiers.

After the final check, Hollister turned to Alistair and Bill. 'It's been requested you two chaps speak to him alone. Not sure I approve, but Brigadier Douglas vouches for you.' He narrowed his eyes at Younghusband, who nodded sharply. 'You have a limited amount of time with him, do you understand? You can ask him questions; whether he answers them is purely up to him. Don't pass him anything, and you have to be finished by 1300 hours, otherwise you'll answer to the Soviet Commandant. And Major Ryovski is a far harder case than I am. Are we agreed? Good. Let's go.'

They passed several guards moving boxes down a flight of stairs and back towards the gatehouse.

'Where are they going?' Bill asked, looking back as the guards disappeared around a corner.

'Happens every three months,' Hollister said, jogging up a flight of stairs. 'Things have become lax here over the years. We allowed the inmates reading materials, some creature comforts. But the Soviets have had a bee in their bonnet since the '40s. Now that Hess is the last man standing, we pack everything of his up and put it into storage when the Soviets are in charge. Damned nuisance, but what can you do?'

They waited for a steel-bound door to open.

'What's he like?' Bill asked, as they entered the corridor.

'A dreamer,' Hollister said, pausing a moment to sign them into the wing. 'You'll see.'

Another corridor took them to a short flight of steps that led up to a narrow room which stretched back into the building.

'Is this the library?' Bill asked.

'It is,' Hollister said. 'Since we've stripped his room in anticipation of the Soviet arrival, this will do to interview him.' He stepped back to allow them to enter. 'Whatever his sins are, try to remember he's an old man, alone in this God forsaken fortress.' He looked at Younghusband. 'Fancy a nip of Slyrs single malt, Major?'

'Don't mind if I do.'

The two majors left the library. A guard took his place inside and closed the door.

Shelving thick with books lined the walls. A table and several overstuffed chairs were the only furniture. A figure sat in one of the chairs, beside a lamp. The electricity flickered and shadows danced over the squared-off face of a man in his late sixties. Silver at the temples tinged his swept-back hair. Noting his visitors, he marked his place in the book and set it aside. He stood, straightened his jacket and approached.

'Rudolf Hess,' he said. 'Who may I have the honour of addressing?' His English was clipped and impeccable.

'For the purposes of this meeting, I'm a man with no name,' Alistair said. 'My friend, however, is from New Scotland Yard. This is Detective Harry Champion.'

Hess didn't offer his hand, instead he merely nodded his head. Bill smiled derisively.

'Please, be seated,' Hess said.

He waited until his visitors were comfortable, before he returned to his chair. Alistair thought that Hess saw himself as their host, and not a solitary prisoner and last remaining figurehead of a vile regime.

'And you, with that odd bundle in your hands. It isn't a weapon, is it? Surely you aren't here to kill me?'

Alistair thought he heard the faintest edge of panic in Hess' voice. He wasn't surprised. The man had already spent a quarter of a century pent up in Spandau, and would spend almost two more decades alone, except for his guards, an overgrown garden, his astrological charts and thoughts of what might have been. Alistair almost pitied the man. Almost.

'It is a weapon. You've held it before.' Alistair pulled the canvas away. It might have been the moonlight shining through the skylight, or perhaps something from within the metal itself, but the gladius glowed. It shimmered like quicksilver, a pulsating vibration that reminded Alistair of a heartbeat.

Hess reached for the gladius, then snatched his hand back. 'Where did you find it?'

'Quietly rusting away in a bank vault,' Bill said.

'I held it once.' Hess' gaze fixed on the blade. 'Took it and held it and flew it across the seas to Scotland.'

'That's why you flew to Britain? To kill Churchill?'

'Kill him? Oh, my dark-skinned friend,' Hess said, almost laughing. 'I didn't want to kill Churchill. I wanted to give it to him.'

CHAPTER TWENTY-ONE
Blackstar

ALISTAIR AND BILL EXCHANGED SHOCKED glances.

'You wanted Churchill to have it?' Alistair asked.

Hess nodded. 'I alone recognised the Führer had placed Germany in a vice. He always planned to invade Russia. And America would eventually come to Britain's aid. History has proven me right. Only a leader such as Churchill could've saved us.'

'By what? Defeating Germany? Your own people?'

Hess nodded, almost eagerly. 'The Russians and the Americans are mongrel races, unworthy of world leadership. If Churchill had taken the Gladius,' – the way he said the word, Alistair could almost see the capital G – 'he would've won enough victories to bring the Führer to the bargaining table. With the European War ended in the West, an Anglo-German alliance would've cemented our joint rule of the world.'

'Why share the spoils? Why not simply give it to Hitler?' Bill asked.

'I offered it, but the Führer rejected anything to do with the occult. I pressed him, and he grew distant from me. After our last meeting, I resolved to take the Gladius to Britain and give it to Churchill.'

'You say it would've led Britain to victory. How?'

'Caesar wielded it, and defeated Gaul and won Rome. Before that, Alexander marched to India with it, sweeping all before him. All the way back to Sumer, it has helped men conquer and build empire after empire. The Gladius is a primal weapon, made from the matter of the universe. It came from the stars to lead men to glory and victory. It draws life from its victims, and transfers it to those who hold it, or those who are linked to it, making them greater than mortal men.'

Alistair thought for a moment, considering what they had learned so far. Putting the pieces together. 'But when you arrived in Scotland, you were disbelieved.'

Hess looked away, his face monetarily lost in shadow. Eventually, he nodded. 'I took it from Himmler's temple in Austria and his Order of the Black Sun.' He sneered. 'His knights were bloodthirsty, degenerate killers. When Himmler realised that I had taken the Gladius with me, he tried, for a number of years, to retrieve it. Eventually, at war's end, he used a military asset in England to steal the Gladius. At the same time, he managed to insert a team of men into Britain.'

'And they nearly killed Churchill with the damned thing,' Bill said. 'But why?'

'The Gladius eats life,' Hess said, matter of factly. 'It also transfers life energies from one living creature to another. At least, that was what my researches indicated.' He paused, and Alistair wondered with a shudder exactly what memories Hess lingered over. Then Hess went on. 'It seemed that Himmler hoped to drain Churchill of his life energy, and direct it through the Gladius to Hitler.'

'That's madness,' Bill said.

'It's the truth,' Hess said, simply. 'I learned all of this at Nuremberg. It pleased me that Himmler killed himself. It was the first honourable thing in an otherwise dishonourable life.' His gaze dropped to the Gladius. 'If it has been stored away in a bank vault, why do you have it?'

'I stole it,' Alistair said.

'Impressive.' Hess spared them a smile. 'For who?'

'On orders of a man in London.'

'The man who would demand such a thing could never be on the side of angels,' Hess said, shrewdly.

Alistair nodded. 'Indeed, this man has nothing but demons on his shoulders. He holds my niece hostage. Her life, for the Gladius.'

'Then hand it back.'

'It's not that simple,' Alistair said. He held the Gladius to the light. Despite its age, the double-edged blade remained wickedly sharp. 'You know why.'

Hess inclined his head. 'Forged in the days of Sumer's might, it has spent the centuries eating the lives of those it slays.'

'And something more?' Alistair asked. His voice was hoarse, and he heard a voice whispering to him.

'You feel it, don't you?' Hess said. 'I did too, on my flight from Germany. It insinuates itself into you, turns your thoughts black. If Churchill had just taken it...' He stopped and shook his head.

'If he had,' Alistair said, 'the world would groan beneath the yoke of a blood-mad maniac.'

The silence was pregnant. Outside, they heard the dim crackle of a storm beginning its death-ride over the city.

'What do you require of me?' Hess swept a hand around the library. 'There is very little I can do for you here.'

'You are a scholar of the occult. You understood the true nature of the Gladius, not Himmler. Tell us how to destroy it.'

Hess shook his head. 'There is no way to destroy it. I tried, once. I wanted to see if the legends were true.'

'And were they?' Bill asked.

Hess nodded. 'The Gladius is immune to the

temperatures found in a furnace. It is resistant to the corrosion of chemicals. It will not bend, and it certainly will not break. Believe me, it cannot be destroyed. It can change shape, though; influenced by the culture it finds itself in. Caesar held it and it became a gladius.'

Outside the library they heard the sound of movement. Hess glanced at the clock on the wall above the mantelpiece.

'The changing of the guard will occur shortly,' he said. 'I advise you to leave before the Soviets arrive. They aren't known for their hospitality.' Alistair saw that Hess had begun to withdraw into himself, his earlier interest replaced by a hauteur that seemed to be his coping mechanism.

'This thing is too dangerous to fall into the wrong hands,' Alistair said, standing up.

'Then I advise you to kill the man who wants it,' Hess said. 'Ah, but there will always be someone who wants it.'

Alistair looked down at the Gladius. 'I suspect you're right,' he said, a feeling of dread creeping over him. What had he said to Bill earlier? They were not here to change the past... But what if they were? What if that was the reason he had been sent back, to put right something that went wrong?

'Then you will have to spend the rest of your life killing them as they come for it,' Hess said.

It was quite a thought.

There was a crash of marching feet and the door opened. Hollister and Younghusband entered.

'You've got three minutes,' Hollister said. He nodded curtly to Hess, who nodded back. 'There's a side door that leads to some backstairs. Hurry.'

Younghusband led the way, and Bill followed. Alistair lingered, looking at Hess.

'I can't say it was a pleasure meeting you,' he said, as

he wrapped the Gladius. He looked around at the library. 'Was it worth it?' he asked. 'The blood and the fire and the endless deaths?'

'If we had won,' Hess said, his eyes distant. 'Then yes, it would've been worth it.'

'You sit here and cast your horoscopes. You search the skies for the future,' Alistair said. 'I can read your future, if you want?'

Hess' smile faltered, a little. 'You have the gift, too?'

'We don't have time for this,' Hollister said, looking anxiously between the two men.

'For this, we do,' Alistair said. 'I have the gift. Well?'

Hess nodded. Straightening his shoulders, he looked squarely at Alistair. 'So. Cast my fortune.'

Alistair stepped close, so that he was only an inch from Hess. His lips brushed Hess' ear. 'You will die here. You will never see the stars except from within these walls. One day, you will slip a noose around your neck and hang yourself in the summerhouse.' He pointed behind where Hess stood. Flinching, Hess looked over his shoulder.

Alistair felt someone dragging him away. It was Bill.

The Gladius.

Alistair felt its malign influence. He couldn't get rid of it soon enough.

Anne parked the car, the tyres shrieking as it came to a stop. Hartigan, his left arm braced against the door, breathed a sigh of relief.

'You should get down to Silverstone one day and have a go against Jackie Stewart,' he said, managing a shaky smile.

'He wouldn't have a chance,' Anne said absently.

She stared out the window at the crowds of people standing in front of the entrance to Westminster. A line of police desperately tried to maintain a cordon as the crowds surged forward.

'Can you feel it?'

'Feel what?' Hartigan asked, though the look on his face told the truth.

'There's something in the air,' Anne said, turning to Hartigan. 'You heard the radio report on the way here. Riots across the country, grotesque figures moving through the night, destroying vehicles and badly damaging property.'

'It doesn't feel spontaneous,' Hartigan admitted. 'Like there's someone behind it.'

'Yeah.' Anne pushed open her door. 'And I think the ringleaders are inside.'

Hartigan followed her into the street. A lone officer confronted them, eventually mollified by the production of ID.

'Good luck getting through that,' he shouted above the hubbub.

'Just keep this lot from storming the building,' Anne said, raising her voice to be heard. She scanned the crowd, looking for a way in. She espied the last person she wanted to be there. 'Magda!' She grabbed Hartigan by the arm. 'Come on, Tom.'

Magda stood looking uncertainly at the huge number of people. She held a handbag tightly. She almost jumped when Anne stepped in front of her.

'What are you doing here?' Anne demanded.

'Father is ill. He's in hospital.' Magda refused to look at Anne.

'I'm sorry to hear that.' Anne reached out and Magda jerked her arm away. 'You should go to him. It's not safe here.'

Magda turned to look at Anne, who felt the full force of her blazing eyes. Red-rimmed, they spoke of a life of sorrow. And something else Anne couldn't put her finger on.

'We should go,' Hartigan said, scanning the crowd for a way through.

Anne nodded. She turned to go, then on impulse turned back to Magda. 'You should come with us, if you're going to stay. It's not safe out here.'

Magda nodded. The fury faded from her eyes. 'Thank you,' she said, as Anne turned and began to force her way through the crowd.

The sound of men marching into the library above followed them. It only faded when they reached the final landing and exited through a door into a clammy stone corridor. They rushed forward and came out into the car park. Their car and driver were waiting. They quickly clambered in, and Younghusband ordered the driver to put his foot down.

'Did you get what you wanted, sir?' Younghusband asked, turning to look at Alistair.

'Maybe,' Bill answered after a moment. Alistair was frowning next to him, his gaze distant. Bill wanted to take the Gladius off him, but he knew Alistair would not release possession of it. 'What is it?' Bill asked.

'He was right.' Alistair lowered his head and rested his eyes on the Gladius. 'We need to get straight back to London immediately.'

'What do you mean, he was right?'

'Vaar.' Alistair tightened his grip on the bundled Gladius. 'Vaar must die.'

'Any sign?' Anne asked, checking her watch. It was almost 3pm. So, around 4pm in Berlin; surely Bill and Alistair were done with Hess by now. Hopefully they were on their way back.

She stood in the Central Lobby, just inside St Stephen's entrance, with Hartigan and Magda. MPs and journalists thronged the large space. Conversations overlapped and echoed, creating a vibrant atmosphere. News of the rioting across the country added an extra edge of hysteria to the chatter.

Anxiously scanning the crowd, Magda shook her head. 'I can't... There's too many people.'

Hartigan and Anne exchanged a look.

'We should —' Anne began, but Hartigan took her arm.

'There,' he said, pointing.

The noise of the crowd dwindled as Arbuthnot appeared. A cheer went up, and applause broke out. Journalists and several cameramen pushed towards him through the crowd, shouting questions.

'How brazen are they?' Anne said.

Flanking Arbuthnot was Vaar, looking deathly pale, and von Werner, whose smile did nothing to soften his facial scars. Behind trailed Vaar's driver and several other hard-faced men, who corralled a frightened girl. Anne looked at Magda and saw her face stiffen at the sight of von Werner.

'Brazen enough to conduct an interview. Look.'

Hartigan pointed to the tight knot of reporters gathered around Arbuthnot. The man preened in front of them, smiling unctuously at the shouted questions. He pointed to a reporter.

'Freddie? Say that again?'

'If you win, what efforts will you make to curb the rioting crisis?'

'Oh, I will win, Freddie, don't you worry about that.' Laughter rolled through the reporters. Arbuthnot's smile lingered, then he assumed a serious pose. 'The British Army is the one bastion we can rely on in these difficult times. The police, I fear, are ineffectual, where they are not corrupt. No, as in Northern Ireland, we will have the army perform policing duties. And,' he said, above the excited babble of questions, 'if any foreign elements are found conspiring against the British people, it won't go well for any of them, including their families. Britain for the British, and damn the rest!' He grinned at the outrage that swept the room. 'Now, if you will excuse me, I have a vote to win.'

Arbuthnot and his group of supporters pushed through the lobby, forcing the crowds to part before them.

Something caught Anne's eye and she turned to see Alistair and Bill enter, frantically scanning the crowd. She went to wave, to get their attention, when a mutter of 'damn' from Hartigan alerted her to trouble closer to home. Anne looked around. Magda had vanished.

A single gunshot rang out.

There was a moment of stillness, then utter pandemonium.

Security ran into the lobby as MPs and members of the public scattered like panicked pigeons. Arbuthnot and Vaar, with the girl in tow, fled towards a door, leaving Vaar's men surrounded by police officers. A gap formed in the crowd.

Her arm extended, Magda pointed a gun at von Werner. Von Werner clutched his chest and stared at Magda in incomprehension. He opened his mouth to say something, when blood spilled over his lips, down onto his chest and then the floor. More blood seeped between his fingers, and then he was on his knees.

'It is done,' Anne heard Magda say, clearly. 'It is done, Mother.'

Von Werner slumped onto his back, staring blindly up at the ceiling.

Anne held up her ID and pushed her way through the watching crowd. She approached Magda, who didn't seem to notice, and gently prised the pistol from Magda's hand. She slipped it into her jacket pocket. She led Magda away, sitting her on a bench against a wall and called over an officer.

'Keep an eye on her,' she said, showing the officer her ID. 'Do not take her into custody, all right? I'll deal with her myself.' The officer nodded and stood guard, eyeing the milling crowd with suspicion.

'Where are they?' Alistair called, running over to Anne, Bill at his heels.

She squeezed Bill's hand, and he squeezed it back. Hartigan joined them.

'They've gone to the party room,' he said. 'You'd think they would call it off, but Arbuthnot was adamant. Vaar's gone with him. They have a girl with them, too.' He looked Alistair up and down. 'Your niece, right? Do you want to…?'

'I do,' Alistair said, grimly. He looked at the others. 'Let's get this over with.'

The Palace of Westminster had stood for a thousand years, expanding in size and function as England, then Britain, came to rule the world. The building exuded history, which anchored it in time and place and gave it the grandeur that befitted a nation that had once been an Empire.

It was also, as Alistair and those who followed him discovered, an absolute maze, riddled with corridors that led up and down stairs, through echoing, empty rooms, before allowing them to re-emerge at the same junction.

'How the hell does anyone navigate this warren?' Hartigan asked, giving voice to Alistair's own thoughts.

'This way,' Alistair said, pointing to a corridor.

'How does a Spanish bank robber…? Never mind.' Hartigan looked at the three of them. 'You're all mad, do you know it?'

'You're in the asylum with us, Tom,' Anne said, smiling.

At the end of the corridor stood a pair of attendants.

'I'm sorry,' one of them said as they approached. 'This is a closed meeting. I insist—'

Anne, Bill and Hartigan brandished their IDs.

'There's been a shooting in the lobby. We have to secure this room,' Hartigan said. 'Unless you want the PM unprotected while a gun wielding maniac is at large?'

One of the attendants blanched. After a moment's hesitation, his companion opened the door, and they entered the room.

The atmosphere was tense. Whether it was the design of the room, which was a long rectangle, or the natural inclination of the participants, but a narrow gap divided those inside. Tall windows overlooked the Thames on one side, and the green patterned wallpaper harkened back to a bygone age. A large painting dominated one end of the room, and a familiar figure stood beneath it, loudly declaiming to the attendees.

The unmistakeable figure of Vaar stood to one side, a young girl standing just behind him. Vaar looked on at the proceedings with an impatient frown.

'We cannot go on with this style of government...' Arbuthnot trailed off as all eyes turned on the intruders. 'You two! How dare you...?'

'We're with Crouch End Police,' Anne said, holding up her ID. Alistair stood at the rear of the group, sizing up the room. 'WDC Ruth Winters. These are my colleagues, DCs Tom Hartigan and Harry Champion. We have reason to believe that... *Vaar!*'

Jeremy Thorpe stood, his deep-set eyes taking in the scene. He had been seated, watching Arbuthnot like a vulture ready to toy with a meal, when the trio of police had burst in. He rubbed his mouth.

'Vaar?' he asked. 'Do you mean this fellow here?' He pointed to the Dominator.

'I do,' Anne said. 'He's a wanted criminal, an associate, we believe, of Arbuthnot.'

Excited chatter broke out.

'What rot!' Arbuthnot called. 'He's merely an advisor in my office. No more a criminal than I.'

'Who you demanded attend the meeting, against all protocol,' Thorpe said, having clearly chosen his side. 'And with a girl, no less.'

'He's not an advisor,' Hartigan said. 'He's wanted in connection with a number of gangland murders, including Sammy Wilberforce just last week.'

'Well then.' Thorpe cast around the room with a look of barely restrained glee in his eyes. 'I believe we should allow the police to do their job, Charlie. After all, you're a big proponent of law and order. I'm more than happy for them to march your friend, and indeed, you, off in handcuffs.'

Something like relief filled the room at the turn of events. Warm laughter followed. Vaar ignored it, while Arbuthnot sputtered in indignation.

'You have it?' Vaar asked, stepping forward, as if deliberately distancing himself from Arbuthnot.

Alistair locked eyes with Vaar and, after a moment, he nodded.

'You can feel it, can't you?' There was a note of eagerness in Vaar's voice that betrayed his need.

'Yes,' Alistair said, feeling the Gladius turn cold in his hands, even through the canvas was wrapped around it. He heard voices again in his head, and saw figures fading in and out of existence; a battlefield superimposed over the curious onlookers in the room. Screams and shouts, the distant clang of metal on metal, all rose and fell like waves on a beach. And he felt a terrible hunger gnawing at him, a desire that needed to be quenched in blood.

'Do it!' The thought whispered insistently to him, in a voice not his own. A cold, terrible voice that would not be denied. How long could he hold onto his sanity and end this nightmare?

'Remember our bargain,' Vaar said. He stepped to one side, fully revealing the Matador's niece. Her eyes widened in hope when she saw her uncle.

The battling figures faded as abruptly as they appeared. In the moment of time it took for Alistair to become aware of his surroundings again, Arbuthnot took his chance to speak.

'Take the damn thing from him, and be done with it! Afterwards, you can have whatever you want.'

'Alistair,' Bill warned.

Alistair looked at his friend and shook his head. 'In the end,' he said, 'there's only really one choice.'

CHAPTER TWENTY-TWO
All the Madmen

ALISTAIR WALKED OVER TO VAAR AND HANDED HIM THE bundle. As Vaar took it, Alistair winked at Bill, who tensed at the signal. Then, Alistair quickly grabbed the girl's arm and hurried her back to stand with the others.

'My reward,' Vaar said, ignoring the rising hubbub in the room. 'Finally.' He regarded the small group, and explained, 'Without access to nuclear energy, I have been weakened. The Gladius will change all that.' He uncovered the canvas with a flourish, exposing the weapon. He gripped it in one hand, and they all saw the transformation in his face.

The light bled away, and shadows grew from the corners. Vaar, his face creasing into a hungry smile, turned on Arbuthnot, who had called for the voting to commence immediately.

'Be quiet, you insect!' Vaar boomed.

Alistair narrowed his eyes. This was the Dominator he remembered. The man he'd fought on three separate occasions... Although one of those times had yet to pass. And maybe never would, if he succeeded in killing Vaar now.

'All here will bow down before me once I have fed.'

With that, Vaar stepped forward and rammed the blade of the Gladius all the way into Arbuthnot. The crunch of metal on bone silenced the room, as did the despairing cry of anguish that escaped Arbuthnot's mouth.

'Holy God,' Hartigan said. 'What's he done?' He started forward, but Anne's hand on his shoulder restrained him.

'Back, Tom,' she said. 'It's out of our hands now.' She looked at Alistair. 'Do you know what you're doing?'

'Half an idea,' he said, nodding to Bill. 'Wait for my signal.'

Arbuthnot's cry rose louder and louder, stilling the room. A glow erupted around his body, which began to fray. Motes of light dissolved into the air, his body disappearing as his despairing wail faded. A chorus of triumphant whispers filled the party room. People began to scramble back from the scene.

Before them, Vaar was transformed. Colour flowed back into his face, and the lines receded. His eyes glowed with energy and he straightened, towering over everyone else in the room. He positively throbbed with energy and, as Arbuthnot vanished, Vaar closed his eyes, his mouth a rictus of ecstasy.

'Now!' Alistair called.

Acting on his signal, Bill and Hartigan sprang forward. Together, the three men charged Vaar.

On impact, Alistair grunted in pain and felt a rib crack. Hitting Vaar was like running into a wall. The Dominator raised his free arm and brushed Hartigan away, as if swatting a fly. Bill ducked under a fist, then stumbled back as the backswing caught him in the shoulder. Alistair, sensing an opening in the tumult, grabbed Vaar's hand where it gripped the hilt of the Gladius.

A shared sense of a howling, voracious darkness filled him, of a sentience that originally lingered in the black gulfs beneath the stars. For the briefest moment, he and Vaar saw the world through the same eyes, both seeing a hunting ground filled with rich pickings that would never, ever satisfy the yearning of the living weapon they held.

Then Alistair, using the surge of energy, smashed Vaar in the side of the head with his fist. Unprepared, Vaar stumbled, and his grip on the Gladius relaxed. Pulling hard, Alistair wrenched it free and stood gasping with it in his hand.

'Get back!' he yelled, as Anne and Bill came to him. 'I'm too dangerous. Take the girl and go.'

Vaar, staring up at Alistair in shock, stumbled to his feet. He bulled his way through the crowd, shoving people as he sought to flee what he saw burning in Alistair's eyes.

'No,' Alistair said, his voice crackling with energy. 'You'll not escape me now!'

The chase took both men through a warren of corridors and rooms. Attendants and other workers within the building scattered before the two running figures.

Vaar staggered up a lonely flight of stairs. He burst through a wooden door, the screech of it against the flagstones outside like that of the damned in hell. He raised his arms against the light, momentarily dazzled. He stumbled forward, then turned as Alistair ran through the door.

They stood on the roof of one of the towers. Across from them, St Stephen's Tower soared into the sky, one of its clock faces visible. The sound of the afternoon street traffic rose to them, a world away from the chaos in the building. Vaar raised his hands.

'No surrender, Vaar,' Alistair said. Distantly, he wondered why his voice sounded like the roaring of a furnace. 'It's never been the Dominator way, so why start now?'

Vaar stood still and straightened. 'You know of my people? How? Who...?' His face creased, and a palpable anger rose in him. 'It doesn't matter. The War Fleet is out there, while I remain on this planet. But under First Master Ordo the Dominators will continue to... *dominate* the lesser races!'

Alistair sadly knew that all too well. He'd been told stories of the Dominators, not least by Edward Travers who had fought them on a planet called Karfel.

Vaar sneered at him. 'There is no shame dying at the hands of a worthy opponent.'

'No, there isn't.' Distantly, Alistair heard someone calling his name, but it wasn't enough to overmatch the whispered voices in his head, demanding to be fed. He tightened his grip on the Gladius and advanced on Vaar.

A hand gripped his shoulder. He shrugged it off, vaguely aware that someone had fallen to the ground. Some instinct made him look, and he saw Anne, struggling to her feet. She shouted at him.

'Don't kill him! You can't play with the timeline!'

He shook his head, trying to free it of the web of voices snagging his thoughts.

'If you kill him, you'll become that thing's slave!' Anne said through gritted teeth. 'Endless death, at your hands. Drop it!'

Alistair couldn't believe what he was hearing. Give the Gladius up? After everything they had done to find it. He shook his head. He saw Anne's eyes, pleading with him. Then he saw the Matador's niece, standing in the doorway to the tower, an arm outstretched.

Something sang to him. Memories. Of the Spanish sun. Of family, gathered at a table on a Sunday after Mass. The sun on his skin, like the kiss of a lover. Conversation and wine and food. The love of his family, gathered in his home. Safe and loved.

And then he saw another. A woman, short with blonde hair. A sense of will as strong as his. Kate.

Against the crying of the voices, Alistair felt his grip

on the Gladius loosen. It seemed to him that it fell endlessly from his hand. When it hit the flagstones, the ringing severed the connection to the voices in his head. He staggered, and the darkness lifted from him.

'Alistair,' Anne said, almost sobbing. 'Thank God. Get away from– Look out!'

Vaar rushed Alistair, bending for the Gladius. Curling his hand into a fist, Alistair cocked his arm and thundered his fist flush into Vaar's jaw. The residual strength provided by the Gladius give him the extra power he needed. Vaar flew backwards, and tumbled over the edge of the building. For a moment Alistair stood there, surprised at himself. Then Anne scrambled past him, and peered over the edge into the Thames.

'He's...' She looked back at Alistair. 'He's gone.'

'He'll be back,' Alistair said. 'And I'll be waiting.'

It had already happened for him, and for Vaar it would happen. One day, almost a decade from now, Brigadier Alistair Lethbridge-Stewart and Director Vaar would meet again.

Exhaustion suddenly rolled over him. He swayed, almost fell, then felt a hand grab his. He looked down, saw that the Matador's niece was by his side, and then folded her into a hug.

'We'll come with you,' Bill said, impulsively grabbing Alistair's arm.

Other than themselves, the squad room was empty. With Hartigan, Bill and Anne had taken charge of the chaos around Westminster. It was late evening, with the press finally decamping to write their leads for the next day's papers, and the conspirators cooling their heels in cells across London, before Bill and Anne had bundled Alistair and Sofia into a car and made their way back to Crouch End Station.

'No,' Alistair said. 'Job isn't finished yet. Have to get

this little one back to her parents.' He patted Sofia on the head and she smiled brightly at them. 'Any news on the golems?'

'After Magda shot von Werner, most of them stopped in their tracks. I hear children have begun hanging Christmas decorations on them,' Bill said with a chuckle.

'Most?' Alistair asked.

'Well,' Bill said, rubbing the back of his neck. 'There are reports some disappeared, marching away of their own accord.'

'Something for the authorities to worry about. Experience has taught me that nothing is ever neatly tidied away. As for Vaar...'

Despite Bill's smile, a haunted look crossed his borrowed face. A memory, one best forgotten. 'He'll hide away, and start again. His gangster life is at an end, at least.'

'And the Gladius?' Anne asked. The sword sat on the table, tightly wrapped in the canvas. 'What if he tries to come after it again? You can't let the Matador have it. He'll likely sell it to the highest bidder, maybe even Vaar.'

'Before, maybe,' Alistair said. 'But we've both had a sense of its power. He'll want it buried as deep as possible. As do I.' He paused. 'What about Magda?'

Anne sighed. 'Her father died this morning. I've had a word with the Crown prosecutor. With Foley's input, there will be no prison time. There's enough going on after Arbuthnot's death that we'll be able to hide what she did from the newspapers.'

'Good,' Alistair said. He looked at Sofia again. He picked the Gladius up and held out his hand to the girl. 'Come, little one, we have a long journey back home.'

'Home?' she said, a smile creeping hesitantly across her face.

'Home,' Alistair said, firmly.

Impulsively, Anne came forward and gave Alistair a

hug. 'Be safe, old man,' she whispered into his ear.

'Always,' he said as she stepped back. Alistair looked first at Bill, then Anne. 'What will you do until…?'

'I can already feel it,' Bill said. He looked at Anne, who nodded.

'Me too,' she said.

'Yes,' Alistair said. 'Well, let me get the Matador out of here. Hopefully I'll see you wherever we end up next.'

'Home, hopefully,' Anne said.

'Yes, hopefully.'

Once Alistair had left the room, Anne turned to Bill. 'How much of this do you think our hosts will remember?'

'It's something I intend to look into when we get back. Anyway, for now there's a lot of paperwork to go through. They'll be busy enough.'

'We may as well give them a head start, see how much we can get done before we're caught in Alistair's wake again.'

They left the room and headed to their office.

'Winters will have a lot to process,' Anne said, brow furrowed. 'I can sense her, just behind my eyes. She's deeply confused about Tom. I think that Hartigan isn't a lost cause. She's strong. She'll make the right decision.'

Surprisingly, they managed to clear most of the paperwork and remained in the station until just after midnight. They left together, deciding to take a walk through the dark London night.

They weren't sure of the time before they felt the pull back into the black.

The Matador's contacts worked quickly. By midnight, he had transport to the coast, where a small boat waited for them. An exchange of signals via torch, then Alistair and Sofia boarded the vessel, which puttered through the shallow waves to a dark shape riding at anchor a mile or two offshore.

'Are we sailing home?' Sofia said sleepily, as their boat neared the trawler.

The Gladius rested between Alistair's feet, while he held the child in his arms. 'You are, little one,' he whispered. He looked up at the stairs, pinpricks against a vast blackness. 'Though I fear I'll be sailing an ocean far deeper than even this one soon enough.'

Boarding the trawler, Alistair and the girl were taken to a cabin. Alistair sat with Sofia for a few minutes until she fell asleep, her face turned to the porthole and a vision of clouds scudding across the star strewn night.

Alistair felt the trawler's motors power up. The deck surged beneath his feet for several minutes, before the engines steadied. He left the cabin and climbed up to the deck. He watched the shoreline reduce first to a distant silver ribbon, then entirely vanish into the night, as the trawler, running lights doused, raced for the French coast.

'Was it a success?'

Alistair turned and recognised the trawler's captain. He smiled and shook his head. 'Depends on how you measure success.'

A faint gleam of teeth came in response. 'I suppose if at the end of every journey you make it back to port alive, then that counts as a success.'

'I suppose it does,' Alistair said, and chuckled.

'What next for you, then?'

'Home, I hope.'

'You hope?'

'That's the best men in our line of work can hope for, don't you think?'

Silence, for a long, long moment.

'Yes,' the captain said. 'A warm bed and welcoming arms. That's all you can expect in this life.'

After a few moments, the captain left, leaving Alistair alone to contemplate the reflections of the moon and stars on the silvery sea.

A little while later, walking across the darkened deck, with each step Alistair sensed the Gladius growing heavier. It seemed to shift within its bundle, as if it knew what he intended. He tightened his grip and stopped at the prow. He glanced down, saw the silvery wake splitting either side of the trawler, and imagined for a moment the frigid depths beneath him. He shivered, then unwrapped the canvas and gripped the hilt.

A jolt shivered up his arm, bone deep and cold as ice. He heard the voices again, snatches of Latin and something far more ancient. Battles raged inside his head, men at arms clashing and fighting and dying, endlessly falling into the blood slick mud, screaming as the Gladius rose and fell, rose and fell, reaping a terrible harvest down the ages.

A terrible compulsion filled Alistair; to return to the cabin, kill the girl, then rampage through the trawler until everyone was dead. Let the trawler beach itself on opposite side of the Channel, then take the Gladius and... what?

With a groan, Alistair shook his head, and the images and sound dissipated like mist under a hot sun. He looked at the Gladius with loathing.

Stepping up to the prow, he raised the Gladius above his head. He faltered as he sensed his mind loosen its moorings, and then he was falling upwards, up and up and up, the world plunging away from him into the inky infinity of endless night. Colours enveloped him, infused him, became him. He saw, without seeing, the trawler an unimaginable distance away.

Before the light gave away to darkness, he watched the Matador pause, seemingly wrestling with himself. Then with a convulsive wrench, the Matador hurled the Gladius into the night, the weapon describing a glittering arc through the air before it plunged into the water with a splash.

And with that, Alistair was gone, adrift in the cosmic winds... into the black.

EPILOGUE

ANNE CAME TO WITH A START. FOR A MOMENT, disorientation filled her head, but slowly things settled and she was able to take in her surroundings. She was sitting in a chair, a blanket covering her legs, a pillow beneath her head. She went to move forward, and felt a crick in her neck.

It was a familiar pain, one she hadn't felt for quite some time. Which meant…

She looked around, and smiled. The room was known to her, but not as known as the man lying on the floor, also wrapped in a blanket. Mid-sixties, skin still handsomely smooth, hair soft brown and grey. Her husband, the way he was supposed to look.

They were back.

Anne stood slowly, mindful of her arthritic old bones, and looked over at Sir Alistair. Comfortably asleep in his bed.

But if she was awake, then…

Bill stirred. Anne helped him to his feet, and after a few groggy moments he too noticed where they were.

'At last.' He kissed her on the lips. 'I did wonder if we'd ev—'

He stopped abruptly as the door to Alistair's room opened and in walked a very surprised looking Fiona and Doris. It was the first time Anne had ever seen Alistair's two wives in one room. As far as she knew, they had both accepted their roles in Alistair's life, any competition or resentments long gone. But still, it wasn't like them to meet up in person.

It was only now, seeing them side by side, that Anne realised how remarkably similar they looked. Both naturally blonde, although these days their hair colour wasn't exactly natural. And both had a mischievous twinkle in their eyes.

Alistair certainly had a type.

Doris immediately took control. She crossed the room and took Anne in a big embrace. 'I was so worried when Fi rang...' She pulled back. 'What happened to you?'

'It's a long story,' Anne said. 'The important thing is, we're all back now, so we—'

'Erm, Anne...?'

She turned to Bill, who was now beside Alistair's bed. She was about to ask what, when she too noticed the problem.

'Shouldn't he be back too?' Bill asked.

Anne rushed over to the bed, Doris and Fiona close behind her.

'Anne, what exactly has been going on?' Doris asked.

Anne wasn't sure where to start. 'We were cast through time,' she decided on saying. 'By that thing.' She pointed at the Gnome, which sat on the windowsill. 'It was just meant to be Alistair, not Bill and I, but we got caught in his wake. Wherever he went, we followed.'

Doris and Fiona took this in like it was just another day at the office. But, she supposed, that's what happened when you married a man like Alistair Lethbridge-Stewart.

'It never ends, does it, dear?' Fiona said.

'No,' Doris agreed. 'And he would insist on throwing himself back into the fray when the UN offered him that job. But would we have him any other way?'

'Well, at least you knew what you were walking into,

Doris.'

Anne smiled. Okay, so maybe they weren't entirely at peace with each other.

Doris ignored Fiona's pointed remark, and looked down at her husband. 'The real question is, if you two were following him, and you're both back, then where's Alistair?'

And that, Anne realised, was a very good question.

The Laughing Gnome continues in...
Lucy Wilson and the Bledoe Cadets

Available from Candy Jar Books

**LETHBRIDGE-STEWART: THE LAUGHING GNOME
— FEAR OF THE WEB**

by Alyson Leeds

Dame Anne Bishop learned a long time ago that for every fixed point in time, this a fracture point, an event that is susceptible to catastrophic changes in the timeline. And when she is catapulted back in time, she discovers first hand that February 1969 is one such point.

The London Event changed the course of human history, and for Anne Travers it set into place a series of events that would see the death of her father barely a year later.

Now, waking up in the body of a woman she barely knows, Dame Anne is faced with the idea that perhaps she can change things – not enough to damage the timeline, but enough to save her father.

Future and past are set to collide, which could have irrevocable consequences for the timeline…

FROM THE WORLD OF DOCTOR WHO

ISBN: 978-1-912535-11-8

Also available from Candy Jar Books

THE LUCY WILSON MYSTERIES: CURSE OF THE MIRROR CLOWNS

by Chris Lynch

The circus is coming to town – and it may never leave.

Lucy Wilson is just about getting used to life in Ogmore-by-Sea. School, homework, friends, and the occasional alien... It's not easy being the new girl in town but, with the help of her steadfast companion Hobo, she's making it work.

But when a mysterious circus opens for one night only, the town suddenly finds itself overrun with invisible clowns and the gang are faced with their biggest mystery yet – the disappearance of Lucy Wilson herself.

Thankfully, they've got help – a mysterious stranger from another world with a special box that moves in time and space.

ISBN: 978-1-912535-10-1